DESERT RAINS

THE DESERT ROMANCE SAGA

JADELYNN ASHER

1

Charlene ran her hands over the heifer's swollen belly, nodding in satisfaction. She straightened and scratched the spotted cow, tagged 52263, between its ears. "She's looking really good, Frank. A few more weeks and we'll have a fine, healthy pair of calves. Keep her in the closest field, okay? I want to keep an eye on her."

Frank patted the cow and attached her lead rope. "Hear that, cow? You did good." The cow mooed, and he smiled at Charlene over the animal's back. "I'll set her loose, then. Anything else you need?"

"Not in particular. Double check those three goldens while you're out there, please. Then Gravy needs a hand setting the seedling trays so they'll be usable tomorrow."

"Yes, Ma'am," Frank replied with a wink. He paused. "I heard through the vine that Ted was coming back soon. Any truth there?"

Charlene strode to the cleaning sinks. She pumped waterless cleaner between her hands and scrubbed from fingertip to elbow. The cleaner stung as it hit a few scrapes, but using it was better for the cows and saved on precious water supplies. "Yep. He arrived back on planet a few days ago and met up with our new technician, but they got held up by a storm down in Granite. If we're lucky they'll make it back today. Otherwise, he'll be back tomorrow morning."

Frank pushed his hat forward, the beaten, black leather having seen better days. A bright blue feather stuck out on the band. "We'll hope fer luck then. You work too damn hard when he's not here."

"I work too damn hard when he *is* here. You all just don't notice."

He grinned, a quirk of broad lips. "Oh, you'd be surprised what I notice, Ma'am." There was a tease in the words, but before Charlene could question him Frank guided the cow out of the holding stall and into the open yard. Charlene watched him go as she toweled off. Frank had been at the Double P Ranch for a bit over 18 months. He was a good hand and a hard worker. Teddy swore Frank was sweet on her, but Charlene wasn't interested and did her best not to encourage him.

Her stomach rumbled, and she wondered if there might still be lunch to be found. She'd missed the general call, busy with her beloved seedlings, and then the heifer had needed to be seen. This time of year, there was always something to do and a scramble to do it before the full heat of a Galilean summer set in.

She pushed away from the sink and her right hip twinged, protesting the use it'd received this morning. Charlene rubbed the heel of her hand against the joint. The pain was all the more reason to return to the house. A second painkiller would do her good and get her through the rest of the day.

As she entered the large open yard between the house and the sheds, Charlene caught the scent of freshly turned earth and the chatter of chickens. The chicken coop was the newest addition to the farm, built just to the side of the modest garden plot which helped to feed everyone. The center of the large yard was spread with ogen straw packed into the sandy ground. It was left open so wagons could be brought in and gatherings could be had without trampling crops or cows. Furrows were building again, and she made a mental note to have the men add more straw and stone after the next storm.

Charlene wandered over to check the chickens, adjusting her thin leather hat to provide more shade from the blistering sun. The heat was oppressive after the cool of the cattle shed and sweat built between her shoulder blades. She tugged the front of her shirt, sending a breeze across her skin. It was still early in the planting season and already too hot. Maybe spending the rest of the day reviewing the books wasn't such a bad idea.

Charlene's musings were interrupted as Tracy flew around the corner of the small chicken coop, very nearly plowing her over. Charlene pivoted to one side, catching Tracy's arm as the teen slipped and slid on the sandy ground. The young woman was recently engaged, and had been unrelentingly bubbly all morning, singing and dancing around the ranch until even Charlene had yelled at her to get out of the way.

Charlene arched both eyebrows. "You're certainly in a hurry, Miss Tracy. What's going on?"

"Mister Walker's wagon is coming up the way! Mister Ted is coming home! They'll be at the house in about 15 minutes. Mama said you'd want to know."

"Of course I'd want to know," Charlene chuckled, amused by Tracy's enthusiasm. It seemed like there wasn't a woman alive who wasn't a little in love with Teddy. Charlene pondered her options, glancing out over the fields. "It's not every day my jail bird brother comes home to roost. Sound the round up alarm and get the men up to the house so they can give Teddy a proper welcome. And tell your mama I'd like slab toast for the men's breakfast. That'll raise a few spirits."

The young woman nodded, running off to the calving shed where one of the alarm units was housed. Her skirts flipped in the breeze of her passing. Within seconds the 'all in' alarm sounded through the property. It was a lower tone than the emergency alarm, telling the men to take a minute and finish up what they were doing before coming up to the house. The emergency alarm meant they should drop it all, and was used for a bad storm or, heaven forbid, a fire.

Deciding she had time while the men gathered, Charlene checked the chickens and refilled their watering tray. She made sure the anti-evaporation lid was firmly in place and the irises the chickens drank through were clear. By the time she made it to the house proper, she was the last to arrive. The eighteen hands who worked at the Double P ranged in age, skin tone, and marital status, but they were all hard workers and currently all men. There weren't a lot of women on planet who wanted to be ranch hands. With Ted and Mister Tyler, the new technician, they'd be back at twenty, which was pretty ideal in Charlene's mind. The cattle still outnumbered them, but that was as it should be.

Missus Davidson and Tracy stood at the top of the porch. Charlene wondered when Tracy had slipped by her, though it was possible she'd caught a lift with someone on a horse. The carts and horses came up to the house around the edges of the cattle sheds in order to keep them out of the gardens and from kicking up too much dust in the yard.

Jeremiah Walker's wagon trundled up to the house, the travelers within greeted by cheers and good natured cat calls. Ever the show-off, Ted stood in the back of the wagon, a large man backed by the sun, whipping his hat above his head and hollering greetings.

Charlene made it as far as the porch stairs before her hip twinged again. She dismissed the idea of climbing up the stairs, even if the higher ground was her rightful place as the boss. Instead, she moved to the left of the porch railing and settled on a large decorative log, amused to watch Teddy's antics as the wagon came to a halt. He leapt from the back of the vehicle with a flourish, followed at a slower pace by a second man Charlene recognized from his employment application as Richard Tyler.

Richard swept his hat off and approached the porch while Ted made the rounds with the men, shaking hands and slapping each other silly; one of the many male behaviors Charlene didn't understand. Somehow it was only a manly greeting if the other man was left with fist-sized bruises on his back.

Under the dark leather hat--it had to be new with how stiff it was--Richard Tyler was a handsome man, much more so than his hiring picture. His hair was dark-blond which would bleach gold under the Galileo sun, curling around his ears and the nape of his neck. He had a strong chin and fine features with pale blue eyes which were highlighted by skin-kissed cheeks and nose. With how clean his white shirt and dark trousers were they had to be as new as the hat. Charlene gave him about three hours before the unbroken boots wore blisters on his heels. He looked like a page from the catalog at Madam Aster's General Store. He took all the merriment in stride. His gaze darted over the men and over Charlene herself, dismissing her dusty appearance, before he approached the porch and the five steps up to where the other women stood.

Richard approached Missus Davidson, bowing over his hat before taking her hand and kissing her knuckles. "Miss Petersmire. It's an honor to meet you at last."

Charlene arched both eyebrows, lacing her fingers on the porch rail and resting her chin on them. She'd never had a new hire who didn't know who she was. Then again, Richard was the first off planet hire she'd ever made. Everyone else came from Ridgeback or Granite, or occasionally as far away as the capital city, Double Fork. She'd seen his picture, but hadn't shared hers. A sour part of her argued he was just expecting a woman in a dress, but she pushed the thought away. She wasn't on Central anymore; there was nothing wrong with the way she dressed for the job she did.

Missus Davidson shook her head, laughing gently. "Not that I don't appreciate the gesture, we certainly don't get much of that around here, but I'm not Miss Petersmire. I'm Missus Davidson, Gravy's wife and the ranch cook."

Richard's gaze went to Tracy and his brow furrowed. "I see, but this can't possibly be Miss Petersmire. She is far too young." He noted Tracy's dismay and caught her hand, kissing it as he had her mother's. "And far too beautiful."

Charlene's amusement soured further at the compliments, as smoothly turned as they were. Tracy was too young and beautiful to be Miss Petersmire? What did beauty have to do with running a ranch? What did this man expect her to look like? Some hardened hag or withered sand rock?

"So, if I might ask, where is Miss Petersmire?"

He had no sooner spoken the question, when Ted stomped up the stairs, catching Tracy and Missus Davidson in a joint hug and spinning them away. "Ah, my two best girls. Please tell me there's something in the kitchen for a starvin' man? My stomach is convinced it's been cut off from my mouth."

"Only if you put us down, Mister Ted," Missus Davidson protested, trying to straighten her skirts. "Landsakes, what a reception today."

Ted lowered them to the ground before realizing he was missing someone. "Hey, where's Char?"

Charlene shook her head and tapped her hat so it fell back on its string to rest against her back as she rose. "Down here, Teddy, in all of my too old, but certainly not too beautiful, number three best girl glory."

A deep frown fell across Richard's face as the hands within earshot broke into hearty laughter. Ted jumped down the stairs in two long strides, grabbing Charlene in a bear hug and spinning her around as well. Finally, he put her down and kissed her forehead. "Now why would you go and say a thing like that? You know you're my number one sister.

Anyone who thinks you ain't beautiful needs his eyes checked, an' that ain't jus' brotherly love talkin'. Right, boys?"

The hands cheered in agreement. Charlene smiled, her ill spirits eased by Ted's good cheer. "Now, now, you know I'm immune to flattery, but you can speak the truth all you want."

Ted squeezed her shoulder, leaning in and whispering, "You're standin' funny. Hurtin' today?"

"Just a little. It's all good." She murmured, before breaking away and holding out a hand to Richard, who had come down the stairs. "Mister Tyler, I presume. I'm Charlene Petersmire. Welcome to the Double P Ranch. "

Richard stepped forward, taking her offered hand. He didn't bow over it as he had Missus Davidson or Tracy, awkwardly shaking her fingers. "It is good to meet you, Miss Petersmire. I apologize for the confusion. Your response did not include a picture, and I admit I thought, given your position, you would be older. I apologize for the assumption."

He didn't look directly at her, as though he was put off by her look or smell, focusing on a point just above her left shoulder. Charlene glanced down at herself, noticing she'd picked up some dirt smudges, and there was a spot of manure on her left boot. That wasn't so out of the ordinary. There might be a little smell, but she wasn't going to sniff her armpits or shoes to make a point. "Is something wrong, Mister Tyler?"

He fidgeted and shook his head. "Of course not, Ma'am. I'm just not accustomed to women in your form of dress. When my sisters wear trousers they are not..." Richard fumbled for words. "Ahem...form fitting."

Laughter roared, reminding Charlene they weren't alone. The ranch hands were obviously enjoying this small piece of theater. Even old Jeremiah was leaning on his wagon, the brim of his hat low, but there was no mistaking the amused shake of his shoulders.

Charlene rested her hands on her hips. Her pants fit well in her opinion, comfortable and durable without too much material flapping around to get caught in machinery.

"I see," She looked over the gathering, raising her voice to carry. "All right, you reprobates. I don't pay you to stand around gawking and laughing. You've all welcomed Ted back, get back to work. Frank, Gravy, help Jeremiah get those boxes down to the seedling lab, we'll need them tomorrow. It's too damn hot to stand around talking in the sun. We'll do a proper celebration of Ted's return at breakfast tomorrow." She saw Richard flinch at the mild curse and decided to cuss more often. She was certain he expected her to behave much more like the society women on Central. His unspoken expectations were too close to the shouted criticisms Carl had left her with, drawing up painful memories.

The ranch hands dispersed, and the Davidson ladies slipped into the house, leaving Charlene, Ted, and Richard standing in the yard. Charlene pushed away her annoyances, trying hard to give Richard the benefit of the doubt. He couldn't know about her past engagement, and it wasn't fair to judge him based on what he didn't know, even if he felt free to judge her based on her trousers.

"Mister Tyler, you'll find a lot of things are different here on Galileo, and I'll hardly be the only woman you'll meet who wears pants. You'll get along better if you put your expectations aside. I don't need anything out of you today. Ted will show you the grounds and your room in the bunkhouse. You'll be doubled up, but I'm sure you can manage. We'll review your duties and the shift schedules tomorrow. They're due to change in a couple days anyway, so it'll be easy enough for you to learn the new rotation with everyone else. Any questions?"

Richard shook his head, though hints of a frown still clung to his lips. "No, Ma'am."

"Good. Go on then." Charlene paused, one foot on the stairs to the house. "And don't call me Ma'am. Charlene will do. Except for Miss Tracy and Missus Davidson, we pretty much stick to first names around here. It's too confusing to try to yell for Mister this and that when we're chasing a cow through a field."

Richard's lips pursed. "I'm not sure I can do so. It goes against every bit of proper training I've had. My mother would pale at the very thought of me calling a woman I've just met, much less an unmarried one, by her first name."

Charlene sighed, forcing herself to walk up the stairs without favoring her hip. Five stairs; it wasn't so bad. "Try, Richard."

He startled and Charlene ignored him. "Ted, get sandwiches for both of you from the bottom locker and get him taken care of. I'll be in the den and I want to hear all your stories." Aware that Richard was giving her a look that was just shy of a glare--at least he was looking at her--Charlene kept moving, stepping through the door and letting it fall shut behind her. "Not young enough or beautiful enough with pants too tight to be proper, huh? Well screw you too, Mister Tyler."

———

RICHARD WATCHED the door slam and frowned. He was uncertain of what he'd done wrong, but very certain he'd offended the woman. He was trying to show her the proper respect due her gender and her position. It wasn't his fault if he expected her to dress appropriate to her role. What kind of woman was offended by being treated well?

Next to him, Ted snickered, "Still glad ya came?"

"I'll make that judgment tomorrow. Your sister seems rather..." Richard tried to think of a description which wasn't outright offensive. He wanted to give both of his new employers the benefit of the doubt. "Prickly."

"Well, we did walk right by her to greet the cook and her daughter first, and then ya stared at her legs like you'd never seen a pair before. She would have slapped you if you'd been staring at her ass."

"Ted! I would not stare at your sister's...er...bottom," Richard protested. He admitted privately Charlene filled out her trousers nicely, but wasn't that exactly the problem? He shouldn't be thinking about how a woman filled out a pair of trousers when it wasn't the woman he was in love with, and certainly not when the woman was his employer.

Ted snorted, "I'd ask ya whether her bottom weren't good enough fer ya, but that just gets right into disturbing territory." He turned away from the house, "Give her a little slack though, huh? We probably just caught her on the end of a long shift. She can be downright pleasant when she's well rested, you'll see. Come on. Jere's got our stuff. We'll get some grub and radio him ta stop back by the bunkhouse and drop it off."

Richard shot a final glance at the house, catching the swing of a faded curtain and wondering if Charlene, no, Miss Charlene--he could at least be polite in his own head--was watching them. Just in case, he bowed towards the window before sticking his hat back on and following Ted across the yard.

2

Charlene was half asleep in one of the big wingback chairs when Ted strode into the parlor, bringing a big plate of currant muffins with him. She forced herself fully awake and shifted in the chair, wincing as she realized, not for the first time, that dozing in a chair was a horrid idea. Ted put the plate down on one of the battered end tables. He took her hands and helped her to twist around until she was sitting forward.

"Did ya get yer second pill today?"

Charlene groaned, pins and needles running down her legs. "No. I got distracted by your return home. Then I started reviewing the figures on the seeds we're going to put in on the top forty. Then it was too late if I wanted to sleep tonight."

"That explains why ya missed the dinner call." He pulled over the matching chair and nudged the muffins towards her. "Eat and talk. Are those the seeds with the accelerated germination you were messing with?"

Charlene picked up one of the breads, pulling the top off and taking a bite. The berries inside were tart in contrast to the soft, sweet breading around them. They were good, but she had little appetite and set it aside after one bite. "They are. I'm convinced if we can get the plants up to size faster we won't lose nearly so many of them during the stormy season. It'd be even better if we can harvest before the big storms hit. These seeds are crossed with those high protein strains which did so well last year, so the hope is to get a fast grower with the higher protein content in bigger yields. If it works we'll be able to get two early plantings in the future."

Ted nodded, eyeing the set-aside muffin. "Sounds like a good enough idea. There's plenty of market for it, even more so before the rains."

"Yeah. The three month travel lock out always puts us behind the growers off planet. If we can beat it, even with part of the crop, we're going to be in good shape."

"Right." Ted handed her the muffin again. "Speakin' of shape, yours is rough. You've dropped weight while I was gone, don't tell me you haven't. I can tell ya hurt. You've been workin' too hard."

Charlene broke the muffin into pieces, making a face at Ted. "Don't you start mother henning me too. Missus Davidson already does enough of that. I'm eating. I'm just not hungry very often. And I hurt all the time whether I work or not. I may as well accomplish something."

Ted frowned, leaning forward and resting his elbows on his knees. "That ain't normal, Char. Maybe we need ta take you back to the doctor and try something different. There has ta be a treatment we haven't tried yet."

Charlene groaned, stuffing the muffin in her mouth and chewing even if she didn't want to eat. She swallowed. "No more doctors. He's just going to say the same old thing, take your pills, do your exercises, don't work so hard, drink lots of water, sleep better, and eat your vegetables. Go to the Pristine Pain Clinic every other week, which just isn't possible. I'm tired of being harassed about it."

"Well maybe if you'd do even some of those things we could stop harassin' ya cause you'd feel better! I feel like I'm watching ya come apart a little at a time, an' I hate it."

Ted's voice rose in frustration and Charlene looked away, chastened. He hadn't been back even a full day, and she was fighting with him. She knew he was trying to help, there was just so little that could be done. She sighed, rubbing her eyes before resting her hands on his knees. "Teddy, I'm sorry. I'm just tired. It's been hard running things by myself, and it's not like I can tell the men that I'm not working on one day or another because my hips hurt."

"Have you ever tried?"

Charlene shook her head. "I don't take excuses from them. I'm not going to give them any either. I can work, but I'm glad you're back so you can take over the heavy lifting, and I can keep to breeding my cows and plants. I promise I will try to do better."

"Mmhm." Ted didn't sound convinced but he didn't push the point. He bit down on another muffin, blowing a few crumbs at her when he spoke. "So what do you think of Rick?"

"Rick?" It took Charlene a minute to figure out who Ted was referring to. "Oh, Richard Tyler. He seems nice enough for all that he's ranch green. I'm just hoping he has the technical skills to go with his manners. I've already got a field generator and a seeder that need to be fixed. We've got to start planting tomorrow, and there's not enough time to get someone else in if he can't manage."

"Well, if'n it makes ya feel better, he patched out and reconfigured a bunch of field generators on the way here. We were down in Granite, and he managed in about 15 minutes with a storm bearing down. Ernest was impressed, and ya know how he can be."

"Huh," Charlene finished the muffin, thoughtful. If Ernest was impressed, it meant something. The old man didn't impress easy. Maybe this would turn out to be a good hire.

"There's a lot Rick don't know about ranchin' and all, yer right about that. He's definitely city bred, but he's a quick study. I think we need ta give him an opportunity with an open mind." Ted covered a yawn before reaching for a third muffin. "That said, I'm knackered. You want any more of these? And can ya get upstairs okay?"

Charlene stretched her legs and decided she could manage. She'd just go slow. One day she was going to build a bedroom on the main floor. "No more, and I'm good. I'll take him out to the misbehaving generator tomorrow and see what he can do." She got to her feet, only wobbling a little, and kissed Ted on the cheek. "Good night, and welcome home. I'm glad you're back."

"Good night, Char. Love ya."

3

Richard rolled over in his narrow bunk, trying to find any position which didn't irritate his stiff, aching muscles. Compared to his restful sleep in Granite, last night had been a nightmare. Combining the thin mattress and the narrow bunk with a body already sore from two full days of wagon travel was wretched. He already missed the conveniences of his father's home on Central. He'd read up on Galileo during the six month transport but details like horse-drawn wagons, which had seemed interesting on paper, were much less interesting in person.

The solid thump of footsteps on the wood floor interrupted his attempts at dozing, and Richard reluctantly opened his eyes. The room wasn't very big, consisting of a bunk on each wall with a narrow walkway between. His belongings were piled up at the foot of his bed and a shared table spanned the distance at the head of the beds for books and other minor necessities.

Frank sat on the edge of his cot, exchanging light weight slippers for heavier pointed-toe boots. Unlike Richard's boots, Frank's were highly patterned with some kind of reptile skin worked in patches along the toe. Richard had met the man--who turned out to be his bunkmate--very briefly the night before, but he hadn't registered much more than swarthy, dark-haired, and a quiet sleeper, the last fact being perhaps the most important. Noticing that Richard was awake, Frank tapped the brim of his worn hat.

"Mornin', Rick."

"Good morning." Richard pushed himself up, swinging his feet out of bed and trying not to groan.

"The ladies are setting up breakfast in the main hall. You'll have to hurry if you don't want to miss out, you know? We're having slab toast in celebration of Ted getting out of the clink."

Richard pulled one of his new cotton shirts over his head, wishing he'd asked about things like laundry and bathing options. Even with all the efforts to conserve water in the red rock environment, he was certain they didn't go without cleaning. He shook his hair out of his face, paying attention to Frank. "Slab toast?"

Frank grinned, "Yep. Thick, chewy toast with a slab of ham tucked inside, dipped in egg and fried. Don't have many pigs around here, so pork products are something Charlene saves for special occasions." He stomped his feet, setting his boots, and rose. "The pisser is out back, but there's a little sink in the dining if you just need washed hands. Hurry up, it ain't like anyone's going to save you a share if you're not there to fight for it."

He clomped out of the room, leaving Richard pulling on pants and thick stockings. He had questioned Madam Aster's wisdom at insisting he buy the socks, but, after a day in the new boots, he was certain her advice was saving him blisters. He hesitated over his coat, feeling odd going in nothing but a light-weight shirt, but the temperature was already too warm. He left it behind.

By the time Richard had made use of the outhouse and returned to the hall he found all the other hands seated around a long table. Missus Davidson and Miss Tracy were making the rounds with a giant platter of slab toast. As fast as the toast hit mismatched ceramic plates, men poured sweet fruit syrups or preserves over them and dug in. If there was grace to be said, Richard had missed it.

He slid into one of the remaining open spaces, the seats just a long bench on either side of the table, and grabbed a plate. As the ladies came by, he received sunny smiles and two pieces of toast. Richard set the plate down, amused by the weight of the thick slabs. "Good morning, Missus

Davidson, Miss Tracy. I had not expected to eat so heartily. If we always eat so I will have to beg someone to alter my pants."

Missus Davidson chuckled indulgently, brushing a wisp of graying hair back from her face. "It's not always this way, but we're at the beginning of the season when transports can get in and the roads are passable. Y'all work very hard, and a man can't work on an empty stomach."

"Try some of the cherry preserves, Mister Tyler," Tracy urged, pointing out a little jar near his plate. "I made them myself." She paused, looking at her mother with a sly smile, and added, "Maybe with a little help."

Obediently, Richard picked up the jar of preserves, the cherries bright red behind the glass. Chunks of the fruit swam in a thick, sweet gel, and he scooped some onto his plate. He cut a piece of toast, dipping it in the preserves and taking a bite. To his surprise, the tart berries went well with the toast, bringing out the meatiness of the ham and contrasting with the texture of the bread. He swallowed, noticing Tracy watching him. "It's most excellent, Miss Tracy. The best cherry preserves I have ever been graced to try."

She started to reply, but was cut off as Ted threw the front door open. "Ya better have saved some for me! It's my party after all." The comment was addressed to everyone and no one, and two of the men who had already cleaned their plates jumped up to make space for Ted at the table. He was followed by Charlene, and Richard finally got a good look at the woman when he wasn't busy taking his foot out of his mouth.

She was younger than Ted, in fact younger than most of the hands, but carried herself with an easy, absolute authority. Her bound up hair gleamed a rich black, which many of the socialite ladies tried to duplicate, but they never managed such sheen without going a little purple. She dressed like the rest of the workers in a lightweight tan cotton shirt and sturdy brown breeches, though she filled out both very differently than any of the men. Richard looked down at his plate, shaking the thought from his head, ashamed at his lack of self-control. She was his employer, and he hadn't even seen Anna yet. He shouldn't be noticing anything about how Charlene wore her clothing. The clothing did not make the man...or the woman.

"Hey, Rick!"

Ted's voice broke through Richard's musing, and he looked up as the large man plucked the bottle of preserves away. "Yes?"

"Char's been trying to get your attention. I know the toast is good, but it ain't *that* good."

Richard cleared his throat and looked at Charlene, whose expression was bemused. "I beg your pardon. I was distracted."

"Seems so." She gave a smile, a few of the men snickering, and Richard wondered if he'd ever go without an audience for his stumbles.

"When you get done pondering your distracting toast, come join me outside. I've got work for you to get to." Her gaze rose to the rest of the table. "As for the rest of you, new schedule comes out in two days. If you need time let Ted know, and we'll work it in. We start planting the top forty today."

A few groans greeted the announcement, and Charlene rolled her eyes. "Oh, knock it off. You've known this was coming all week. We've got to get the crop in if you want to get paid. Ted will take first shift with the seeder that's working, and, if our new tech genius can get the other one going, we'll start a following shift. The sooner we have seed in the ground, the better."

She walked out and Richard glanced at Ted while the men doubled down on feeding their faces.

"Is the planting really that bad?"

Ted swallowed a bite of toast, chasing it with a slug of milk. "Naw. These guys just like to bitch and moan to give Char a hard time. It's hot work, but crops in now will be ready to harvest before the rainy season."

Frank cocked his head to the side. "We trying new seed again? I know the stuff from last year had to hold over the rains, but we got paid good for it. Seems we'd stick with what works, you know?"

"We'll be doing a combination of crops. Top forty and west forty get new seed with a faster germination time. The central fields will use the stuff from last year. We'll hedge our bets to make sure we've got a crop no matter what."

"Good enough." Frank headed out, and within a few minutes most of the men had cleared out along with Missus Davidson and Tracy.

Richard finished the last of his toast, stacking the plates that had been left behind. He wasn't sure where they went next, but it seemed rude to leave everything for Missus Davidson to clean up. Ted was still mopping up preserves with the last bite of toast and watched Richard stacking.

"If ya keep Charlene waiting much longer she's going to think yer avoiding her. She ain't that bad of a taskmaster."

"I'm not avoiding her. It just seems rude to leave all of this for the women."

"It ain't. Cleaning up is what we pay the Davidsons for and fixing the seeder is what we're paying ya for." Ted pushed back from the table, licking a smudge of berry from his thumb. "So stop stalling and get working."

Richard rolled his eyes. "Yes, Sir." He left the rest of the dishes behind and walked out, finding Charlene leaning in the shade of the front porch. "Sorry to keep you waiting."

She looked up, watching him under the wide brim of her much abused hat with dark, amused eyes. "No problem."

4

Charlene tried not to be impatient waiting for Richard. She couldn't blame him for finishing breakfast, but there was a lot to get done today, and she wanted to get to it. When he finally joined her, she pushed away from the wall.

"Sorry to keep you waiting."

"No problem." Charlene walked away from the bunk house, trusting him to keep up. "This way. Teddy tells me you worked on a field generator down at Stacia and Harold's place. The ones we've got are from the same batch, so it should be a straightforward repair. Then we've got a seeder that needs some loving care, and it needs to be out on the fields today."

He chuckled. She liked the sound, a warm laughter that invited her to be amused too. "I've never had a job where I was very literally hands on the first day. I suspect this position will represent many firsts. The field generator is a simple enough design that I'm sure I can assist, but I haven't seen a seeder before."

"We'll call it on the job training or maybe a test of your skills. You did say you hadn't found many machines you couldn't figure out quickly."

"I did indeed, but I didn't know I'd be immediately called upon to defend my claim."

"I expect you'll survive. How much of the ranch did Teddy show you last night?" Charlene asked, angling towards the cattle sheds and corral.

"Not much, admittedly. I was tired so I took advantage of the bed as soon as possible. I was, however, surprised to see that you are both farming and running cattle on one ranch. I understood from my reading most establishments focused on one or the other." Richard didn't look at her as he spoke; his gaze for his surroundings and the red rock cliffs in the distance.

"Depends on a lot of things. If you're a smaller place, it makes sense to focus because you don't have the land to do both or what you've got is more suited to one or the other. Most of those create relationships with someone doing the other so they can exchange feed grain for meat or a milking cow. We're lucky here. The Double P covers a good amount of flatland, and we back onto a series of canyons where we can run the cattle to forage on their own for about half the year. They're down here for calving right now. We'll drive them back out and get them settled on range in about six weeks. The soil is good, and we get rain shed from what comes off the hills. It means dodging flash floods, but it's worth it for the greater range of options."

Richard nodded, and she wished he would at least look in her direction on occasion. She felt like some automated tour-guide sprouting off facts and figures that didn't begin to cover the reality of ranch life. How hard it could be and how lovely all at once.

He peered into the larger cattle shed, watching as Gravy and Frank drove the cows in for their morning feed. "Did you grow up here?"

"Yeah. Teddy and I were born and raised here. I went off planet to college and came back a few years ago after my parents passed to take over running the ranch."

This time he did look at her, his brows raised in surprised. "Where did you go to school?"

Charlene shrugged, turning towards the open fields beyond the corral and gesturing for him to follow. "Calibara College on Central."

Richard whistled low, admiration in the sound. "Truly? I applied to Calibara, twice in fact, but didn't make it in. They're very elite."

"I have a knack for biotechnology. They wanted to see what could be done with the genetic modifications to whetin I proposed in my admissions essay. It was a really good fit. I loved being there." The scholarship money had made it possible to go without draining her parents' funds. Charlene remembered how proud they'd been; their little girl going off to Calibara. It'd been the talk of the town for months.

"I'm surprised you came back instead of leaving the ranching to Ted. He seems content with it, and you must have had other offers which played to your strengths."

Charlene snorted. Richard looked away at the indelicate sound. "Good heavens, that never would have worked. Don't get me wrong, Ted loves the ranch. He's a hard worker and very smart when it comes to practical matters--well, except women, but that's neither here nor there. However, when it comes to keeping books, and rotating orders, and all the other details which make a ranch run from an organizational perspective, he's a disaster. We tried for a couple months while I was taking my finals and lost several thousand credits. If we wanted to keep the ranch, it needed us both here. So I packed up and came home."

They walked in silence for several moments, crossing the top of the field to stay out of the furrows. Charlene was having a good morning, and her joints handled the motion without pain. Then again, she'd remembered both of her pills and started the morning with a full breakfast. She would never admit how stressful it had been without Ted, and how refreshing it was to have him home and sharing the work.

"That must have been a very difficult decision. I'm certain any number of corporations would have hired a Calibara graduate. I know my father would have, even if he didn't begin to know what you specialized in. Just having the diploma would have been enough to inspire interest."

Charlene was glad to get more than a sentence out of the man. The choice to come back to Galileo had been one of the hardest things she'd ever done. She nodded, stepping over a water spigot and gesturing at the white tower several yards away. The field generators were six foot tall columns spaced about every twenty feet through the fields. They were designed for fire suppression and to create an ionic shield which protected the fields from the worst ravages of Galileo's ion storms.

"That's where we're headed. And, yes, it was difficult. There were some really good opportunities and wonderful people I left behind." She shrugged. "But I don't really regret it. I don't think I could have lived with letting the ranch die. The Double P was my parents' passion, and what started as saving their passion became mine. My biotech work continues here, and I can see firsthand the results, which is gratifying in its own way."

They approached the tower, and Charlene tossed him a key. "That one is yours. It unlocks all the field generators and keys the fire suppressors, so don't lose it."

Richard unlocked and popped the panel, swinging it aside so he could get to the controls. "So is there something in particular the tower isn't doing that it should be?"

"Yeah, the pass-through is off. When we activate the grid, or it comes up automatically, everything around this unit comes right up and starts talking back, but this one is usually a full minute to two minutes behind. It's annoying, but, more importantly, it sets off alarms when the nearest three towers can't get a hook up. Then we have to power those three down, wait for this one to completely wake up and bring them back up to get everything in sync. The whole thing wastes about 15 minutes and since the towers host the fire suppression pumps that's just too long. Daria, the woman who used to do this job, thought it was related to a watering program we used to centralize some of the operations. It failed spectacularly, and we turned it off. This tower never forgave us."

He nodded, gently pulling back wires to get a better look at the insides. "I'm not as good with programs, but I've done enough dabbling to deal with the basics. I'm better with the physical hardware." Richard checked the status screen, tapping a few buttons and watching the input and output numbers. The tower hummed as he sent power through the system. The generator rose to its full ten foot height, and Charlene did her best to wait patiently. Far in the distance, cattle bellowed and lowed, and she heard the rattle of the old seeder chugging its way up to the north forty.

Richard continued to poke at the guts of the tower, and Charlene startled as a snap of electricity arced between two of the highest points. Another couple of minutes and he pushed the wires back into place and closed the panel over the top, running his fingers along the seams to make sure the seal was proper. He had fine, manicured hands, and Charlene found herself watching the motions of his fingertips.

"I believe I've fixed it. There was a process running when the unit powered up that isn't associated with the normal start up. At least not with the ones I saw on the other generators I looked at. I've disabled it and everything pings back much faster now. We'll have to power up the other towers to make sure they all see each other, but the response numbers are coming back immediately versus a 90 second delay."

Charlene blinked and checked her watch. It'd taken him less than ten minutes to fix something they'd been futzing around with for six months.

He smiled, smug, but charming. "Do I pass?"

She laughed, offering him a hand up. "For now. We'll see what happens the next time we power up. If the tower falls over or shorts out, I'm taking it out of your pay."

He closed his hand over hers, accepting the help though he didn't pull very hard. "What's next? Didn't you say there was a problem with a seeder?"

Charlene released his hand once he was fully on his feet. "Yes. I expect that'll take longer, but I'm not going to guess at your timing. If you finish all your repairs this fast, Frank and Gravy may get some help mucking the shed after all."

Richard raised both eyebrows. "I'll give the seeder my best efforts. My Uncle had an old tractor which my cousins and I took apart and reassembled one summer. If the seeder is similar, even if on a larger scale, I should be able to manage." He paused. "And I do hope you're kidding about shed mucking, Miss Charlene."

"Why ever would I be kidding? It needs to be mucked and three hands will make it go a lot faster. Tomorrow we've got to recheck the expectant heifers and disinfect their feet, so the mucking has to be finished today."

"I understand the issue of timing, but I'm uncertain what that has to do with my tasks. I don't remember mucking sheds being part of my job description."

He looked horrified at the very idea, and Charlene held back a sigh. She knew this had been going far too easily. She rested her hands on her hips. "It's part of everyone's job description, Richard." She emphasized his name, not bothering with his title. "We all have specialties, and we attend to those first when we can, but then you fill in the time with whatever needs to be done."

Richard pursed his lips, crossing his arms over his chest. There was a stubborn set to his chin as he spoke. "And whatever needs to be done includes shoveling cow manure?"

"Sometimes, yes. It also includes weeding, running pipe, sitting watches, installing fencing, and chasing errant cows. There are dozens of things that have to be done every day to keep a ranch working. We run a small crew, so everyone has to pitch in and help everyone else in order to get everything done." Charlene scowled, fighting back her temper. How arrogant did a man have to be to think he was above mucking with everyone else? "What did you expect?"

"I expected you'd have respect for my skills and use them more effectively than manual labor. I'm certain that even if something isn't broken now it's coming. If I spend my time working on upgrades and finding problems before they occur it's much more efficient." His tones were reasonable, but Charlene saw a line of irritated tension around the man's mouth.

"Look, I understand what you're saying. It might be more efficient, and I'd love to get ahead of entropy, but I need a tech *and* a working hand. I can't pay for half of your time to be sitting around designing systems we may never be able to afford, or increasing some output somewhere at the cost of not having the planting done for lack of labor."

"Miss Charlene, you can certainly hire cheap local men to do the manual labor and provide me with the opportunity to optimize my technical skills."

"No, I really can't. I need you to prioritize to do what you do best *and* to be available for other chores." Charlene fought to keep her voice even, but annoyance leaked through. "Everyone else chips in. It won't take long before folks notice you getting out of the hard work, and I'll have eighteen other men all wanting to know why they can't be dismissed from unpleasant work too. I told you everyone has a specialty and not a one of them is scooping shit. Doesn't mean the shit doesn't build up and need to be scooped."

Richard scowled, a hard expression even with the sunburn on his nose. "You might have put that in your offer of employment. It certainly would have affected my considerations."

"So you're saying that you wouldn't have come if you'd known you had to do real work? That you weren't extra special just because you know how to speak technology?" Charlene said, leaning towards him. "Maybe that's how it works back on Central where being a self-centered jackass is applauded, but out here we take care of our own and we don't back off just because what's being asked isn't what we love to do. Ted spoke so highly of your helping folks down in Granite, I thought you already knew."

"Granite was an emergency situation. Besides checking a few cisterns, I directly put my skills to work. I don't see it as being the same. I also don't see any reason for name calling. It's neither necessary or attractive to be a self-righteous, vicious shrew. I do not know how someone as pleasant as Ted could have such a crass and unpleasant woman for a sister!"

The words struck home and Charlene looked away, sucking in a deep breath and reaching for calm. The dust and water scent of turned earth drifted to her. She closed her eyes and counted to ten before speaking again. "*Mister* Tyler, let me make a few things crystal clear. The position of technical service hand is a combined position. It primarily requires someone to look after the upkeep of the mechanical and electronic equipment on the Double P Ranch. Furthermore, it is required that the hand be willing to do odd jobs as required of a general hand, including manual labor when his primary skills are not required. The technical nature of the job comes with a higher wage even when working on labor issues. If you don't want the job then I guess it's good to come to that conclusion now. I've already paid to bring you here, including a signing bonus. As it seems I share responsibility in the misunderstanding of terms, I won't require you to repay those funds, but if you choose to terminate your contract I cannot pay for your transport off planet."

"Cannot, or just won't?"

Charlene heard the snarl behind his civility and wondered how she'd managed to hit such a chord. It wasn't like she was asking for something unreasonable. "Pick your favorite, but the Double P won't be picking up your tab home and most of the work you'll find in Ridgeback or Granite is going to have similar expectations and limitations. If you can get Jeremiah to take you back down the Double Fork, you might find something more to your liking, but he'll charge you for the ride."

"Of course he will."

Richard went quiet and Charlene didn't turn around to look at him, she was too angry. It wasn't just the attitude, which was enough, but the fact that she'd have to start looking for a technician again. She'd already lost six months waiting for him to show up in the first place. Not to mention he hadn't fixed the seeder yet, and she really needed it in the field today. Maybe she could see if Tracy's young man could learn on the job. He'd need something more than he was getting on his father's place if he wanted to build a house for her, and he had a head for machinery.

"You're contracted for a minimum of six months, Mister Tyler. I don't think that's so much to ask."

"It's a badly worded contract, Miss Charlene. I'm certain I could make a convincing argument before a judge if you wanted to press the matter."

"Sure. Judge Frebon oversees every case from Granite to Ridgeback. He also owns the Triple Cross Ranch a few miles up the road from here. I've seen him muck a shed several times, once in his going to church clothes. I'd love to get his opinion on the situation."

Behind her Charlene heard Richard blow out a long breath, muttering something about 'unfair advantage.' "This isn't helping. Miss Charlene, I think we're both letting our frustrations get the better of us. You cannot afford to return me home and, honestly, I cannot afford the transport on my own. As well, there are other factors which require I remain on Galileo. So, I propose a compromise. I will stay on and do the work you're asking of me. However, if I find a better way to do something, or if a technical task arises which I feel supersedes weeding or mucking, I am allowed to pursue it. Six weeks should be enough time to earn a ticket off planet and to measure if the work is as bad as I feel it is going to be. It will also give you time to look for another hire. Then, we'll revisit this issue. If I hate it, you'll release me from my contract, and I'll stay long enough to train a replacement."

Charlene considered the offer, frowning. She was still annoyed, but he was being reasonable and giving her time to address the situation instead of just storming off, even if she'd accused him of being a selfish jackass. She turned to face him and held out her hand, though this time she didn't look at him directly. "Done."

He shook her hand and started off, his long-legged stride carrying him across the field faster than hers. "Show me where the seeder is kept, and then I'm sure you have more important work to do than watch over my shoulder. If I get finished quickly, I'll find Frank or Ted and ask them what else needs to be done."

He was dismissing her and Charlene's temper reared again, but she squashed it down. "Fine." She jogged a few steps to get in front of him and led the way to the equipment shed, considering her options for a trainee and hoping that in six weeks she would see the last of Richard Tyler.

5

Richard paused at the door to the bath house, peeling off his mud-caked boots and setting them on a thick straw pad by the side of the door. For more than a week after his arrival, he'd been plagued with blisters, but time—and an herbal blister gel Missus Davidson had graciously supplied—had toughened up his heels. Now, three weeks later, his boots were broken in and more comfortable than his day shoes.

He pulled off his previously white shirt, flipping it wrong side out and shaking it away from the door, sending clumps of red dirt flying. He beat the worst of the dirt off his pants with a flat, flexible rod, trying to keep as much mud and sand as possible outside. After experiencing several of Galileo's odd hit and run heat storms, Richard had learned if he wanted to keep his shirts unstained, he had to get the soil off quickly and set them to soak. Even then most of his clothing had taken on a faint reddish-brown cast that would have caused his mother dismay.

With at least some of the dirt removed, Richard pushed the bath house door open. He stepped inside, setting the bundle of clean clothing on a counter meant for the purpose, and dropped his soiled shirt into the first stainless steel sink in a line of three. The rest of his clothing followed. He filled the sink with just enough water to cover the cloth and added a scoop of cleaner.

As he watched the soap sink, Richard was amused at how routine many mundane tasks, like doing his own laundry, had become. He still wasn't a fan of mucking the cattle, and sometimes felt like his talents were not being used to their fullest, but true to her word, Charlene had allowed him to experiment with efficiencies without giving him grief. He suspected he owed her an apology for their first angry conversation, but she rarely spoke to him, save in passing, which he found mildly disappointing. There was something about her that was intriguing, even when she was giving someone a dressing down. Something he appreciated more when her ire wasn't directed at him.

Richard stepped into the shower stall, working the knobs and bracing for the blast of cool water. No one wasted water by waiting to start until it was warm, not that it was particularly cold either. Ted had told him that come the rainy season, when the distant hills picked up some snow, everything in the cisterns would be much cooler, but for now they were just lucky to have as much water as they did. It'd been a good spring.

He washed quickly, trying not to wince as he scrubbed sweat and grime from his sunburned skin. He'd already peeled once, but he'd burned again and resigned himself to being continually red and tender from the waist up. Frank suggested, with much waggling of eyebrows, that a few hours of nude sunbathing would even out his coloration and toughen him up. Richard decided there were portions of his anatomy he didn't want to risk being sunburned, odd tan lines or not.

Despite his discomfort from sunburn and hard worked muscles, Richard admitted he was getting stronger and leaner. Jobs which had been difficult the first week were, if not easy, much easier. It wasn't that he'd been in poor shape before, but walking around the park, ball games and the occasional horseback ride did not prepare one for the realities of ten to twelve hour days on a ranch.

Richard dipped his head under the shower and rubbed soap into his hair, reminding himself to ask Missus Davidson about a haircut. He couldn't imagine what Anna would say to see him sunburned and shaggy like some historical savage, though he would settle for her seeing him at all. He'd sent several letters down to Ridgeback attempting to make an appointment, but she was always caught up in some event or another on her father's behalf. Her mother had passed shortly after landing on

Galileo, and while Richard couldn't begrudge Anna's father the comfort of his daughter's assistance, he did wish she would make time for him. After all, she was the true reason he'd come.

He fumbled the faucet off, shaking out his hair and letting the water drip down the drain. Even with good stores in the cisterns, everyone worried about water, especially as the fields demanded more and more of the precious resource. Richard had learned the sandy soil of Galileo didn't hold moisture for long. If it wasn't gathered immediately it was lost.

Richard stepped out of the shower and grabbed a towel from the general pile. The water evaporating off of his skin felt refreshing and he enjoyed the relief from the heat as he toweled off his hair.

Through the fog of the fabric he heard the door open, and he pulled the cloth off his head to see Charlene, a flush racing up her cheeks. Richard lowered the towel to cover himself, certain she would flee the room. To his surprise, she met his gaze with an eyebrow arch, an admiring smile playing in her dark eyes, before she turned her back on him. "Sorry. Ted said you were washing your clothes. I didn't stop to think you might be…" He heard a chuckle in her voice, "Cleaning everything else."

Richard's cheeks warmed, and he was grateful his complexion was already red enough it wasn't noticeable, even if she had been looking. "Well, there is a certain efficiency to washing yourself while the clothing soaks."

He grabbed his bundle of clean clothes, inwardly groaning as the shirt slipped off the pile onto the floor. He was not bending over in nothing more than a towel. Leaving the shirt behind, he retreated to a dry shower stall, putting the wooden wall between himself and Charlene as he pulled on undergarments and pants.

"So, were you looking for me? If Ted told you I was out here, you must have been. Is there something I can do for you?" He told himself to shut up. It wasn't like a pretty woman hadn't ever seen him naked, but those events had been limited to his infancy and people he intended to sleep with.

"Oh…" Charlene sounded distracted, and he wondered what she was thinking. "Yes. I wanted to let you know that Edwin, Miss Tracy's fiancée, will start coming over three times a week to shadow you and learn whatever you can teach him."

Richard frowned, pushing his hair out of his face before coming out of the stall and hanging the towel. As much as he'd wanted to leave a few weeks ago, he wasn't certain now. "Making preparations to be rid of me, Miss Charlene?"

She frowned and sighed. "Not specifically, Richard. No. You're doing good work. Teddy has no complaints and neither do the others, but you asked for the option to leave in another couple weeks, and if you do I need a fall back. Even with a few weeks shadowing, Edwin can't replace you, but it would be something while I looked for another technician."

"And if I decide to stay?"

Charlene shrugged, and he noticed she was holding his shirt, drawing the soft fabric between her fingers. "That would, obviously, be better, but it still doesn't hurt for Edwin to learn. I figure helping her sweetheart build his skill set is a good way to take care of Miss Tracy no matter what you choose, and it gives us a backup for times when you're away or if you get sick."

Richard considered her answer and saw good sense there. No matter their personal head-butting, Charlene was dedicated to taking care of not only her ranch, but the people on it. It was an admirable attitude. "I'd be happy to help him learn, then."

"Thank you. I appreciate it."

He was aware she was looking at him again and felt the lack of his shirt. He wasn't sure if he should be embarrassed or enjoy her lingering gaze. It had been a long time since he'd had a woman look at him with the appreciation he saw in her eyes. Richard smiled and held a hand out. "Can I have my shirt back?"

"Nope."

He blinked, surprised. "Um? I beg your pardon."

Charlene quickly held up a jar of one of Missus Davidson's ointments. "That is…I noticed the sunburn, and we're out of burn spray, but we have a really good cream. I thought you might want help getting the spots you can't reach." She took a deep breath. "Think of it as a goodwill gesture to say I'm sorry for the things I said the last time we spoke. I would prefer not feeling like I need to duck you on my own ranch."

Richard smiled. The gesture was thoughtful, and maybe they just needed to start over again. "I think we both could have handled things more gracefully. So I will forgive you if you offer me the same kindness."

She nodded. "I'm pretty sure I can manage that."

"Well, then I admit, I would be beyond grateful for the assistance. This burn itches terribly. I truly should be more cautious."

A bright smile crossed Charlene's lips, and Richard found himself staring. She really was an attractive woman with a mouth made for kissing. She was also brash and stubborn, but truly lovely.

"I'm not surprised. You've already gone red once. You've burnt a more tender layer of skin, but this should help the itching and protect it from getting worse. If you put it on before you go out in the morning it'll help block the sunburn in the first place."

She gestured to a stool she'd pulled out from under one of the sinks, and Richard obediently sat. "I wasn't aware of the preventative aspects."

"Hah…because most of the men ignore them. It would be far too sensible to prevent pain rather than treating it."

Charlene's fingers brushed the nape of his neck and an electric shiver ran down Richard's spine, making him jump. Charlene laughed, not a girlish giggle, but a woman's rich laugh. "I haven't even started and you're tense as a cow about to be branded. Do you need me to get Teddy to help?"

"I'd be just as happy if you didn't. He might think it was appropriate to tie me down."

She started laughing again. "Maybe that's not such a terrible idea. I am certain I can find a rope."

Richard found himself laughing along. She was flirting with him, and despite his attachment to Anna it was flattering to be appreciated. "Now, Miss Charlene, if you want me to stay still you must not say such things."

"I suppose this is true. You'll have to forgive me, Mister Tyler. I don't mean any harm. I'm just rather in a mood tonight. I shall do my best to hold my tongue. Now, hold still, this will be cold."

Richard straightened his shoulders, resolving not to jump as she smeared the cream across his ravaged skin. He wondered if there was someone who benefited from Charlene being in a playful mood. He couldn't remember her showing favor to one hand or another. Then again, she was the owner, and he might be reading too much into her comments.

The cream was cool and, as promised, drew the pain and itching away from the burn. Charlene never pressed too hard, brushing and smoothing her fingers over his back without agitating the skin. Part of him argued they should keep talking, should do something to fill the silence, but he was enjoying the experience. He had expected the brisk application and teasing he had received from his sisters as a child, not such a gentle intimacy.

Richard opened his mouth to speak, but Charlene found a particularly sore spot and the words turned into a sigh of relief. Tension Richard didn't know he was carrying eased from his body, and he leaned his head forward and closed his eyes, the actions garnering a chuckle he was sure was smug.

Once she'd finished with his back and shoulders, Charlene covered both of his arms from shoulder to fingertip before kneeling in front of him.

"Keep your eyes closed," She murmured.

He made a non-committal sound, but didn't open his eyes as she applied cream to the burnt tips of his ears and his face. Her fingers skimmed over his cheek bones and nose, and Richard inhaled, catching the scent of lilac under the stronger scent of the sunburn cream.

She addressed his throat and collar bones, tilting his head one way, then the other before urging him to sit up enough to run her fingers over his chest. Her hands lingered on the line between chest and stomach, then she leaned away, and Richard opened his eyes. Her gaze was intense on his face, and he tried to find words, but they fumbled around his mouth and nothing came out.

Charlene brushed his hair back from his forehead and took his hand, putting the jar into it. "I think you can reach everything else."

Richard cleared his throat, forcing himself not to stare at her lips. He had to try twice before he could speak. "I think so, yes."

Charlene chuckled, rising to her feet. "Missus Davidson would have time to cut your hair in the morning if you'd like. It's a chapel day down in Ridgeback. You don't have a shift, so you'd be welcome to come if you want. Even if you aren't particularly religious, the sermon is worth listening too, and you can meet more of the folks who live in town."

Anna. Surely Anna would attend chapel. The thought of finally seeing her cooled the heat rushing through his body, and Richard smiled. "I would like that very much, both the hair cut and the trip to town. Ted has spoken highly of Sheriff Reid's preaching. It would do my mother's heart good to know I've not become a complete heathen."

"It's settled then. Wagon leaves at eleven." Charlene handed him his shirt. "I'd wait to put this on until the cream has completely soaked in."

"Thank you, for the advice and the attentions."

"It was my pleasure."

6

Charlene sat on the edge of her bed, rubbing lilac infused lotion into her legs. Once she was done, she pulled each leg into her chest, stretching knees, hips, and ankles one joint at a time. Her joints cracked and popped, making terrible grinding noises until she got them loosened. The process hurt, but without the morning routine she would lock up and stumble at random moments. Not that it wasn't still possible for her traitor body to send her down a flight of stairs, but the stretching helped.

She shifted to shake out her fingers and wrists and caught the scent of Missus Davidson's sun cream. Charlene rubbed her fingers together, her thoughts drifting back to the night before. When she'd gone looking for Richard, it had been with the intention of dropping off the cream, introducing the idea of Edwin, and complimenting his work. She hadn't expected to catch him fresh from the shower, and the offer to rub sunburn cream on him had been a spur of the moment decision. She could still feel the warmth of him on her fingertips, the soft flow of skin and firm muscle. She might have overstepped, but she wasn't really sorry.

It felt strange to be taking so much time over her morning preparations, which were usually much more hurried, but she and Ted had worked out a schedule to give her one morning a week down time. She'd spent the last one reading and lazing about in her pajamas and this one getting ready for church. It was a nice change of pace.

Charlene pushed to her feet, crossing to the small closet and pulling it open. She hesitated over her usual church gear, a pair of wide-legged tan breeches, which almost looked like a skirt, and a matching blue silk blouse, and pulled a dress from the back of the rack. The pale green fabric was soft against her fingers and still in perfect shape despite not being worn frequently.

She slid the dress on over her under garments, smoothing it at the hips to get the skirt to lie flat, then turned towards her mirror. The fit wasn't perfect. In four years she had lost weight from some places and gained muscle in others, and the precisely tailored bodice hung looser than it once had. On the other hand the flowing skirt, studded with tiny white flowers, looked amazing and showed off her legs nicely.

As Charlene studied herself she began to doubt the wisdom of dressing up. Really who was she trying to impress? Richard? The other men? She gave herself a shake. Who said she had to impress anyone? There was nothing wrong with dressing up for herself. It had always just fallen to the bottom of the list because of the effort required, and today, dress or not, she felt pretty.

Confident in her decision, she fished silk stockings out of her small dresser, smoothing them on and adding a pair of dress flats. The bodice was an issue, but a wide belt hid some of the extra fabric, and she was pleased with the result. The dress sleeves were shorter than she usually wore, and Charlene dug up a lacy shawl which had been left on the ranch by one of Ted's paramours. It seemed a shame to get rid of such a lovely garment just because Ted couldn't remember who had last worn it.

She kept her hair simple, catching it up in a pony tail and adding a white ribbon which matched the shawl and belt. Charlene tried to remember if one was supposed to wear white before or after the rains and gave up. Being fashionable wasn't the point.

Humming softly, Charlene scooped up her hymnal and nearly skipped down the stairs without her knees or hips protesting. She even jumped over the last stair, landing with a soft thud.

From the kitchen door Missus Davidson laughed, adjusting the wide calico bonnet she wore for travel. "Well now, you seem to be in a good mood, m'dear." She moved forward, gesturing for Charlene to spin around. "And you look lovely. Is there a special occasion?"

Charlene smiled and shrugged. "The sun is shining, the seedlings are growing, and we're going to chapel. I don't see any reason to be in a poor mood."

Missus Davidson nodded, smiling her approval. "Those all sound like good reasons to be cheerful to me."

"Indeed," Charlene walked to the door, pulling it open just as Ted stepped up onto the porch.

He looked her over and blinked in surprise, then looked past her. "So sorry, Pretty Lady, but have ya seen my sister around? She's about yer height and build, but she'd never wear a dress because silk stockings and skirts are hot and were created by the Devil himself."

Charlene leaned forward, giving Ted a fierce smile. "Teddy…bite my butt." She leaned back again, and Ted burst into laughter.

"Ah, now there's the sister I know and love."

The laughter added to Charlene's good mood, and she lifted her chin as she swept past him down the stairs and into the yard. She came around the corner where two wagons waited, the first belonging to Gravy and the second hired out with Jeremiah for the short trip. Nearly a dozen men were lounging about in various attitudes of going-to-church clothes. Charlene knew a few of them would only make it as far as the bar or the brothel, but she didn't begrudge them their amusements as long as they were back home and functional by their next shift.

Conversation died down as one by one the men noticed her standing there, or someone nudged them to make them notice. Someone whistled low, a sound cut off by an *oof* as he was elbowed in the ribs. Charlene rested her hands on her hips.

"All right, if anyone has anything to say out with it."

No one spoke, and she raised both eyebrows.

"Oh, come on. I know you're dying to tease me. Go ahead and get it out of your systems."

Richard looked up from where he stood next to the gate of the wagon. It was properly lowered for a change, and someone had arranged boxes to sit on. He removed his hat and gave a bow, the only one among them wearing a proper dress jacket despite the heat. "We're speechless because you're so lovely, Miss Charlene. I can't imagine anyone having the lack of manners required to tease you." A smile slid over his lips as he continued. "Not to mention your mountain of a brother is standing behind you glowering."

Charlene spun around, coming nose to chest with Ted as the men laughed. Ted put on his very best innocent look and offered his elbow. "I have no idea what Rick is talkin' about. I never glower. May I see ya to the wagon, pretty sister of mine?"

She took the offered arm and patted Ted's hand. "Why, I'd be delighted, mountain of a brother."

They crossed to the wagon, and as Ted guided her into the bed she caught a couple looks of admiration, though she watched Richard more closely than the others. Even if she had convinced herself the evening before was nothing but a pleasant diversion, she admitted she wanted him to notice.

She settled onto one of the boxes, tucking her skirt so the wind wouldn't catch it. The men loaded into the two wagons. Richard was pulling up the gate when Kevin, one of those staying behind, came tearing around the barn waving his hat.

"Charlene! Wait!" He yelled, running up to the wagon. His face was red from the run, and he had to catch his breath before speaking. "Sorry, but that heifer, 52263, is dropping her twins. She's gone down once. I got her back up and into the shed, but she's bawling something awful. I need ya!"

Charlene swore under her breath, and Ted stood up. "I can help, Char. You go down to church."

"No." As grateful as she was for the offer, Charlene knew she'd worry the entire time if she went. The cow was one of her breeding projects. It would break her heart if the twins didn't survive. She had to stay. Not to mention she was the one on call, it was her responsibility. Damn responsibility.

Charlene stood up, stepping around the men to get out of the wagon. "It's my turn. I'll take care of it. The rest of you get going, you don't want to be late. I expect you back by dark. Teddy, give my love to Matilda and apologize to Sheriff Reid for me, please."

Richard caught her arm as she reached the tail gate, lowering her to the ground so she didn't trip. "Are you sure more of us shouldn't stay?"

Charlene shook her head. "No. She's likely still hours away from a delivery, and I won't deprive everyone else just because I need to stay. Kevin and I can handle it. Go on and enjoy Ridgeback."

He nodded reluctantly, and Charlene broke away, looking to the flustered young hand. "Keep an eye on her, Kevin. I'll change and be right out."

Charlene didn't look over her shoulder to see if Kevin was following orders, but she heard the creak of the wheels as the wagons got underway. She sighed, pulling off the shawl as she went into the house and wadding it into a ball. She was disappointed she had to stay behind, but such was the reality of ranching.

It took far less time to wriggle out of the beautiful clothing than it had taken to get into them, and in frustration she tossed the dress in the bottom of the closet. Within a few minutes she was on her way to the calving shed.

7

The wagon moved along at a good clip, but Richard kept looking back at the ranch. He admired Charlene's dedication to her work and the cow that needed help, but he'd seen the disappointment in her expression. He gathered dressing up wasn't something she did often, though he couldn't imagine why. She looked lovely, even if the sparkling eyes and smile from the night before lingered with him more than the dress.

They came to the junction where the straw-packed ranch road met the rubberized main road, and Frank jumped down from the wagon, pulling the gate open. Jeremiah guided the ride through, waiting for Gravy and the second wagon to join. To Richard's surprise, Frank pushed the gate closed and waved them on before wordlessly walking back down the road.

Richard raised an eyebrow, turning towards Ted who shrugged. "Guess he ain't feeling religious after all."

It was a simple dismissal, but Richard wasn't certain, and the way Ted kept looking back said he wasn't either. However, there wasn't anything wrong with a man changing his mind, and Richard put Frank's behavior aside. It wasn't any of his business what the man did with his off day.

With the wagons loaded, the trip into town took the better part of an hour. Halfway there a breeze kicked up, taking the edge off the heat and making the trip much more pleasant. The town of Ridgeback was tucked into a wide valley carved out from between high mesas of rusty red rock. Easily twice the size of Granite, the sight of the little city quickened Richard's pulse with anticipation.

As the wagon descended into the valley, Jeremiah stuck to the outskirts, circling the city rather than trying to cross the busy streets. The chapel proved to be a large gathering hall built at the foot of one of the red cliffs. With its whitewashed exterior, it stood out against the stone, nearly glowing in the midday sun. The windows were wide, filled with stained glass which displayed the six days of the traditional creation, with the seventh portrayed in the reliefs on the wide double doors.

Jeremiah joined a queue of wagons and carriages pulling up to the chapel doors and letting their passengers off, then parked in a wide field to the south of the building. Richard struggled with the pin on the tail gate, wishing Jeremiah would put the faintest effort into keeping it clean, and descended from the wagon. While the other men unloaded, Richard went to Gravy's wagon to assist Missus Davidson and Tracy so Gravy could park.

Missus Davidson smiled, squeezing his hands and murmuring her thanks before joining several other women all waiting for their husbands. Ted was an immediate draw, mostly of young women, but some of the men stopped as well to shake his hand and ask questions about his time in prison on Pristine.

Richard had heard the story several times now about how a girl and a gun led to Ted spending six months in the federal prison on Pristine, but the man was happy for any chance to tell the tale again. Listening to Ted, it sounded like prison was a vacation, and after his weeks on the ranch Richard conceded the point.

He shook his head, amused at how Ted's jovial manner took in everyone around him. The man would be a stellar politician if he wasn't so honest. The thought made Richard chuckle, and he turned away, drawing closer to the church and looking up at the large pane of stained glass. The panel showed waves crashing against a distant shore, and Richard felt a twinge of homesickness. The last time his family had been to the sea was only a week before Greg's passing, the last time his brother had left the hospital. The only sea he saw on Galileo was filled with sand.

"A credit for your thoughts." A soft voice intruded on Richard's musing and he spun, his heart jumping into his throat. Like a vision from his memories, Anna Reches stood a few feet away, the sun filtering around her with angelic light. She wore a dress of pale pink crepe wrapped around her like a blush against her fair skin. The sleeves were short, but she made up for that with lace kid gloves and a wide white umbrella with a lace overlay. Her golden hair was twisted up around her head in an ornate halo that left a single thick curl to rest over her shoulder.

"Anna...Miss Reches." He breathed her in as he spoke her name. Richard took two steps and caught her hands. He bowed, lifting her knuckles to his lips. "You look ravishing. I cannot say how much I've missed you."

Anna laughed, a sound as light and airy as the lace she wore. "My darling Richard, it has only been a few months. Surely you could not have suffered so."

"Every day." The rose of her perfume tickled his nose, and Richard reluctantly released her hands, unexpectedly flashing on the spicy scent of sweat and lilac. "You've denied so many of my requests for audience that I was beginning to doubt you wanted to see me at all."

Anna shook her head, the thick curl bobbing across her shoulder. "Not at all. I have merely been very busy with Father's business affairs. It has been very difficult for him since the loss of my beloved mother, and it only seems appropriate I attend to his needs. I knew you would understand."

She smiled, and Richard's concerns flowed away in the light of her expression. He could hardly fault her for being a good daughter. "Of course, though I hope now we might be able to arrange more frequent visits."

"I am certain of it. I've told Father all about you, you know. How hard you've been working to establish yourself, and how wonderful you were to me during school. He says he would like to meet you." Anna brushed the tips of her gloved fingers against his cheek. "I think you two will get along well, and just maybe we can find you a position which doesn't include standing out in the sun so much. I've never seen you so brown, though I must admit on you it is very attractive."

Richard smiled, leaning into her hand. He wished her fingers were bare, but she was terribly concerned about keeping her hands well cared for and never went without gloves. "Is that so? Attractive enough to earn a welcome kiss?"

Anna nodded before laughing and pulling her hand back. "Oh yes, but there goes the preacher. Chapel is going to start, and we must not delay. I fear kisses will have to wait."

Disappointed, Richard held back a sigh, but the crowd was moving into the building, and it would be inappropriate to sneak away, as much as he wanted to. He straightened and offered his arm. "Then allow me to escort you inside. I hear the preacher here is very good."

"Oh, indeed. Preacher Reid never disappoints." She took his arm, resting her fingers delicately at the crook of his elbow. "I am truly glad to see you again, Richard. It feels like I've been waiting for my life to start, and finally here you are. Change is in the air."

Richard covered her hand with his, leading her up the stairs into the church. "I am glad you feel so. Like the preacher, I will do my best not to disappoint."

8

"Hell and damnation, you stubborn cow!" Charlene swore, bracing herself against the cow's shoulder and shoving. "Kevin! Get her on that other side! We need to get her head into the gate."

The cow bawled, hooves shifting on the straw bedding as she pushed back against Charlene's efforts. Charlene's shoulder creaked, and she shifted for better leverage, damning the slick floor. "Kevin!"

"I've got her, just another second." It wasn't Kevin that answered but Frank's smooth voice, confident as he encouraged the animal. "Come on, cow. In ya go."

The animal stumbled a few steps, nearly taking Charlene with her, and her head slid into the gate. Charlene leaned against the cow's side, breathing hard, running her hand along the animal's flank. She watched Frank secure the lead, Kevin standing behind him, looking distressed and sheepish. "Thanks. Frank, let's get an injection of anti-inflammatory ready. I don't want to give it to her until after the birth if we can help it. Kevin, push those bales in on either side, just in case she goes down again. It'll be easier to get her back up if she's not on the floor."

Charlene felt the heave of a strong contraction and watched the cow shift uncomfortably. "You can do it, girl. Just take it easy. Let's get those babies here healthy and strong, okay?" The words were half encouragement and half prayer. "Don't you collapse on me, you hear? Kevin, as long as Frank's here, why don't you make a round of that near pasture and make sure no one else has decided to follow 52263's example?"

"Yes, ma'am."

As Kevin left, Frank came around 52263, still in his church clothes which had picked up dirt and pieces of straw, and carrying a stack of towels. "I've got the injection and more rags. I'm not seeing hooves yet."

Charlene nodded, pushing off of the cow. "Yeah, she's not presenting, but she's in full labor. We'll give her a few hours to progress, and if she doesn't I'll send someone to see if Dr. Platt can come up and help us with a c-section."

"Then I'll get comfy," Frank nodded, pulling over a rolling table and setting a stack of towels and the medications in easy reach.

"I'm surprised you're here. Weren't you going to chapel? You're going to miss the brimstone and hellfire sermon."

Frank chuckled. "Yeah, but it occurred to me that an extra pair of hands might be more needed here. Putting the good word into action, you know. I know Kevin's never birthed a cow, much less twins."

Charlene smiled, thankful for the help. Kevin was doing his best, but he preferred crops to cattle and was the newest of the hands besides Richard. Having Frank around wouldn't get Kevin out of helping, he needed the experience, but it would ease the process. "Fair enough. You sure you don't want to go change? It could be a long wait and everything in a calving shed stains."

"Eh, I'm not worried. Confidentially, the pants have a hole in the pocket and the back of the shirt is already stained." He removed his vest and bolo tie, setting them on the table next to the towels. "Though I'll admit less layers are more comfortable."

Charlene nodded, fetching a set of rolling stools from one of the supply areas and bringing them back. "May as well be comfortable while we wait, or at least as much as possible. I have the feeling this is gonna be a long one."

"Sounds like a good idea." Frank pulled over his stool, settling unexpectedly close. For a moment neither of them spoke, Charlene's attention on the uncomfortable cow. It was Frank who broke the quiet.

"You know, you looked awful nice this morning. I think most of us were sure you didn't even own a dress. I can't remember ever seeing you in one."

He was teasing, and Charlene snorted, glancing over her shoulder. "I have two of them, actually. Missus Davidson sewed me another dress a while back." She chuckled and rolled her shoulders, trying to keep them loose. "I've never worn it."

Frank tapped his fingers on the edge of the stool. "Maybe you should. Wear it, I mean. It'd shock the boys, and I'm sure I could win a bet if I knew when you were going to do it." His voice lowered, husky and close as he said, "And I have to admit the sight of a pretty girl helps distract a man from his sorrows."

Charlene pressed her hand against the cow. She knew Frank was complimenting her, but his observation, no, not the observation but how he said it, made her uncomfortable. Frank was a decent enough man and maybe even a friend, but her feelings didn't go any further. She did her best to brush the compliment off, wishing she hadn't sent Kevin to do the check. "I'm certain you don't have that many sorrows, Frank. You'd find more pretty girls in town than here. However, shocking the boys was fun. I may try it again in a year or two. I wouldn't want the novelty to wear off."

"I'd be disappointed if you waited so long." Frank said, and Charlene didn't look at him. She didn't want to see what emotions were in his gaze.

"As much as I hate to disappoint, I don't think it's gonna happen."

"Charlene."

Her name was a breathy whisper, and she felt Frank so close behind her they were almost touching.

"Look at me."

"Frank, this really isn't the time for this."

"Maybe." His breath brushed her ear, his right hand resting on her hip. "Or maybe it just makes you uncomfortable to think someone might see you as something besides the boss."

Charlene sighed. She didn't want to have this conversation. She didn't want to ruin her relationship with a good hand. Damn dress. "Maybe it does, but I am the boss and this isn't a good idea. I think you should scoot back a few inches."

Frank chuckled. "Or maybe you should scoot closer. You're a beautiful woman, Charlene, and you deserve a man who knows it, you know? I've tried to tell you before." He drew one finger down the line of her neck. "I won't hurt you."

Charlene's gut tightened, and she slid her fingers along the cow's under side, finding a thin band of stretched skin between udder and belly. Silently, she apologized to the animal and gave a sharp, twisted pinch. The result was immediate and stronger than she'd anticipated as 52263 bellowed and bucked, jerking against the headgate.

The bale closest to Charlene tipped and a hoof lashed at her head. No longer thinking of where Frank was or what he was doing, she shoved herself backwards, trying to get away from the powerful kick. She went off the back of her stool, feeling her elbow connect with something solid. Frank's outraged cursing gave her a good idea of what.

She tumbled to the ground, scrambling up on her knees. "We have to calm her down!" Charlene looked up and found Frank cradling his face, his left eye watering and already starting to swell.

He shook his head, snarling. "Damn you woman! Your cow, your problem!" He stomped off, not bothering to pick up the rest of his clothing or even help her off the ground.

Charlene stared at him, surprised at the suddenness and depth of his anger. She grabbed the stool, using it to get to her feet. 52263 was calming on her own, though the lunging had made the tips of the calves' hooves appear. Charlene rubbed the cow's neck, loosening the headgate a little to keep it from chaffing. "Well…that's that." She sighed, resting her forehead against the animal. She would need to talk to Frank, and apologize for hitting him in the face, even if it was an accident. However, she wasn't going to do it now. She'd give him a chance to cool off first. "No more dresses for me. It's just not worth the trouble."

9

Richard didn't remember much of the sermon. The Sheriff was a powerful speaker, but, sitting next to Anna, Richard found himself distracted from what the man was saying. She hadn't taken her hand off of his arm, and occasionally her fingers drifted over the crook of his elbow, sending warm tingles through him despite the jacket. He believed she was happy to see him, but now that he was here, he wasn't sure what he was supposed to say or do. Were they picking up from where they'd left off? Or was it too fast to resume a relationship maintained through electronic comm messages and slow letters?

A murmured *amen* ended the service, and Richard rose when others around him did, guiding Anna to the door. He'd lost track of Ted, but that was a minor issue, and one easily solved as all he had to do was look for the tallest man in the crowd.

Once they were clear of the building, Anna opened her parasol and looked around, making a soft 'ah' noise before tugging Richard towards an air car parked amongst the closest wagons. The sleek, silvery vehicle looked out of place between horses and wooden carriages, with the attitude of someone who didn't care if they fit in and maybe preferred if they didn't.

When they were a few feet away from the car, one of the back doors opened, a man rising from the dark, air conditioned interior. Richard was sure the man wasn't as tall as Ted, but there was an air about him which made him seem larger, absolutely in command of himself and everyone around him. He was dressed in a crisp white shirt and black overcoat with a tucked cravat pinned with a dark red gem the size of Richard's thumb. Leather gloves covered his hands so smoothly they had to be tailored specifically for him. Black trousers rode over polished black shoes, all topped off with a flat-topped black fedora, banded in matching red. Everything about him spoke of money and power.

Anna let go of Richard's arm, running a couple of steps and leaning up on her toes to kiss the man on the cheek, saying, "I wasn't sure if you were going to make it back, Father. Did you hear any of the sermon?"

He smiled indulgently and shook his head. "Not today, though I am sure the preacher would be happy to read me a list of my sins some other time." He turned his gaze to Richard and offered a hand. "Donovan Reches. You must be Richard Tyler. It is good to meet you finally. Anna speaks of nothing else."

Richard forced a nervous smile as he shook Donovan's hand. "I'm certain that's an exaggeration, sir. I know how busy she is, but I'm happy to hear she mentions me."

"Often. I believe my daughter is very fond of you, Mister Tyler." Donovan drew Anna to his side. "We've little time to speak today. I'm certain you understand the demands of business life, but I would like to get to know you better. Why don't you join us for dinner at the end of the week? The project we're working on will have slowed by then, and we can take the time to properly enjoy a repast. I am certain Anna would like to show you her gardens, and our cook makes an excellent veal steak."

"That sounds delightful, Sir."

"Very good. You are up at the Petersmire Ranch, yes? I will send a car for you."

Richard paused, arching both eyebrows, and said, "I wasn't aware the air cars worked that far out from a major power grid. Yours is the first I've seen since leaving Double Fork. There don't even seem to be many motorized vehicles beyond tractors and seeders."

Donovan laughed, and Richard was certain the man was laughing at him. "My cars work out as far as I instruct that they should, son. These back system ranchers may prefer physical power, but I settle for nothing but the best." He nodded to Anna, "Say your goodbyes, my girl. We've things to do."

Anna smiled, lowering her parasol and placing it into the car before stepping forward and offering her hands to Richard. He took her hands, kissing the back of each. He was glad to see her and didn't want to leave so soon.

Richard straightened and Anna leaned up, kissing his cheek. It was a whisper brush of her lips, just as soft as he'd remembered.

"Be safe, Richard, until we meet again."

"Until we meet again."

He squeezed her fingers a final time, and she drew away, settling herself into the car. Donovan gave Richard's hand another shake before he too entered the vehicle, closing the door behind them.

The air car rose to full travel height and slipped away, dodging wagons and settling into smooth motion over the street. Richard watched them go, only turning back to the church when he could no longer see the silvery car. His turn brought him nose to chest with Ted. Richard startled, surprised Ted had gotten so close without being seen. Richard stepped back and Ted looked down, drawing his gaze from the town beyond. He grinned.

"I saw that."

"Saw what?"

"You getting comfy with Anna Reches." Ted chuckled, wiggling his eyebrows. "First day in town and you're getting kisses before I am. It just ain't fair."

Richard laughed. "Maybe I'm just better looking than you are."

Ted snorted. "Bullshit. Gravy and the women are headed back to the ranch. The rest of us are gonna go catch a drink or three and maybe find some female companionship. Ya coming?"

Richard considered the offer. It was tempting, but he'd never been much of a drinker, and he'd just watched the female companionship he desired drive away. "No thank you. I'll catch a ride back with Gravy. Someone should check on Miss Charlene and her cow."

"Good enough. See ya in the morning."

10

Richard jumped out of the wagon as Gravy pulled up to the ranch house. He was the only extra in the wagon, and, once he was out, the Davidsons continued on toward their small home a few miles away.

He strolled to the bunkhouse, pondering his options for dinner. Missus Davidson generally left stew and sandwich makings in the cold lockers if there wasn't going to be an official dinner. Richard was certain he could come up with something. Stepping into the building, he heard the low whine of a guitar and thick singing which didn't sound entirely sober.

Curious, Richard tracked the sound and found, to his surprise, it was coming from his room. Frank was draped in the corner of his bed, a long Spanish guitar cradled on his lap, and a mostly empty liquor bottle leaning against his leg. His fingers plucked at the strings, finding a mournful melody. His eyes were closed, the skin around the left one swollen and purpling beautifully.

"Frank?"

Frank's fingers paused on the strings, and he peered up at Richard. "Well look who it is."

"Are you all right? What happened?"

Frank snorted, feeling around until he found the bottle and draining it in a long pull. "Women, Rick. Women be crazy, ya know?" He squinted, peering at the bottle. "Empty. What good is an empty bottle? Be a pal and find me another one?"

Richard frowned. "I think you've had enough. I can get you some water, and you'll need some aspirin."

"Hah. Aspirin is fer pansy boys. Real men don't need... Real men get what they want, ya know?" Frank pushed the guitar onto the bed and staggered to his feet. "Real men don't get overlooked fer a cow. Damn cow."

Cow? Frank had mentioned a crazy woman; was he talking about Charlene? If something had gone wrong with the labor wouldn't Frank still be in the calving shed? "Did something happen to the cow? Is Miss Charlene all right?"

"I'm sure she's fine." Frank snorted, digging around in the trunk at the foot of his bed. "Got a mean right elbow. She can defend herself against some cow." He slammed the trunk shut in a sudden reversal of mood and stalked by Richard, ramming into his shoulder. "Go check if you don't believe me, Central Boy. I need a drink. I'm going into town."

Richard frowned, but didn't try to stop the man. It wasn't his place to pry into whatever was eating Frank, and he had as much right as anyone to ride in. The front door banged shut, and Richard peeled off his church clothing, carefully packing hat and coat away and exchanging his formal shirt and trousers for the comfort of his everyday wear.

His gaze lit on the half-full jar of sunburn cream, and Frank's words nagged at him. Something had happened while they were away, something which had resulted in a black eye and drunken singing. The thought bothered Richard and even though he wasn't on shift he decided to check on Miss Charlene, just to be sure everything was all right.

11

Charlene blotted sweat off her forehead with her forearm, shifting on her stool and watching the monitor change as she ran the ultrasound paddle across the cow's middle. Both calves still had heartbeats. They just weren't beating fast enough, a common problem with twins. She set the paddle aside and picked up a packet of long, sterile gloves. The cow was doing pretty well for her first time, but it'd be better if they helped her. These calves were the latest results of a breeding program Charlene's parents had begun, and she'd expanded based on her father's notes. If everything went well, the animals would represent the start of a completely new breed. She just needed Kevin to come back from eating.

She rose from the stool and yelped as her left knee collapsed, sending her tumbling. Charlene caught herself against the cow, dropping the sealed gloves so she didn't end up on the ground at the animal's hooves. She used every swear word she knew and made up a few, shifting to rest on a straw bale and pulling herself up across it. She slowly bent and extended her leg until her knee popped and slid into place, sending a tingling rush of painful pin pricks between her knee and foot.

Despite how well the morning had started, crouching over and climbing under a cow was a strain, and she yearned for a pain killer and a bath. Charlene banged her head against the cow a couple times and sighed. She hated the disease that was eating her joints away, but she'd be damned and double damned if she let it rule her life.

The shed door open with a grinding sound, reminding Charlene it needed to be cleaned and greased again. She set the packet of gloves on the bale, shifting her weight onto her knee which seemed like it was going to behave, at least for now, and rose. She picked up the calving ropes, routinely attaching them to the hooves which were emerging from the cow. Break time was over. "Kevin? Get over here, huh? I need another pair of hands."

To her surprise it wasn't Kevin who came into the birthing corral, but the much broader form of Richard Tyler. Charlene blinked and tried not to think about him without his shirt on, or his britches for that matter. She had a cow to focus on, and he was one of the hands. She had to behave herself. She took a deep breath and tightened the ropes, letting them dangle and reaching for the gloves before offering him a smile. "Hey there. I didn't think the wagons would be back for another few hours."

He stopped near the cow's head, scratching the laboring animal between the ears. "Mister Walker's wagon won't, but Gravy and Missus Davidson wanted to get back. I thought I'd come along."

Charlene pulled the package open with a crinkle of plastic. "I'm surprised Ted didn't insist on showing you around town and trying to drink you under the table." The cow shifted, and Charlene shoved her back. "Stop that."

"I've never been a big drinker." Richard paused, catching her gaze, his brow creased with concern. "Though Frank seems to be working his way through a bottle or three and looks like someone punched him in the face."

Charlene sighed, shaking her head. She considered trying to dismiss the incident, but it wasn't as though word wouldn't get around. She might as well make sure at least one person had the right story. Or at least the version she preferred. Frank didn't deserve the pummeling Ted would give him if he knew everything. "Did he say what happened?"

"Not specifically, but he mentioned you had a strong right elbow." He walked down until they were looking at each other over the back of the cow. "Did you hit him?"

"Yes, but it wasn't nearly as dramatic as it sounds."

The concern look deepened, accompanied by a frown and tightness around his lips. "Maybe it's none of my business, Miss Charlene. I know you are a very capable person. However, did he do something which required punching? Not to be indelicate, but he didn't lay hands on you, did he?"

Charlene blinked. "Oh heavens, no. He hit on me and tried to kiss me, but it didn't go further than that. And don't you dare even mention that to Teddy, or he'll beat Frank black and blue."

"Miss Charlene, if he touched you against your will he deserves to be beaten black and blue, whether it was just a kiss or something more forceful. If he hurt you Ted will have to stand in line."

He was so earnest Charlene couldn't look away, captured by the intensity in his gaze. She had no idea if Richard had ever thrown a punch in anger, or at all, but she was certain he meant what he said. It was a nice feeling knowing there was someone besides Ted who cared what happened to her, but she didn't want to start a fight between the men.

"Thank you, but let's not cause an incident. I didn't even really mean to hit Frank, to be honest. He leaned in, I was paying attention to the cow and she kicked. In trying to get out of the way, I belted Frank in the face. I only realized what had happened when he was staggering out, and Kevin has been in and out fetching things so I've not been able to leave the cow to check on Frank." She paused as the look on Richard's face faded, and almost wished she could bring it back, but not at Frank's expense. She didn't want to be courted or kissed by the man, but she didn't want to fire him either. He was a good hand.

Richard nodded, some of the tension easing from his expression. "Well, he went off to town, so I'm sure things can be discussed later. Just... know you don't have to be afraid of him, or anyone else."

The cow shifted between them and snorted, shaking her head in the gate. Charlene reached down, pressing her hand against the cow's side, grateful for the interruption. "I'll keep it in mind. Kevin isn't back still, and she can't keep laboring like this. We're gonna have to help her. Would you give me a hand?"

"Of course." Richard took a few more steps until he was at the back of the cow and came to a quick stop. "Miss Charlene, why is there a rope dangling out of this cow? That doesn't seem, um, normal." He looked surprised and a little pale, studiously not looking at the liquids already staining the straw.

"It's attached to the calf," Charlene pulled on the long gloves one at a time, keeping them sterile by touching nothing except for the other glove and the bottle of birthing lubricant. "We're going to pull when she pushes and see if we can't help get them out."

Richard's mouth worked, but it took two tries before the words came out. "You want me to pull a calf out of a cow with a rope?" He seemed to be trying to convince himself that he'd misheard. Charlene grinned, amused by his discomfort.

"That's the long and short of it."

He stepped forward and then stopped again. "There seems to be a lot of…erm…fluids involved."

Charlene broke into laughter, nodding towards a couple of heavy leather aprons hanging on the fencing. "You can have an apron if you want. The miracle of life is amazing, but it is not clean. I never think about what this must look like to someone who's not done it. I promise it's not hard. You just pull nice and evenly on the rope and I'll take care of the truly icky part." She paused, raising both eyebrows and wiggling her gloved hands at him. "Unless you'd rather wear the gloves."

———

RICHARD SMILED and inclined his head. There was a challenge in Charlene's gaze, and despite his desire to fetch Kevin and leave this messy business to someone else, he picked up the apron. He didn't dare think very hard about where she might be putting her hands that required gloves of that length or material.

Dressed in cotton trousers and a man's shirt streaked with dirt and some dark liquid, Miss Charlene was a very different picture from Anna in her lace and ruffles, though no less appealing. Richard surprised himself with the comparison, and dismissed it, pulling on the apron.

"I'll leave the glove work to you, if you don't mind."

Richard took in a deep breath, the scent of manure mingling with the hay and the faintest whiff of lilac. Why did that scent keep following him? He reached for the ropes, grateful when he found a plastic handle on each end.

Charlene leaned against the cow, and he heard her counting. She looked at him and nodded. "Okay, on my mark just lean back into your heels and pull as straight towards you as you can, maybe upward a bit. Nice and easy. Once the head and shoulders are out the rest will come really fast, so be ready."

"People have been breeding cattle for how many centuries and there still isn't a machine to do this?" Richard knew there were machines to help with human births, so why not cows?

"They're expensive and the mortality rates are awful. There are a lot of limbs here to juggle, and if she gets tore up inside, infection sets in fast. I don't want to lose either the mama or the babies. There she goes. Pull."

Richard leaned back into his heels, bracing himself and pulling steadily on the ropes. They moved slowly, give an inch and take half an inch. He didn't watch what Charlene was doing, but more liquid splattered near his feet, and he focused on the red rope. Why red? Why in the world would someone use red rope in this bloody scene?

"Harder, still steady, don't jerk the rope, but harder. We've almost got her!"

Charlene's voice was excited, and Richard wrapped his fingers tighter around the grips and pulled. The ropes resisted and then, as he'd been warned, there was a sudden give like pulling a plug from a dam. Richard tumbled backward, landing in the straw just before a heavy, wet body half collapsed on top of him.

He looked down at his chest where the calf's floppy head rested, seeing it trying to breathe through nostrils covered with a film of liquid. A wet rag hit his shoulder. "Clear her nose and get the gunk off her. Her mama's busy, and I'm going to need you again. The other one is right here."

Richard didn't question the orders, mopping the calf off. It seemed like it couldn't be alive, it was so heavy and wet. He cleaned its nose again, uncertain if there was a way to give mouth-to-mouth to a cow, but it sucked in a rattling breath and then another. The calf blinked, looking at him with dark-brown eyes before sneezing a wet gob of something onto his face and trying to stagger to its feet.

"She's getting up, what do I do?" Richard did his best to stabilize the wobbly creature, amazed by what had just happened. Charlene was right, it was not clean in any way, but it was powerful. Life in his hands.

"Get her over to her mama and make sure she starts suckling, then get back here. They don't usually come too fast after each other, but there's always a first time."

"What about the rope?"

"We'll get it in a minute. I have another set."

Richard helped the calf slide across the floor, the animal near frantic to get to its mother. He wasn't sure the best way to get it to suckle, but the process seemed instinctive. Within a minute the baby was attached to a nipple and making slurping sounds that Richard decided meant success. He hurried back to where Charlene was ripping open a second pair of gloves with her teeth.

"She okay?"

"As far as I can tell, yes."

"Good. We'll let her drink until we get the second one here and then swap her to a bottle."

Richard grabbed the ropes, this time with more confidence. "Why a bottle? Isn't it best they bond with their mother?"

"Yeah, but it's hard for one cow to have enough colostrum for twins, so we'll give them extra formula to make sure they keep up weight. Don't worry, they'll get plenty of time to nag her."

There was that teasing smile again and Richard laughed. "Nagging? Is that what it's called between cows?"

Charlene squirted more lubricating gel onto the gloves, her eyes dancing. Despite the ick factor and the stress, this whole process brought a lightness to her which he enjoyed. "Oh yeah. Just wait until you hear how these little ones can bawl. It's definitely nagging."

She bumped the cow with her hip. "Okay, cow, let's work together one more time, huh?"

"Doesn't the cow have a name?"

"52263. Cow and Damn Cow."

"Those aren't names. That's a number and two generic things that apply to all cows."

Charlene gave another smile. "The ranch is 30 years old. We've gone through about 25,000 head of cattle in that time. How do you keep track of that many names? The numbers are easier to remember since they're part of the cow's tag, though I admit I've named a few, especially when I was little."

Richard tilted his head, missing the brush of the hair Missus Davidson had cut off this morning. "Like what?"

"Sunshine. She was a beautiful golden-tan cow who gave the best milk and was so tame I could ride on her. Pretty sure she never went where I wanted her to, but I didn't care. She was mine and I loved her. It broke my young heart when we sent her off planet to market. Okay, she's contracting again, start pulling."

The second birth took longer than the first, and they had to pause twice to let the cow—Richard had a hard time thinking of it as 52263—rest. Finally, the dark calf slipped free, and Richard lost his feet for a second time, even though he was braced for the arrival. The male calf was larger than his sister and more robust, snorting mucus and stumbling to wobbly feet with a miniature bellow.

Charlene released 52263 from the headgate. The cow began licking the two calves, switching back and forth between the pair of them.

"Well, that's a good sign." Charlene tossed her gloves into a red bin before retrieving an oversized baby bottle from one of the storage rooms. While she was gone, Richard glanced at his pocket watch, surprised at how long they'd been in the shed.

"It's been some time since we began and Kevin never returned. Should we be worried?"

Charlene glanced up from where she crouched, getting the first calf to take the bottle. "Good question. He was working a back to back so one of the other men could go to town. I wonder if he fell asleep somewhere." Her stomach growled audibly. "And he was supposed to bring some dinner out to share."

Richard stripped the apron off, folding it over and setting it aside as he didn't know where else to put it, and scrubbed his hands. Now that the excitement was over, he noticed Charlene was pale, looking pinched and painful. She'd been dealing with the cow for hours before he arrived and that was hard work. "Since you know what else needs to happen out here, why don't I go get you something to eat and see if I can find him?"

"That'd be nice. If we can just get these two settled, then once Ted gets back he can take over."

"Think he'll be sober enough?"

Charlene shifted until she was kneeling in the straw, the calf half across her lap. "Honestly, Richard? I don't care even a little if he's sober enough. We did the hard part. He'll just have to check on her every couple of hours. He can do that even if he's stumbly."

Richard nodded. "Seems fair enough. I won't be but a few minutes."

He thought he saw her wince as he left the shed, and Richard hoped she hadn't been hurt during the process. He couldn't remember anything happening which would account for injury; possibly her feet were sore.

Richard found Kevin asleep at the kitchen table, a half-eaten sandwich on a plate near his head and an open book under his hand. Curious, Richard glanced at the book. The pages were covered with equations, some printed and some in a narrow scrawl. As he looked closer Richard realized the book was a practice manual for college entrance testing.

He nudged Kevin in the side. "Wake up, Kevin."

The hand muttered in his sleep, and Richard nudged him again, harder. Kevin's eyes fluttered open. He blinked, pushing his head off the table and rubbing his cheek where it'd gone red. "Wha? Er…" He suddenly came fully awake and jumped up, slamming his knee into the table. "Damn! Ouch. I'm sorry. I'm coming!"

Richard grinned, resting a hand on the man's shoulder. "Calm down."

"Dammit, I fell asleep. How long was I out? The calves! Charlene's gonna kill me."

"It's possible. You did leave her hungry."

Kevin rubbed the heels of his hands against his eyes. "I'm so sorry. I didn't mean ta."

Richard started digging through the refrigerator, pulling out cold cuts before searching for the bread. "The two are here safely, so I'm sure you can explain everything in the morning." He nodded at the book. "That's a lot of studying. Does Miss Charlene know you're applying?"

"I…erm…not yet. I don't want her ta think I don't like the ranch, but I want more." Kevin looked sheepish, "I know she went away for school. I'm hopin' she'll understand."

"She will, but that's a conversation for tomorrow. Go get some sleep."

"Yes, Sir." Kevin picked up his book, carefully closing it after marking his page with a scrap of paper. "Thank you."

Once the young hand was gone Richard finished the sandwiches, checking the cooler and coming up with a wedge of berry pie Kevin had overlooked. Richard wasn't sure if Charlene liked pie, but it seemed a decent guess, and he loved it. With his hands full he had to back into the shed, catching the door with his shoulder. "Miss Charlene? Come give me a hand, and we can eat."

His call went unanswered, and Richard picked up his pace, worried something might have gone wrong in his absence. He came around the corner into the birthing pens and came to a stop. The cow was still fussing over the larger of her offspring, but the little female calf was curled up across Charlene's lap, and they were both asleep. In sleep the woman the hands called 'fair but tough' looked anything but tough. Her features were vulnerable and soft, her dark hair curled across her neck against sun-bronzed skin.

Richard stared at her for a few minutes before he finally found someplace to set the untouched food. He could carry her back to the house, but she might be happier out here until Ted got back, and she'd kill him if something happened to the new calves while they were both away. However, she couldn't sleep like that without getting terribly stiff. Richard remembered Ted saying something about keeping cots in the sheds and searched until he found one folded up and hung on the wall. He unfolded it and covered it with a blanket from the same location before he knelt next to Charlene. He shook her gently.

"Miss Charlene. Let's get you moved to somewhere a little more comfortable."

She muttered, a soft sound of protest, and Richard chuckled. The poor woman had to be exhausted to react so little. He shifted and got an arm under her shoulders and knees and pushed to his feet. She was lighter than he expected making it easier to carry her across the slick straw.

Richard set Charlene down on the cot, and she curled on her side, never fully waking. He gently pushed her hair out of her face, letting his fingers linger on her cheek for an instant before he shook himself and went to sit on the stool near the monitors and eat his sandwich. He was still there when Ted walked into the shed nearly an hour later.

The big man looked over the scene, both eyebrows raising towards his hairline. "Wow. I leave for a few hours and look at the mess ya made. Everyone looks to be here safe and sound."

"Messily." Richard muttered with a grin. "Not sure I want to be involved in that particular aspect of ranching every day."

"Eh, most of the time it's not too bad. Often they even drop out in the field and all we have to do is check on them and clear up whatever mess is left. Bet her afterbirth ain't passed yet, that's the really gross part." He moved to Charlene's side, kneeling and shaking his sister harder than Richard had.

Charlene shifted, startling and half waking. "Wha?" She pushed up on one hand, and immediately collapsed, making a soft, terribly pained noise which brought Richard to his feet.

"What's wrong?"

"Hey, Char… It's okay." Ted crooned as Charlene wilted in on herself. Richard wasn't certain, but he thought she might be crying.

"What can I do to help?" Richard didn't know what was happening and hated being unable to help. The sound of her cry cut him to the quick. He remembered that sound from when Greg had been in the hospital, the desperation of someone in a deep pain.

"Nothing." Ted's cheerful features tightened as he wrapped an arm around his sister. "She just needs a few minutes. I maybe shouldn't have shook her."

"Ted."

"It's a long story. She's got a condition and it's not my thing to talk about. She'll be all right. Just wait here and let me get her to the house, then I'll come back and take over."

Ted didn't wait for Richard to reply, sweeping Charlene up like she was a doll and striding out of the shed. Richard stared after them, sitting back on the cot in the silence. He wanted to know what was wrong, and even more he wanted to help. He had watched his brother's steady decline over the months and didn't want to picture Charlene like that. She worked hard and took little for herself. She deserved more.

12

Despite the water restrictions, Charlene stood in the heat of the shower until she shriveled and the water poured cold. She ached from head to heel and wanted nothing more than to curl up in her bed and stay there, but she didn't have the luxury. However, she could limit her list to some pressing paperwork which had been gathering and a trip to go check on the new calves after her pain killers kicked in.

The thought of the new calves made her smile, and she fumbled the water off. They were both starting off robust and healthy and the rest of the season should prove their viability. Father had wanted to breed cows that did better in the heat and made better use of the ogen and whetin mix they were fed. If all went well, these two, and a few others to be born in a couple months, would be the pinnacle of his hopes.

She dried slowly, trying to stretch out as she did. The muscles around her left shoulder spasmed, and Charlene pressed her fingers over the shaking tissue, squeezing as hard as she could until it stopped. She hated spasms; they were a sign she was dehydrated and low on potassium, and once one muscle started the others followed suit. It was going to be a long day.

Once dry, Charlene wrapped up in a soft blue robe, light enough to be comfortable but fuzzy enough to be comforting, and made her way to her desk. She paused at the window, watching as Richard crossed the yard towards the cow shed. He'd been a great help last night, and she was certain she wouldn't have been able to get both of the calves safely born without him. She'd wondered if he was going to make it through the entire process with how green he'd looked, but he'd showed more grit than she had given him credit for.

She had a faint memory of Richard lifting her off the stall floor, of the musky scent of his sweat and soft fingers on her face, but she wasn't sure how much was real and what her dreaming mind had come up with. She'd never before considered courting one of the hands, worried about creating claims of favoritism. Not to mention, after Carl she'd concluded all men were selfish idiots, but it was possible Richard could be the exception on both counts. At least if he was interested.

Richard disappeared from her view and Charlene settled at her desk, slowly sorting papers into piles of what needed to be dealt with in what order. The computer was starting up, and she had just opened the first letter when Ted came into the room with a breakfast tray, not bothering to knock.

"Good morning."

Charlene pulled the paper out of the envelope, arching both eyebrows. "Teddy, you really need to learn to knock. What if I was still naked?"

"Then I'd close my eyes." Ted paused, finding another chair and pulling it over where he could sit and set down the tray on her desk. "Though it ain't like you've got anything I ain't seen before."

"Ew…" Charlene let the letter drop onto her lap, reaching for a biscuit which was already spread with butter and honey. "I'm going to pretend you didn't say that." She took a bite, enjoying the balance of tender and flaky which Missus Davidson always seemed to manage. For a change she was ravenous. "Have you seen the calves this morning?"

Ted snorted, leaning back in the chair and folding his hands across his belly. Today he wore a brown shirt with little green checks, and his hair was finally growing out from the awful prison cut. "I have. I sent Rick and Frank in with extra feed and vitamins for the mama and bottles for the calves. Frank wasn't overly excited, but I expect that's cause he's hung over." He paused, "And because someone punched him in the face. Rick gave me some story about a misunderstanding, but I want to hear it from you. Do I need to fire Frank? Or pummel him?"

Charlene managed to swallow, the honey no longer as sweet as it had been. "No. It was a misunderstanding." She repeated the story she'd told Richard, keeping the details vague, and concluded, "I really didn't think he'd go off drinking because of it. It was an accident."

Ted hrmphed, crossing his ankles and getting more comfortable. "I suppose, though I don't like it. He shouldn't have been hitting on you, and just goes to show Dad was right about asking a woman before ya kiss her."

"And do you always ask before you kiss a woman?"

"No, but when it backfires and I get slapped I always think that I should have."

Charlene poured her tea, nodding. "Well, I can't say you don't deserve to get slapped sometimes, Teddy. You are incorrigible."

"I suppose." He sat up a little. "Oh, I was meaning to ask you. Did you shift some of the seedlings from the lab? I went to check that tray of sprouters this morning so we could do that second planting along the fire line and they weren't there."

The tea pot chinked gently against the cup, and Charlene set it down. "No. I didn't touch them. I spent the whole day with 52263 and never got out to look at the seed at all." Her brow furrowed with concern. "Gravy is the only other person with access. He might have pulled them this morning to get in front of the work."

"Yeah, I can ask him."

Silence drew out while Charlene drank her tea. She could feel Ted's gaze heavy on her and finally she looked back at him. "What?"

"I was just thinking. What's the deal with you and Rick?"

Charlene felt herself blushing, though she did her best to hide it with another bite of biscuit. "What deal?"

"The one where he's watching you sleep and getting slathered up with sun cream. Then you're wearing a dress and hitting Frank. That deal."

"How did you know about the sun cream?" A few crumbs fell from her lips, and Charlene brushed them away, ducking the real question.

"I'm not dumb, Char. Ya come looking for Rick and I sent ya to the bath house. When he comes back from the bath house he's all lotioned up. Ya can't tell me he's flexible enough to rub lotion on his own shoulder blades." Ted paused, then added, "And if he is I don't wanna know. Stop dancing around the issue. Do you like him?"

"I…" Charlene stopped herself, setting aside the last bite of biscuit and rubbing her palm against her leg. "He's interesting, and his ideas for our systems upgrades are unique and actually doable without completely destroying my budget. He's become a good hand and is willing to take on new tasks, but still doesn't give up that air of civility. So, yeah, I like him."

"Have ya kissed him?"

Charlene blinked, staring at her brother with wide eyes. "Not that it's any of your business, but no. Good heavens, Teddy, why would you go and ask that? I don't even know if he likes me in return. Things haven't gotten that far."

"Maybe things should continue not to get that far," Ted said, sitting up in the chair. He no longer looked comfortable, but troubled, and Charlene didn't feel sorry for him. He'd started this conversation. It wasn't her fault if he didn't like something he was hearing.

"Why would you say that? If there's something you want to tell me then talk, or, buggered joints aside, I will kick you in the shin."

Ted shifted again, leaving a dirty smudge on the arm of the chair. "It's like this. I saw him all cuddled up with the Reches girl during church services. Arm in arm. Later Rick was talking with Donovan Reches. Maybe it's all coincidence, but he seemed to know them well. She kissed him before she left, and he didn't mind that at all. Ya know I think Rick is a good match here and belongs on the Double P, but I don't want him breaking yer heart neither. Not to mention Reches is a belly crawling gutter snake, and seeing any of our men that friendly with him just don't sit right."

Charlene sat still, feeling like she'd been punched in the gut, and her breakfast turned to stone. She didn't have any claim on Richard, but it was unfair to have even the idea of him yanked away before she could explore it. And by Anna Reches. Was there really no man on the planet who could resist her? Charlene admitted Anna was beautiful, and she had money and charm to spare, but in the last year she'd also tried to buy controlling shares in the Double P and to convince Charlene to sell off the patents behind her seeding methods. Everyone knew the Double P produced the best ogen on planet, but they didn't know why, and that was a secret Charlene intended to keep.

She realized Ted was watching her with a worried expression and she sighed. "You're not wrong."

"Are ya mad? I know I'm not supposed to interfere with yer love life, even if I still think punching Carl would have been satisfying, but I can see there's chemistry between you and Rick and…well…I don't want no one getting hurt."

"Yeah, I know, and telling me is the right thing. I'd rather know now not to pursue anything than to find out when I open my big mouth and stick both feet in it." She tried for a smile, though it was weak. "And besides, I shouldn't be thinking about courting a hand anyway. I already turned Frank down. It'd cause trouble to encourage Richard."

Ted took her hands, squeezing them gently and knocking the paper off her lap in the process. "Maybe so, but ya should court someone. It's hard to see ya so lonely."

"Oh, I'm not so lonely, Ted. I've got you, and the boys, Tracy and Missus Davidson, and don't forget the cows. I've got a full life, and let's be honest, not many men are going to want to marry a broken woman."

Ted growled. "You ain't broken."

Charlene smiled, patting his hand before bending down and picking up the paper. "Keep saying that when I'm forty and you have to build me a wheelchair ramp." She glanced at the letter, finally reading more than just the opening salutation. Whatever Ted said about the chair was drowned out in the sudden racing of Charlene's heart. "Oh hell and damnation…"

Ted blinked, startled, "What?"

"It's from the Keeles. They're asking we close their loan and pay back the last of the money."

"Well, yeah, at the end of the year. We expected that. You said we should have plenty after harvest."

Charlene dropped the letter on her desk, rubbing her forehead. "That was my plan, yes, but they're activating the early termination clause. They're leaving planet and want to be paid before they go."

"So how long do we have?"

"Until the rains," Charlene murmured.

"We won't have enough harvest by then. We can maybe sell off some of the cattle, but even those won't fetch best price until they've had time on the range."

Charlene tapped her fingers on the arm of her chair. "We might. That seed we put in the upper and west forty. If I did everything right, and we get lucky with the weather, it'll be ready before the rains and we can get top price if we get to market first. It'd be enough."

"That's a lot of ifs, Char," Ted warned, shaking his head and running his hand over his hair. "A lot of ifs."

"Yeah it is, but it comes with the ranching. We rely on good rains and good work and no accidents every year. Sometimes it's better and sometimes it's worse. This isn't any different, just more pressure. Richard had an idea for re-piping that field which would help the yield. I'll talk to him about it. We'll do our best and hopefully we'll get a little bit of a miracle."

13

If Richard believed in portents, he would have reconsidered his dinner with Anna and her father. But, despite the gathering of dark clouds on the horizon, he was looking forward to the evening. The last few days had been rough with a lot to be accomplished. He'd managed a trip down to Granite to purchase a beautiful butterfly clip for Anna and been talked into staying far too long to meet Madam Aster's newest grandchild. Right after he returned, Miss Charlene had given him free rein to design a new watering system, listing what she needed for the north and west forty. The field drained a little oddly and the tie ins to the fire suppression units were a unique challenge. It was only in the last hour Richard had broken away to prepare for his dinner, showering quickly and brushing his coat until it was as black as when he first bought it.

His cheeks burned, raw from the fast shave, but he'd learned Missus Davidson's sunburn cream worked just as well for razor burn. He hummed happily and shifted to balance on one leg with the other foot on the sink so he could polish the toe of his shoe. The door to the bath house opened and he rubbed harder to get the red dirt off the shoe without looking up. "I'll be done in just a moment."

"No rush. Nothing wrong with the view."

Charlene's tones were wry, and Richard whipped upward, pulling his foot off the sink and nearly falling into it. "Miss Charlene." He cleared his throat. "It seems you always catch me under odd circumstances."

Charlene chuckled, crossing the room to the soaking sinks. Her arms were filled with stained clothing and canvas cattle covers, all of which she dropped into a pile in the sink farthest from him. "Seems like it. There used to be an occupied sign for folks to hang on the door, but that disappeared a long time ago."

"You could make another one easily enough."

She picked up a shirt and started the water at a trickle, using it to loosen up the dirt. "I could, but then I'd either miss out on…odd circumstances…or be doing it on purpose."

Richard wasn't certain how to respond. He watched her work in silence, realizing they hadn't really been alone since the calves—he'd silently named them Autumn and Bruiser—were born. Not that they hadn't spoken, but it had all been focused on the needs of the upper and western forty and asking if he wanted to help ride the cattle out to pasture – he didn't. She spent more time at the house and less in the fields, and he thought back on that pained cry.

"Miss Charlene?"

Charlene looked at him, slapping the shirt against the side of the sink several times and tossing it into the next sink. "Uh huh?"

"Perhaps it's out of place for me to ask, but are you all right? You weren't injured when we were birthing the cattle, were you?" He watched her closely and saw tension pull her shoulders tight before she shrugged.

"Not as such. It was just a really long day."

"But that's not all, is it?" He wasn't sure why but he wanted her to confide in him, to know he would help her if he could.

She sighed and pulled up a piece of canvass, tossing a hunk of manure into the trash with her bare hands. "You're not going to let this go, are you?"

"I will if you ask me to, but I admit I'm curious and I want to help."

"You're kind, but there's not much to be done." She waved a hand towards the corner of the room. "Hand me that washboard, please."

He complied, handing her the metal and wood contraption and silently urging her to say more as she rigged it on the side of the sink.

"Heavens, Richard, stop looking at me like that. It's not like I'm dying or anything. I'm just kind of broken. It's a degenerative joint disease. I was diagnosed with it about twelve years ago. There are a few therapies for it, but all are expensive and all off planet. Some days are pretty good and some days I hurt like hell, but I manage."

The information settled in Richard's brain, and he considered many little moments over the weeks when she'd moved oddly, or obviously pushed through discomfort. It also explained the way Ted watched over her so closely when Charlene wasn't watching. Maybe she was just as tough as the hands said, though he wasn't sure they knew about this. If they did, it certainly didn't change their expectations of her abilities or respect.

"The men...they don't know, do they?" The question was out of his mouth before he could censor it.

Charlene shrugged, lifting the canvas and flipping it before drawing the cloth down the board. "A few do. Gravy and his wife. Ted, obviously. It's not something I bring up with the rest. I need them doing their work, not wondering if I can do mine."

Richard picked up his hat, running his fingers along the brim. He thought of times he'd pushed more work on her than he had to because she happened to be there, and his guilt rose. They should be more careful with her. Not that he doubted her abilities, but he'd been raised to use resources wisely, and not to increase a woman's burden. If she collapsed because she was taking on work she shouldn't have to, it'd be tragic. But she'd never accept that line of reasoning, and he tried to tread carefully. "I can see that, but if they knew, we could do more to help you. There really isn't a reason you should be participating in a lot of the manual labor. I'm sure if you just explained..."

"Explained what? Oh, I'll lecture you all on pitching in and doing things you don't want to do, but I'm going to take myself up to the house and drink lemonade because my knees ache? I can just imagine how that would go over." She slammed the canvas down and took a deep breath before pouring soap into the mass.

"They don't need to know. They don't need to doubt my dedication or have an excuse not to do what I tell them to. Half of the men here are older than me, and it's been hard enough convincing them I know what I'm doing whether Teddy is here or not. I gave up everything for this ranch, and I *am going* to see it successful. So you can keep your mouth shut, and I'll keep muddling along and we'll be fine. I'm not a problem to be solved."

Anger competed for worry in Richard's gut and anger won out. "Right until something really bad happens and no one is in a position to assist because you're keeping us all in the dark. You're being stupid and stubborn! Like the perimeter walks. There's no reason for an owner, any owner, to be doing those, much less you. No one is going to think any less of you. They probably wouldn't think anything of it at all. You don't have to do everything!"

"Well there certainly ain't anyone else stepping up," she snapped, and thunder rumbled overhead in emphasis.

"That's not true. You're just too proud to let anyone help you shoulder your burden. I've even seen you brush off Ted. You don't know people wouldn't step up, and you're not giving them a chance. Maybe they're all afraid you'll punch them in the face for helping, or trying to get close to you at all."

Charlene scowled, crooking her finger at him and glaring. Her dark eyes snapped with ire, but he didn't regret pushing the issue. She needed to hear it and maybe if Ted couldn't get through to her, he could.

"I'd hate to dirty up your pretty duds, but come on over here and we'll see how my punching hand is doing today."

Richard took a step forward, angrier than he'd been in years. He wanted to grab her, but he wasn't sure if it was to shake her for being obstinate, or hold her until she accepted she wasn't alone. He admired her independence, but this was foolish pride.

The bath house door jerked open, carried by the wind, stopping either action. Frank stood in the doorway, blinking and looking between the two of them. Finally he pushed the door close.

"Hey Rick, there's an air car here for you, nice one, you know? We've got a storm closing fast too. I'd run or you're going to be muddy from tip to trot." He fished a leather packet from his vest, offering it over. "Got some papers that need ta be dropped off with Mr. Reches, if you don't mind."

Richard battled down frustration and huffed out a breath. He took the packet and slid it into an inner vest pocket, never looking away from the maddening woman. He'd sort where the papers needed to go in the car.

"I'll do that, Frank. Thank you for the information." He bowed ever so slightly to Charlene before putting on his hat. "Good day, *Miss* Charlene."

Richard stormed out of the room, slamming the door behind him with a satisfying rattle. Maybe she deserved the pain she brought on herself; sooner or later she might learn from it. He berated himself for the thought as soon as it occurred. He didn't wish such a thing on her and was ashamed he'd thought it, but she was certainly making things worse on herself.

The first drops of rain began to fall, and Richard spotted the silver air car waiting in the yard. He slipped into the car as the storm picked up, pushing his maddening concerns from his mind. He was resolved to have a good time tonight, and if all went well, maybe he wouldn't be on Galileo much longer—at the very least, not at the Double P.

14

Charlene frowned when the door slammed, turning back to the heavy canvas and working the soap into it. The stains were never truly going to come out, but the process of scrubbing them was good for her temper, even if her hands would smell like the harsh lye soap for days.

Frank stepped next to her, though she noticed out of reach, and pulled up a separate canvas cover. He began removing the big chunks of dirt and refuse. "Did I interrupt something?"

"Just a difference of opinion, nothing that's a big deal." Though it felt like a big deal. Why did it hurt when Richard corrected her? And why did he have to look so good going to see another woman? Even if she was resigned to not being able to court him, it didn't mean she wanted someone else to have him, especially a high society trollop. He hadn't said where he was going, but everyone knew he had a dinner with Anna Reches. The men gossiped just as much as women, the language they used was just different, embarrassingly so.

"That piece of cloth seems to be taking quite a beating for something that's not a big deal."

Charlene looked down at the canvas and snorted. "Eh, it can take it. Soap can't be harder on it than cow shit." She glanced up, her gaze lingering on Frank's eye. The bruising had faded, but there were still a couple of dark spots right under his eye and yellowing around the sides.

"Frank, I'm sorry about hitting you in the face. I know I've already said that once, but I really do mean it. It wasn't my intention. "

Frank nodded, reaching over and squeezing her soapy hand. "Forget about it." He took the canvas from her to rinse, leaving her the next one to wash. "I should have been more careful around a laboring cow, so maybe just bad timing all the way around, you know?"

"Maybe so," Charlene reached for the soap as Frank continued.

"I'd still like a kiss one day. I meant what I said about you being a beautiful woman. I've tried to say this before, but it never worked out. You've never heard me, but I want you to listen. I want to court you."

Charlene's stomach dropped, and she closed her fingers on the soap cup, looking away from him. "Frank, I don't think…"

"Don't. Don't just dismiss me off the cuff." His voice was hard, but he softened it like he was speaking to a spooked animal. "I know I'm nothing fancy like Rick there, and I don't have a lot to offer just yet. But I can make you happy. I know the business here, and you need someone to run this big ranch with. Someone who won't go away like your brother did."

"That wasn't Teddy's fault."

Frank shrugged. "Maybe not. Maybe not this time, but what about the next time? Or what if he marries some cute little girl and decides to go off planet? Or, heaven forbid, if there's an accident? Things happen on a ranch. No one knows when it's their time to go, you know?"

The soap cup fell from her suddenly nerveless fingers. Charlene grabbed for it, but Frank got there first. He pushed the cup back into her hand, curling his fingers around hers. "That's an awful thing to say," she said.

"I'm not trying to scare you. I just think you should think it out, Charlene. You know I love Ted like a brother, but things happen. Think of your poor parents in that accident. No one could have seen that coming. And Ted is prone to being Ted. I don't want to see you all alone. That was a rough six months while he was gone."

His tone was easy, but Charlene couldn't help the chill running down her spine. She pulled her hand away, frowning deeply. The way he spoke of the deadly accident and equally as casual that something might happen to Ted chilled her. She didn't think he was threatening her, but it still left her cold.

Rain pelted the rooftop echoing through the bath house, and Charlene plunged the canvas back into the cool water. "I'll...I'll keep it in mind. I have things covered here. Why don't you take Kevin and check the gather drains around the house? They mudded over last storm and I'd like to see if they're working now."

Frank hesitated, his eyes intent on her face. His hand raised to touch her, but fell back and he tipped his hat. "Yes, ma'am. Think about what I said. I'll see you at dinner."

The door closed behind him, and Charlene stared into the dirty water. She wasn't going to cry, not over Frank and not over Richard Tyler. She'd manage with them or alone. She kept repeating the words to herself, even as her sight blurred and tears dripped into the water.

15

The ride into Ridgeback was much faster by air car than wagon, a fact Richard did not appreciate as much as he might have under other circumstances. He didn't take the time to explore the various switches and buttons, his insides turned up in knots of anticipation and annoyance. Anticipation for where he was going and annoyance for where he'd left. He was trying to help, and he didn't understand why Charlene wouldn't let him.

Rain pelted the car and lightning cracked overhead, but Richard didn't pay attention to either, absorbed in his thoughts, and by the time they reached the turn off to Ridgeback the storm had passed. The driver of the air car said nothing to disturb Richard until they pulled to a stop in front of a large metal gate.

"We're here, Sir." He pressed a button on the steering wheel and the gate opened on a hedge lined walk of smooth paving stones. The car easily maneuvered up the way, coming to a stop in front of a manor twice the size of the bunkhouse at the Double P. Tall white columns held up a vast veranda which wrapped around the red brick home. Baskets and planters burst with greenery and brightly colored flowers from the desert-hardy paintbrush to roses Richard hadn't seen since leaving Central. He couldn't imagine the care it must take to keep so many varieties watered and healthy.

The car stopped at the steps and the driver got out and opened Richard's door, something Richard noticed he hadn't done in the rain. Richard nodded to the man, pushing aside everything but having a wonderful evening from his mind.

He walked up the steps, the tingle of a large electronic dust door playing over his skin at the top step. A quick glance showed him where tiny shield generators were worked into the masonry all around the veranda, creating a field to protect the precious flowers.

Richard double checked the box with his present was still in his coat pocket before striding to the double doors and knocking.

The doors opened with a surprising burst of cold air which made Richard glad for his coat. The woman on the other side of the door did not smile at him, and given the way her lips were pursed he wasn't sure if she smiled at all. She stared through him with eyes like two chips of dark flint. "May I help you?"

Richard straightened his shoulders, trying not to picture her as a watch dog with a studded collar, and gave the woman what he hoped was a charming smile. "Richard Tyler, here to see Miss Reches. I am expected."

"Hrmph." She turned on her heel, a motion which made her brown skirt flare ever so slightly. "Follow me."

Richard wondered if it bothered her that the skirt had more humor than she did, but he didn't comment, following her through the house. If she had given him the chance he would have taken a better look around the manor, which was luxurious by Central standards and downright opulent compared to anything he'd seen on Galileo. It was a casual display of wealth meant to impress and intimidate. For all of his parents' wealth, they'd never rubbed it in everyone's face.

Footfalls were lost in the deep carpets, the silence broken only by the passing *tick* of a tall grandfather clock. The house was beautiful, but sterile, empty of the babble of noises Richard experienced each day. On the ranch, the only place you were ever really by yourself was walking the perimeter, and even then there were the sounds of the cows and the birds, life in all its glory.

After passing down three hallways and through a dining room set for three, the housekeeper came to a stop at a second set of double doors. She pushed them open to reveal another wide porch, sunshine-dappled by tall trees and pleasantly warm after the cool house.

At their arrival, Anna looked up from where she was perched under an umbrella on a wooden bench, a slim book in one hand, though he didn't believe she'd been reading it. Reading for pleasure had never been Anna's preferred distraction, but it gave her a way to watch people without them realizing it, which she enjoyed.

She set the book aside, turning her face up to him. "Richard. You're finally here." Laughter played in her eyes and she rose to meet him, offering her gloved hands before kissing each of his cheeks. "I have been absolutely anxious waiting for you. The hours have crept by. And did you see the awful storm? I was afraid it would ruin everything."

Richard laughed, tucking her hand in the crook of his arm. "I know I'm not late. I came as soon as the air car arrived and the storm didn't even slow us much."

"Yes, yes, but that doesn't mean I wasn't anxious. I've thought of nothing else all day long. I want everything to be perfect, and you've not even complimented me on my dress yet." She stepped back from him, striking a pose so he could admire the creation of peach crepe and lace overlay, studded with tiny seed pearls in perfect contrast with her pale skin and the golden ringlets curling around her neck. Her corset was cinched tight to enhance her curves, even if it meant her breath was shallow.

She was picture perfect, and yet Richard found himself thinking that Charlene would never wear anything so binding or obviously useless. The thought was distracting, and he ignored it, turning a smile on Anna.

"You look perfect. Though I am certain you don't need a fancy dress to accomplish such a thing."

Anna blushed prettily and took his arm again, drawing him down off the porch into the yard. "You always know precisely what to say to brighten my day. I can't believe it's been months and months since we were last together. Having you here, it feels like it's only been days."

"Well, it has only been days since chapel, my darling." Richard teased, intending to make her blush again. Just the two of them, walking hand in arm made him feel like she was right and it'd only been days since they'd walked together every afternoon.

She smiled up at him, watching him through her lashes. "Such a tease." With a soft tug she led him deeper into the grounds, passing between two young maple trees. Richard felt a brush of moisture and heard the babble of the small waterfall before he saw the rock formation and the pool at the bottom of it. Colorful fish swam in the deep waters and decorative benches had been artistically placed around the water and along the thick foliage of the cottage garden.

It was beautiful, and Richard caught his breath, not at the beauty, but the sheer waste of resources. He'd spent all day calculating and recalculating ways to make the water in the cisterns and whatever was brought in by storms, fewer and fewer in number as the weeks went by, last until the rainy seasons. His figures even had to account for the cattle that would be leaving versus the birthing mothers who were staying. He knew Missus Davidson and Miss Charlene used the water from steaming off vegetables to water the few flowers near the house and to add to the drainage which supplied the house garden. This was the first time he'd seen someone on Galileo treat water as though there would always be more.

Anna laughed, misinterpreting his expression and pulling him to the edge of the pool. "Isn't it wonderful? It's like the one behind the clock tower on campus. I told Father I was determined to recreate the effect, though everything was a chore. They have all these ridiculous rules and regulations about water use and didn't want me tapping into the city watershed. Fortunately, it wasn't overly hard to get around that, though getting the fish here was a chore. They kept dying and all these cats would prowl around, coming right into the garden and knocking over the trash bins."

"You didn't eat the fish?"

"Heavens, no. They're awful for eating, or so the cook assures me. They are very pretty, though I'm thinking of clearing out this lot and trying another variety in red."

Richard pushed down his astonishment, reminding himself how many things he'd taken for granted before coming to Galileo. As sheltered as Anna had always been, it wasn't likely she'd even considered the waste she was creating. She simply wanted something and had enough money and persistence to see she got it.

He patted her hand, walking around the pool to examine the waterfall. "It's very beautiful."

Anna tilted her head. "Is something wrong, Richard?"

"Not as such, no. I had just forgotten, I suppose, how different Galileo is from Central. All of this is like a little piece of home in the middle of the desert." Richard crouched by the stone, running his fingers through the water. It was cold, the perfect temperature for the non-native fish. Near his feet a small panel showed the time and two temperatures, ambient and liquid.

"Yes. That's why I like it. I can escape here and pretend I'm back on Central where things are civilized." Anna drifted along the edge of the pond, sitting on a bench and patting the seat next to her. Obediently, Richard rose and joined her, pleased when she leaned her head against his shoulder. He slipped his arm around her back, supporting her without pulling her too close.

A moment passed with nothing said save for the murmur of the water, then Anna rested her fingers gently on his leg. "I really do hate this planet, you know. It's so dry and hot and the people are so…" She shuddered delicately searching for a word. "Well, they're certainly not our kind of people. They're almost savages. Have you seen the women? No sense of fashion. Some even wear men's clothing, if you can believe it. I keep hoping Father's business deals will come to an end soon, and we can go home. I have a life to live and plans for my future."

Richard raised her hand to his lips, his skin very dark against the white of her gloves. He kissed her fingertips. "And all these plans, do they include me?" Even as he asked Richard felt a twinge of doubt. He didn't hate Galileo. He was doing work which challenged him and made an immediate difference to people's lives. It was certainly the most satisfying work he'd done. He didn't dislike the people. Once he got over his initial expectations, he found them refreshing.

Anna's lips turned in a light smile, and she lifted her face to his. "What do you think?"

He shifted his arm more fully around her, brushing his fingers along her cheek before kissing her lips. She was pliant in his arms, her lips warm and soft, yielding to him without demanding. The kissing was pleasant and welcoming, but, to Richard's astonishment, boring. He felt no fire, no racing heart or pounding in his ears. There was no encouragement in her touch or desire in her kisses. He wasn't sure if there was something wrong with him, or if it had always been this way and he'd just had enough passion for them both.

Richard drew back, still touching her cheek, and Anna leaned into him, her eyes closed.

"Mm. I've missed that too." She murmured.

"Perhaps I should leave you young people alone, but the cook informs me that we are minutes away from dinner being ruined." Donovan's amused voice carried across the garden, and Richard dropped his hand, flushing guiltily. It seemed he couldn't do anything with a woman without interruption, and he couldn't imagine any father would be impressed finding his unwed daughter kissing a man he'd never met.

He sprang to his feet, helping Anna to stand as well, and turned to meet their host. "I am sorry to keep you waiting, Mister Reches. We lost track of the time."

Donovan laughed, watching them from the garden entrance. "Not at all, my boy. Anna's mother and I were famous for holding up events in order to take a little time for ourselves. I can hardly fault you. Though Anna should go freshen up and let us speak for a few minutes. Despite her dire warnings, the cook will keep our supper warm."

"If you'd like, Sir." Richard escorted Anna back around the pond, certain Donovan wanted to discuss Richard's intentions towards Anna, which was a more complicated question than it once was. If he'd been asked when he first came to Galileo what he wanted, she would have been the beginning and ending of his answer, but now he wasn't sure.

When they reached Donovan, Anna removed her hand from Richard's arm, leaning up to kiss her Father on the cheek. "Do not scold him too much, or keep him too long, Father."

"Of course not, darling girl, but it is a father's prerogative to speak with his daughter's suitors privately. Now, up to the house. We shall join you presently."

She laughed and Richard watched her slip out of the garden, drifting like an errant flower blossom across the groomed landscape. Once she was out of sight he turned back to Donovan, who was watching Richard instead of his daughter. "She's a good girl, my Anna, her mother in miniature and a great comfort to me. Not to mention, as I have recently learned, a very savvy businesswoman. I believe she is very fond of you."

"And I of her."

"Good. Your attentions please her and what pleases her pleases me." Donovan walked along the pool, forcing Richard to keep up with his pacing. Richard expected talk of the kiss, prepared to apologize, but Donovan surprised him. "She tells me you are working at the Double P Ranch. It's a location I've particular interest in. What do you think of the work going on there?"

"It's…a solid job and I find it challenging. Very different from what I would have been doing on Central, but in a good way. I have had to use my skills in ways I'm certain my professors never considered."

"What have they got you doing then?"

Donovan's voice was so casual it broke Richard out of the pattern of polite response, and he frowned, answering more carefully. "Mechanical repairs mostly. Upkeep on field generators and suppression units, new programs for water use, other ranch work as needed. I'm sure you understand that when a job needs to be done, everyone participates." Richard didn't miss the irony in explaining a concept to Donovan which Charlene had had to explain to him. He'd come to Galileo with expectations which now embarrassed him.

"Of course, that's just good work ethic. I'm glad they're keeping you busy. I've been impressed with the owners. They're hard workers and tough negotiators." He plucked a flower from the hedge, casting it into the pond and watching the fish scramble to taste it before he continued. "Miss Petersmire is a particular challenge. I have never met a woman who was so inflexible in her business dealings. Not even Anna could thaw her disposition."

"Sir?" Richard knew he sounded sharp, but he didn't like hearing Donovan criticize Charlene or the ranch.

"Oh, do not worry, Mister Tyler. I have no ill will towards either of them. I have to admire the skill which creates crops and cattle of such quality, but I think they're not making the most of it. What good is holding the patent on a method if you're unwilling to license it to anyone? With the right business deals, they stand to make a fortune and could leave behind that little plot of land and this planet which doesn't appreciate the genius behind what they're creating."

Something about the way Donovan spoke set Richard's nerves on end, pulling on every protective instinct he had. He expected questions about Anna, not about the Double P and its owners. "I think they're both happy to stay where they are."

Donovan turned towards Richard with a hard little smile. "Exactly my point. It shows a complete lack of ambition. If they lack the ambition it stands to reason they should be willing to work with someone who will take their product and make something of it on their behalf. The improvements to the ogen seed alone are worth a fortune in the right markets, and rumor has it they've improved even over last year's crop. It seems like you are in good favor there. I would like you to be my emissary, young man, and convince them to see reason. I would even hire you on to manage their account. It would be a business forward move for them and for you."

"Sir, even if I thought they would agree to something you've most certainly presented before, I'm not qualified to be an account manager, nor is that where my interests lie." Richard protested. Even in the cool of the garden he felt too warm, uncomfortable, and wishing he could go home. He stopped on the thought. When had the Double P become home?

Donovan's gaze grew sharp, and he pushed a breath through his nose like a bull. "Perhaps you should think about it this way, then. Anna likes you and expects you to offer for her hand, maybe even tonight. She is my joy and has always been well taken care of. Some might even say I spoil her, but that is also a father's prerogative."

"When she marries there is a manor set aside for her outside of Paradise City on Central. It was her mother's childhood home, nothing so dowdy as this place, but perfect for her and for the grandchildren I expect. I have to know that whatever man carries her over that threshold is a man capable of keeping her in the style she is accustom to. She isn't going to be the wife of a ranch hand or minor technician, browning her fair skin and disgracing herself by walking around in trousers. It would be shameful, and I will not let it happen. You have potential, Mister Tyler, and a good family name. It's a good match, but only if you show that you have worthy ambitions and deserve my girl."

Richard's stomach dropped. He didn't expect to live on Galileo permanently, but nor was he planning on immediately returning to Central or changing his occupation. While he understood the value of family land, he didn't wish to be beholden to his father-in-law for their home. He wanted something he and Anna could create together, a reflection of their goals and dreams.

The distant sound of a bell broke the silence, and Donovan turned to the garden entrance. "That will be the cook warning me that the food truly is in danger of souring. Think on what I've said and what you want. I am not such a harsh taskmaster, and if you worked for me there would be plenty of time left for your own pursuits. You might even surprise yourself by enjoying it." He stood in the grotto entry, the backlighting making him a dark, foreboding shadow. "Come along. We mustn't keep the women waiting."

"Yes, Sir." Richard brushed past Donovan into the sun-dappled yard, no longer intrigued by the beauty or disturbed by the waste. It was a lovely poisoned trap, a cage of elegance in the desert heat with Anna as the bait and he the unwary prey. He didn't want dinner, his appetite had fled, but as his host was also the provider of his transportation, Richard walked into the house.

16

"Okay, Char, it's on full! What're we getting down there?"

Charlene crouched at the end of the watering row watching as the water indicators turned from red to blue. The stripes across the furrow were brilliant, a much easier way to know how far the water was flowing versus having to walk down the rows and push back the soil at checkpoints. She waited until the last stripe went through its color change before straightening and waving back to Ted. "All the way down. The flow rate is spot on."

"Hot damn!"

Happier than she'd been in days, Charlene jogged to the top of the field where Ted was monitoring the numbers on a new portable monitor Richard had set up. It was based on the units the local children used for games, but he'd rewired it to pick up data from the sensors attached to the watering tape on each row.

Ted turned the monitor so Charlene could see it, and she gave a little whoop at the numbers. "That's half the rate of the flood method and still better than the tape alone. We'll have to watch the absorption, but as long as that's constant this is huge."

"We'll have ta watch for runoff. Stage two is something about gravity feeding to the other fields, but Rick didn't get inta details and says that won't be ready for another week."

Charlene nodded, watching the number go up and down. She could almost see the thigh-high grasses sucking the water up, or at least she told herself she could. The last week had been dry and hot with the extra challenge of a constant wind. It'd been a huge fight getting water to all the right places, and some of the plants were showing the effects. They weren't dying off, which at least proved the seed, but they weren't maturing fast enough to beat the rains either. The worst possibility was to come to seed during the rains when they'd both miss the first delivery date and have to force the hands to harvest in the gale. If Rick's watering system could keep the water where it needed to be, and they came around with another round of Charlene's latest fertilizer mix, it was still within reason to expect the harvest in time.

"Yer going to have to give Rick a bonus fer this, you know." Ted's tones were oh so casual, and Charlene shot him a look, arching both eyebrows.

"Yeah, that seems only fair. How come you're looking at me like I'm going to protest?"

"It just seems like you and Rick are back to avoiding each other. I thought we got past that, 'r are ya at odds all over again?"

Charlene shook her head, kneeling and checking one of the leads into the irrigation tape where she saw a glitter of water. "We did, but that was two weeks ago, and it was stupid."

"He was stupid or you were stupid?"

Now that was an interesting question, and Charlene gave it a long thought. "I think we were both stupid. He was trying to be helpful. I was hurting, and jealous, and stubborn. Then he was belligerent and stubborn, and there was punching talk before he ran off to dinner with the Princess."

Ted snorted. "Punching talk, huh? I thought I was supposed to do the punching around here. It's the job I signed up fer." His voice gentled, "I thought you weren't gonna pine after Rick. As long as he's chasing Reches it's only gonna hurt ya."

"I'm not pining," Charlene sighed, scooping up a handful of sandy soil and letting it pour through her fingers. Ted let the silence hang and, after a moment, she relented. "Okay. Maybe I'm pining a little. He's clever, kind, and physically appealing, and he's making a difference around here. I know he really cares about the ranch and it's really hard *not* to like him."

"Except when yer avoiding him."

"I'm not, though, Ted. I've tried to catch him several times to apologize and tell him how much I appreciate what he's doing, and he keeps slipping away. I got so desperate I sent a note and a piece of pie with Tracy a few nights back. I got back an empty plate. I have no idea what an empty plate means in male speak, except he knows Missus Davidson made the pie, and I didn't poison it. So I've stopped trying and left it to him to decide if he wants to talk to me. As long as it isn't interfering with his job." She shrugged, brushing her hands off on her pants and pushing to her feet. "It's not like I can really complain."

Ted rested his hand on her shoulder. "Ya want me ta talk ta him?" He grinned, wiggling his eyebrows. "I could punch him if ya think it would help?"

Charlene shook her head, laughing at his eager expression. "Naw. I appreciate the offer, but I'll give it a little longer and see what happens. Maybe if I'm giving him a bonus he'll talk to me long enough that I can figure out what's going on."

"Right. And, hey, who knows, maybe Miss Reches will develop some horrible face blotches or something, and Rick will come to his senses. Then ya can chase him around all ya want. As long as I never know about it, because ew."

She squeezed his callused hand. "Now, now, it's not nice to wish blotches on people, though I can't say I'd feel too bad if she turned purple for a while." Charlene gave a half-hearted smile. "Okay, enough. If you've got this, I need to make a round of the cows, we still have a couple who haven't dropped yet, and then check on 52263's brood. Gravy branded them yesterday, and if they're healing up good I can let them back out with their mama. See ya at dinner."

"Pretty sure I can watch water drip down irrigation tape all on my very own. See ya, Char."

———

RICHARD STOOD in the doorway of the little control shed, watching as Charlene walked away from Ted. He knew he should have been out there showing them the nuances of the new system, but every time he saw Charlene he felt guilty and conflicted. Donovan had followed their initial meeting with a packet of papers showing his vision of how Charlene's patents could be used and the potential money to be made off the patents and the ranch itself. The numbers were ridiculous.

He'd leafed through the packet out of idle curiosity, not because Richard had any intention of becoming an account manager, and found a set of smaller papers in the middle of the pile. He knew what they were immediately. He'd seen plenty of medical reports. His mother had insisted he read Greg's medical record for her because she didn't understand most of the language the doctors used, but wanted to know what was happening to her son. Richard had become something of an expert at parsing abbreviations and doctorese.

The identifying information had been scrubbed from the report—which didn't make it any more legal—and Richard was halfway through the document before he realized he was holding Charlene's medical history from the pain clinic on Pristine. He knew he should have stopped reading, but curiosity drove him forward. He read the whole thing twice and felt like a cad. Charlene's disease was worse than he'd believed from her description. Her joints were literally fusing, gathering calcium deposits which broke off when she moved. The gathering, breakage and reabsorption of the minerals caused a nerve conduction issue and damage to both the joints and the surrounding soft tissue. No matter what she said about good days, she was always hurting. She just didn't complain about it.

The notes showed she was on medications to help with pain and to break down the calcification faster, but they weren't cures. Without better options she was living on borrowed time before the damage outpaced the medication and destroyed her mobility, but the treatments were expensive and nothing was available on Galileo. The nearest planet with any kind of pain center was the one on Pristine, and even the options there were outdated.

More disturbing than the information about Charlene was what the papers meant. The obvious reason for sending Richard the medical documents was to convince him that selling the patents or the ranch itself was the best way for Charlene to get the treatments she needed. It was deplorable and said a lot for the kind of man Donovan must assume he was if he thought this would change Richard's opinions.

Richard's opinion of Donovan was already tarnished by their discussion in the garden, and after this the only true worth he saw in the man was the fact he was Anna's father. And there was the rub which kept him from telling Donovan exactly where he could shove his suggestions and ideas. How much did Anna know about her Father's business dealings? How involved was she? On top of that, supposing they did work out a relationship, would she stay with him if Donovan didn't approve? If she was innocent, was it his duty to enlighten her? And if she wasn't, then how much of her affection for him was honest, and how much a part of getting him to do as her father wished?

As Charlene disappeared into the lower fields, Richard stepped back into the control shed, settling in the hard backed chair and checking the feedback screens. When he started work on this project, the shed had contained the single tie-in for the flame suppression units in the field generators as well as shovels and buckets for putting out fires, earning it the title of the fire suppression shed. It wasn't a particularly impressive title and the system was inadequate for what it was being asked to do.

Over the weeks, Richard had begged, borrowed, and bartered for various pieces of equipment, patching together a stronger over all system and turning the shed into a control center for multiple operations. From the outside it still looked like nothing much, a large privy, but it had turned into Richard's center of operations and private retreat.

Richard stared at the numbers, but they didn't register past his concerns. He'd received a letter from Anna this morning stating that she'd be off planet for some time as part of a charity endeavor. She'd invited him to come along, but he declined.

He wasn't sorry she was away. He remembered waking up the morning after seeing her and feeling dissatisfied. For months, seeing Anna again had been the focus of all of his efforts. He'd wanted to prove to her he was dedicated to the future he'd promised, and to show her father and, well, everyone really, he had something worth offering independent of family connections and wealth.

Now that he'd seen her, he was faced with a sobering truth. She didn't need him to provide for her, and it would be a while before he could even begin to afford the luxuries she surrounded herself with. Worse still, no matter what she said, he knew she didn't truly want him. Not enough to put aside other things to see him, not enough to show her passions when she kissed him, and certainly not enough to leave her life of luxury for whatever life dealt him.

The realization was painful, and he'd spent awhile feeling sorry for himself and hiding in his work. Then Charlene had sent him a slice of pie, making him realize how much effort he'd put into avoiding her, not that he really knew why. Richard leaned back, fishing a much fingered paper from his pocket.

Charlene's script was neat and tidy, the message simple with an open humor.

~I'm sorry for overreacting. I behaved badly. I hope you will accept this piece of humble pie. The humble for me and the pie for you.~

Pie was a treat Missus Davidson made once or twice a month and Richard's favorite dessert, not that there was any way Charlene could have known. The pie was cherry and delicious. He knew he owed her an apology too, but he didn't know where to start which wouldn't lead to all the other troubles on his plate. He stopped himself at the excuse. No matter what happened or didn't happen with Anna, he needed to talk with Charlene about his behavior and stop putting it off.

He shoved the note back into his pocket, glancing at the screens again and focusing on the unit in the corner, the only display which told him nothing about the ranch. Instead it showed a wireframe prototype of his new obsession, a portable pain treatment device. If he could make it work it would be the ultimate apology, but given how much time it was going to take, a verbal one was going to have to do for now.

17

T he sun was setting by the time Charlene finished her rounds of the cattle, having to walk to the back of the pasture land to find two of the cows she was concerned about. The pair were escape artists, and she had decided she was going to have to send the men out to search for them when she found them in a dusty waller. A lot of prodding and yelling got them moving further in field, but it took forever and by the time she approached the calving shed Charlene was exhausted and filthy.

She noticed a wagon parked outside the door and pushed past it into the shed. Covering a yawn, she headed for the stall where they kept calves which were ill, or recovering from medical procedures or branding. "All right, you two, let's get you…"

Charlene trailed off as she realized there were people with the calves: Frank, who might have reason to be there, and Jeremiah, who certainly did not. Charlene's steps slowed and she frowned.

"Frank? What's going on?"

Even as she asked the question she knew something was wrong. Frank's expression was guilty, and Jeremiah dropped a large syringe, stomping on it. Her gaze darted to the calves, both showed signs of sedation.

Frank moved in front of the smaller calf into the open door to the stall. "Charlene, let me explain."

"I'm pretty sure there's no explanation for why you're sedating my cattle, except that you're trying to steal them."

He held up his hands, frowning. "It's not that simple."

Charlene started backing away. "It never is."

There was an 'all in' alarm next to the door of the shed. She didn't fool herself that she could take Jeremiah and Frank if the situation turned violent. Frank looked to be disarmed, but Jeremiah often carried a knife, and she couldn't see if he had it now.

"Charlene, stop. Let's work this out, you and me. I know about your medical issues. I'm doing this to help you."

"I've heard that before. I'm pretty sure no one who says that means it." She kept moving, afraid to turn her back on him. He was following her fast, not quite running, but with the slinking grace of a hunter. She didn't like being seen as prey.

"Last chance. Come and talk to me, let me explain everything. I keep trying to talk to you, to make you see what's best. If you keep walking away you're going to force me to hurt you."

Charlene bit down on the fear clawing her belly, channeling her inner Ted. "Bite me. I'm not forcing you to do anything. If you hurt me it's because you choose to. I'm not letting you take those calves. Get the hell off my ranch!" One more step and she bent down, scooping up an empty wash basin and slinging it at him before breaking into an all out run.

She slapped the alarm just seconds before Frank's body slammed into her, driving her to the floor. Charlene couldn't get her arms in front of her fast enough and hit the side of her face as she landed, her vision dotting with the impact. Frank's legs closed around her thighs, and he wrenched her arms behind her back. Charlene heard the wail of the alarm, knowing it was echoing through the ranch. It would bring help, but that wouldn't be worth much if Frank killed her. She thrashed, trying to push Frank off.

"Jeremiah! Just bring the little one. Hurry!" Frank yelled. He lunged upward, dragging Charlene awkwardly to her feet. "You just couldn't let anything be easy, could you? I would have been good to you, you know? I've always wanted you and wanted you to want me. We could have had a good life, but you had to throw me over for that city boy. I saw you looking at him, rubbing him down, sending him pie. Never sent me a piece of pie, did ya? I earned a chance, and you wouldn't give me that.

Well, now I'm going to be the boss and you're going to give me what I want. Jere, grab a rope. She's coming along."

He was snarling, and Charlene didn't understand half of the words. She only knew she had to keep fighting.

Jeremiah scowled, his arms full of calf. "We don't have time fer her! Jus' stuff her in the storage closet!"

"No. She's seen us. We need her to keep Ted off of us. We can ditch her on the road."

Frank pushed Charlene into a stumbling walk and after two steps she threw herself backwards, stomping his toes with the thick wooden heel of her boot. Frank swore and Charlene stomped again, wrenching away and getting a few steps before he grabbed onto her waist and dropped her again.

As she fell, her right hip wrenched with a terrible sound, and pain shot from hip to the arch of her foot. Charlene's leg went numb. She landed hard on the concrete a second time, screaming.

———

RICHARD JOGGED across the yard to where the other men gathered. The piercing wail of the 'all in' emergency alarm continued to sound, and he pushed his hat back as he looked for Ted, who was easy to spot in the crowd.

"Ted! What's going on? Which alarm was tripped?"

Ted looked over after sending a few men up to the house to check on Missus Davidson and Tracy, others to the fireline. "I ain't completely sure. Breaking folks up ta figure it out."

"I just came from the top forty, and didn't see anything between here and there."

They were shouting over the noise, and Ted sent a few more men to check the west forty. "All right then. We'll take the cattle sheds and pasture."

Richard nodded, scanning the crowd again and moving to Ted's side. He spoke quieter, but still pitched to carry. "Ted, where's Miss Charlene?" He was hoping Ted would say the woman was at the house, but Ted's worried expression destroyed that hope before his words.

"I don't know. No one has seen her in hours."

"I'm sure she's all right."

She had to be.

"Yeah, she's likely just with one of the cows. But I'll be happier once I've laid eyes on her."

Ted nodded, leading the way to the cow sheds.

As they approached, the alarm got louder underlined by the unmistakable sound of a woman screaming. Ted broke into a run with Richard hard on his heels, hitting the door of the shed with his shoulder. The hinge gave way, and they shot into the room as the screaming abruptly stopped.

Richard had only a second to process what he was seeing, the image searing into his brain. Jeremiah had Charlene half in his lap, his hand clamped over her mouth while Frank sat on her legs, tying her wrists in front of her. At least he was trying. She was thrashing like a wild cat, blood dripping down her bruised face from a gash above her eye. A few feet away the calf, Autumn, lay in a heap. Richard couldn't tell if she was even alive. Rage burned through Richard, a hot protective drive, and he found himself stride in stride with Ted, bearing down on the startled men.

"Take Jere." Ted ordered, even as he caught Frank by the back of his shirt and threw him off Charlene, sending him skidding across the concrete and into a piece of metal fencing. Ted pursued Frank. Richard stopped paying attention to them, his entire focus on the man holding Charlene.

While Richard had never been much of a fighter the weeks of ranch work had given him strength, and anger fueled by adrenaline did the rest. Jeremiah saw him coming and threw Charlene to one side, rising to meet Richard's charge with a short, sharp blade.

Richard jerked to the side, the knife catching his clothing and grazing the skin of his ribs. It hurt, but not enough to slow him down. He punched Jeremiah in the ribs, hitting as hard as he could and watching for the silver flash to come around again. Jeremiah stumbled back several steps, bringing the knife up and weaving it through the air.

"Come and get it. Make yer bleed like a stuck pig, boy."

A yelp followed the tough words. Richard saw Charlene smash a metal pipe into Jeremiah's legs, doing her best to help even with her hands half bound. Richard jumped forward, grabbing Jeremiah's wrist with one hand

and hitting him in the face with the other. The pipe swung again and Jeremiah crumpled. Richard rode him down, banging Jeremiah's hand against the floor until he released the knife. Jeremiah tried to knee Richard in the groin, but Richard turned aside, slamming an inelegant punch into Jeremiah's face. He hit the man again and again until the skin of his hand bruised and split. Charlene caught Richard's arm, trying to hold him back.

"Stop," she said thickly. "Richard, you can't. You're killing him."

The words permeated the red haze of fear and rage, and Richard blinked, his gaze focusing on the bloody mess he'd made of Jeremiah's face. His hand throbbed. He jerked back from Jeremiah's groaning body. Part of Richard was pleased, knowing the man richly deserved the punishment for laying hands on Charlene, and the rest of him was horrified. He was shaking, and he wanted to walk away, but he couldn't. Instead he turned to Charlene, reaching towards the cut next to her eye. He saw the blood on his hands and stopped before he touched her, instead loosing the dangling rope from her wrists.

"Charlene, are you all right?"

"No. But better than I could have been." She swallowed and scooted further away from Jeremiah. "Keep Ted from killing Frank, and...check the calf?" Her voice went quiet and Richard saw the tears gathering in her eyes as she began to shake.

He ignored her request, sitting on the ground next to her and drawing her into his arms. "They'll wait. Believe it or not, you're more important than the cow."

She buried her face against his chest, blood staining his shirt as they clung to each other, and she sobbed. Richard stroked her back, whispering nonsensical words of comfort until Ted joined them. Charlene sat back, wiping the tears away with a dirty hand.

Ted dropped to his knees, pulling Charlene out of Richard's arms and crushing her to his chest until she protested.

"Teddy. Teddy, you're hurting me."

He released her, tilting her face to look at the cut.

"Oh damn, look at ya. Ya need stitches. But, hell's sake, Char. I thought we were gonna lose ya."

Charlene pushed his hands away. "I...I thought so too. They wanted a hostage." She rubbed her cheeks again, smearing blood and tears. "We need the Sheriff and Doctor Kirtlin. Emergency channel."

Ted nodded, reluctance in every motion, hugging her again before he got up. "I'll send some of the men in to watch over Frank and Jere, not that I think they're going anywhere. Rick, get her up ta the house? Missus Davidson is a good nurse an' someone's gonna get gangrene sitting on this floor."

"I'll take care of her," Richard promised, noticing Ted too had blood on his hands. Richard suspected very little of it was Ted's.

The big man strode out of the shed, and Richard looked at Charlene, standing up and offering his hands. "Let's get you out of here."

"Wait, what about the calves?"

Richard sighed with a wry smile. He was still shaking from the adrenaline, two men were battered on the floor, and she was worried about the cows. He took the couple of steps to Autumn. The cow looked up at him and bawled, conscious if not moving yet. "Autumn is fine, and Bruiser is tougher than she is. The folks coming to the shed can get them put away, all right?"

Silence met the report and Richard spun around, afraid Charlene had passed out. She was still awake, though her hand was pressed to her lips. She made a funny little noise, and Richard realized she was laughing. "What?"

"You…" She shook her head, the near-hysterical laughter a strange contrast with her haggard appearance. "You named my cows."

Richard smiled, sheepish. "Well, yeah, I did. I know what you said, but it just seems impolite not to give something you helped birth a name." He returned to her side, "Now will you please let me take you to the house?"

Charlene nodded, the laughter draining away. He saw her struggle with the words before she admitted. "I…I don't think I can walk that far. I'm pretty sure I can't get up without help."

He knew the admission cost her pride. Richard dropped to one knee, catching her up in his arms. "You're just saying that so I can look manly and impress everyone who sees us. We know you're tougher than all of us put together. Except maybe Ted, and, as he is the size of some of the bulls, it's not a fair contest."

"I can take Ted. I know where he's," She caught her breath as he lifted and rose to his feet, "ticklish."

Charlene slid an arm around his neck, doing her best to support herself. Richard tried to keep his pace smooth. Even then she bit her lip, and he knew he was hurting her.

"Is there something I can do to make this easier?"

She shook her head, grimacing as they went down the two shallow steps out of the shed. "Not at the moment. Get to the house where I can stretch it out."

Richard nodded, ignoring the curious looks and demands for explanations from some of the hands as he carried her across the ranch yard. Ted could decide what everyone needed to know. Richard's focus was to get Charlene somewhere she was safe and comfortable. He took the stairs to the porch as quickly as he dared, her short nails digging into his shoulder.

He wasn't sure how he was going to manage the door, but Missus Davidson was watching for them and cleared the way. Her face was furrowed with worry, and when she saw the blood the lines deepened. "Quickly, into the parlor."

Richard followed her instruction, lowering Charlene onto a three-cushion couch which had been covered with a white sheet. She hissed softly, waving at her left leg. "Grab my ankle and pull as straight as you can until I tell you to stop."

He hesitated, and Missus Davidson nudged him. "Do as she says. I need to get the rest of my nursing supplies."

She hurried out of the room, and Charlene slid herself further up, hooking her arms over the head of the couch. Richard positioned himself at the opposite end. He pried her boot off, setting it aside before grasping Charlene's ankle. "All right, tell me when to stop."

———

CHARLENE FORCED herself to take a deep breath, knowing she was breathing too shallowly and too fast. She hurt in too many places to tell what was really damaged beyond her face and her hip. Richard's hands wrapped around her ankle and she dug her elbows into the couch cushions. "Just pull straight and steady."

He tried to smile as he started to pull, but it was strained. "Just like birthing a cow?"

"Not...not as...messy."

Richard kept pulling, and Charlene grabbed the cushions, her eyes filling with tears. She was certain someone was driving a branding iron into her hip joint, wiggling it around with sadistic glee.

"Hell and damnation!"

"Do you want me to stop?" Richard asked, easing up the pressure.

"No! Don't stop! We're so close." Charlene pulled back against Richard's grip and twisted to one side. The ornery joint held for another moment, and then she felt a slide and the pain receded to a dull throb. She collapsed against the couch in relief, and Richard released her, coming to kneel at her side. His face was lined with worry, and she touched his cheek before she remembered he wasn't hers to touch.

"Is it better now? Is there something else I can do?"

Charlene swallowed and shook her head, dropping her hand. "I'll limp a little for a day or two, but it'll be fine. Thank you. Thank you for helping me, both with this and with Jeremiah. I…" The thoughts of the shed and how close things had come surged up, and she choked back a sob.

"It's all right, Charlene. Cry if you need to." He took her hand and squeezed it. "I promise I won't tell anyone." He blew out a breath, "I am so sorry we weren't there faster. And sorry I haven't been fair to you. I've owed you an apology and since my pride didn't know how to apologize, I've been avoiding you."

"Pride is a weird thing. It's all right." His grip was warm, and despite his blood-splattered appearance there was no one else she wanted with her more. "Can't guarantee it won't happen again either, but at least I know I can apologize with pie."

"Anytime."

She looked at him, trying to think of something to say then found a faint smile, "Hey, Richard?"

"Yes?"

"It's been six weeks. You gonna stay on the ranch?"

He stared at her before bursting into tired laughter. "Yes, Charlene. I'm gonna stay on the ranch. We can't leave Teddy to take care of things while you recover, so I can't in good conscience go too far."

It was the answer she wanted to hear, and she released a breath she didn't remember holding. "Good."

Richard looked up as footfalls drew near. "Missus Davidson is coming back. You let her patch you up and get some rest. I'm going to go check with Ted and make sure the calves are all right, okay?" He patted her hand gently, laying it to rest on her belly. She didn't want him to go, even if everything he said made sense.

"All right."

He allowed Missus Davidson to take his place. "If you need one of us, just send Miss Tracy and we'll be here."

Charlene nodded, closing her eyes while Missus Davidson blotted the blood off of her face. Richard had fought for her. She'd seen the rage on his face, the way he threw himself at Jeremiah. He'd been almost as mad as Teddy. Maybe…just maybe Anna Reches didn't own Richard's heart, and maybe Carl hadn't really shattered hers.

18

The rest of the night passed in a blur of action. Richard managed to change into a clean shirt and wash his hands before the Sheriff arrived. From there he answered questions, helped unload several trays of seedlings from Jeremiah's wagon, and load the very battered and sullen Frank and Jeremiah into the same wagon for transport to Ridgeback.

Doctor Kirtlin came down from the house, verifying both Frank and Jeremiah were stable enough for transport and insisting on checking both Richard and Ted before she left. She sprayed his ribs with something which stung before numbing and pronounced the cut superficial. As a precaution she splinted Richard's fourth and fifth finger, suspecting a hairline fracture in his ring finger, and made him promise not to take it off for at least five days. Something in the thin, black woman's manner reminded Richard of his mother, and he agreed to keep the splint on, the bandages fresh, and not to hit anyone in the face for at least a week.

The doctor reported that she'd put half a dozen stitches in Charlene's forehead. On top of the obvious bruises and cuts, Charlene had a concussion and wasn't to be out in the sun for more than an hour at a time until the stitches came out. Richard and Ted both agreed to keep an eye on her, and, satisfied, the doctor headed back to town with Sheriff Reid.

Richard's final, self-appointed task was to check on the calves. He found them both in the stall asleep and none the worse for the whole evening. He made a mental note to release them out with their mother in the morning and staggered to his bunk, mostly asleep before he hit the bed.

19

One at a time the kernels of ogen grain dropped between Charlene's fingers, bouncing into the white piece of cloth on her desk. She was certain they felt drier than the last batch, but she didn't get her hopes up. She scooped up the handful, placing half of them into a petri dish and slipping it into one of the little machines which dotted the parlor, turning it into a makeshift lab.

The machine hummed, and Charlene split the grain that was left into two more plates for other operations. The last six weeks had been a mixed blessing and curse with Ted and Richard taking very seriously the instructions from Doctor Kirtlin. None of the men would allow Charlene to do much more than walk around the ranch and pull the occasional weed, or give a cow a good scratch. Sooner or later she was gently, or not so gently if Ted was involved, ushered back to the cool of the house. She protested, but he just pointed to her stitches and repeated the doctor's orders of no more than an hour until the stitches came out.

Charlene knew that much of Ted's stubborn protection came from a place of love. The moments in the calving shed had scared him badly. She hadn't been on planet the day their parents had been killed, and Ted had been left with the task of identifying the bodies and preparing for the funeral himself. He never talked about it, but she knew it bothered him and in the heart of the big man was a deep terror over losing anyone else.

The machine beeped, and she moved the tray to a second slot and started it again. The first week of her medical leave had been frustratingly boring, which she'd complained about when anyone would listen. She'd talked to Ted about going down to the seedling shed where at least she could run tests on the grain samples, but he'd refused saying he didn't believe she'd stay out of trouble out there. Shortly after she'd given Richard an earful, her research equipment had appeared in the parlor, and after three days she had enough equipment and samples to get to work. She sent him two pieces of pie in thanks.

Charlene dropped a few kernels into a clean mortar, breaking them down to dust before pouring them off into a small tube and filling it with water. She shook the tube and added in the strip of test paper before turning her attention back to the machine. It beeped again, and she tried not to hold her breath as numbers flooded the little output screen.

In four weeks, give or take, the rains would set in and all travel off planet would come to an end. They had to harvest no later than two weeks if they were going to make the transport to the Pristine market and pay the Keeles, but harvest required the moisture level in the kernels drop under 20%. The last three tests had all stubbornly remained over 30%.

She scanned the output, checking all of the other numbers first before letting her gaze drop to the all important humidity output. 18.1% Charlene let out a whoop of joy, jumping up and banging her knee on the desk in the process. She didn't even notice the bang as she grabbed the shift roster, locating where Ted should be before running out of the house.

Charlene made it to the equipment barn in record time, shouting for Ted as soon as she hit the open double doors. He looked up from the pile of tools he was degreasing, his brow furrowing with concern. "Char?" He came around to meet her, "Are ya alright?"

She laughed and grabbed him around the ribs in a happy hug. "I'm perfect."

Ted blinked down at her, bemused. "Well, I could've done told ya that."

There was a rattle of wheels, and Richard pushed out from under the tractor, looking up at them from the creeper. "Miss Charlene." He rolled off of the device and rose, rubbing ineffectually at the grease on his shirt and face. "I didn't hear you come in."

Heedless of the grease or any sense of impropriety, Charlene hugged him too. It took a second before his arms came around her, awkward at first before settling into a gentle squeeze. She liked being in his arms.

"Not ta be a spoil sport, Char, but exactly why are we gettin' the huggin' an' dancin' around routine?"

Charlene leaned back, barely noticing the flush on Richard's cheeks. "18.1! That's why. The grain is dry enough to harvest, and young enough the quality is excellent. I'm still waiting on the protein report. It takes longer, but I'm certain it'll be good. We'll need to make sure the watering lines are pulled, and we need three days to let the field dry completely, but then we can get the combine going. We've got a full two weeks to get it gathered and down to the transport. I can arrange with Mister Tuttler to..." She paused midsentence, watching the men look at each other. Neither was smiling anymore. "What?"

"The combine, Char, it ain't ready for the harvest." Ted began.

"Well, get it ready. It was in good shape when we put it to bed last year. It shouldn't take much between the two of you. Even if it pushes us out another day, it's not that big of a deal. We can get through most of a field in a long shift."

Richard frowned and said, "Unfortunately it is a big deal. We're out at least two weeks, maybe three. There are parts on order which we can't fabricate, and we haven't found anyone with a spare."

Charlene's brow furrowed, pulling the stitches, and she rubbed them. "What happened to the combine that it needs more than routine maintenance?"

"It's mostly fixed. I didn't want ta worry ya."

Charlene stepped closer, her voice gone very soft. "Theodore Joseph Petersmire. What. Happened. To. My. Combine?"

Ted hunched his shoulders, looking like a very large puppy with his tail between his legs. "Frank and Jeremiah, far as we can figger. Day after they were hauled off we started findin' problems all over the ranch, pipes jerked out of alignment, one of the field generators welded shut, all the belts in the combine slashed, the thresher beaten in two, couple of busted fences, and mudded over water lines."

Charlene staggered, and Richard caught her by the shoulders, guiding her to a chair. "How in the hell did they manage all of that?" she whispered, her stomach turning. Jeremiah hadn't ever been her favorite person, but since he was only on the ranch for deliveries she'd put up with him. But Frank…she'd trusted him. He'd been one of *her* men, and he'd betrayed her trust, damaging the very ranch he'd talked about wanting to run.

Richard shook his head slightly. "We don't have any proof, Miss Charlene, but it is my supposition Jeremiah brought in extra help who did the damage and slipped away when he and Frank were found out and arrested. I've talked to the rest of the hands, and I believe their outrage was sincere. They would not have done harm to the ranch. We've repaired most of the damage, but there are still a few things which have not been addressed."

"And neither of you thought to tell me about this?"

"It was thought, given your injuries, we should wait."

Ted crouched next to her, resting a hand on Charlene's knee. "Don't get mad at him. I told everyone not to tell ya. I didn't want ya ta be worried about anything but healing."

Charlene rested her hand on top of her brother's. "That's an excuse for the first few days, Ted." She met his gaze, angrier at him than she'd ever been in her entire life. "It's been almost SIX weeks."

"I was doing it for your own good."

Charlene didn't think about hitting him before she did it. Unlike Frank she didn't hit Ted in the face, instead hitting him hard enough in the chest that Ted fell back onto his butt, staring at her in shock. Charlene stood up, looking down at her brother who usually loomed over her. "I love you, Ted, but you do not get to make decisions based on what you think is for my own good. I am not a child, and you are not my father. You're my brother, and you're my ranch manager. I expect you to trust me enough to bring me information, even the nasty stuff. I have lists of equipment vendors, and contacts who can expedite the process of getting us parts."

"How was I supposed to know that?"

"I've offered to show you a million times, but you laugh it off as paperwork stuff. If I had to stay in the house, making comm calls would have been the perfect way to help, you idiot." Ted's expression turned sheepish, and Charlene shot a glare at Richard. "What about you? Did you think this was for my own good?"

Richard looked between them before answering, and she heard him trying to strike a neutral tone. "I don't think my opinion in this case is relevant, though I may have mentioned we should make a report. I'm not going to take sides as I would rather neither of you hit me. I think at this point it's much more important to create a plan for how we can meet the needs of the harvest and then discuss better ways to share information at all levels."

His voice was gentle, the kind of voice Charlene used with a spooked cow. She arched a brow at him. "Are you managing me?"

"Maybe a little," Richard admitted, his smile tentative. "But I'm also being honest. We can either deal with the past or the present, and if we delay one for the other we'll miss our window of opportunity. So I think we need to know what our options are now."

Ted shifted, but didn't bother getting up. "If Char will give me the lists I can see if we can get parts here sooner, or she can. It don't much matter who does it, but someone should make comm calls as soon as they can. It really comes down to finding anyone on planet with the right size belts."

Charlene nodded, fighting to focus through her anger. She gave Richard a bit of leeway for not telling her because he'd been told not to by his boss, but Ted should have known better than to hold back information. She got bumped on the head, that didn't mean she couldn't still think. "Yes, but even that is jumping too far ahead. The first step is to pull the pipes and get the field drying. That has to happen no matter what other solution we come up with."

She looked around the big barn, chewing her lower lip. "We can start the harvest anyway. We've got sickles, scythes, cradles and the hand threshers somewhere. Likely in the upper deck here. Even if we can't get all of it in before the shipping deadline, we can ship whatever we have. If we have to store the rest we can, but we have to get it out of the fields before the moisture drops below 13 percent and before the rains come in. With the field generators we can take a storm or two, but not the fall rains."

"How fast is the hand harvest?" Richard asked.

"Three acres a day, maybe as many as five if I can get extra hands and we stagger the shifts. We've got 80 acres between the two fields and 18 days at best before everything has to go to transport. It's possible to do it all by hand, but it means doing nothing else and one storm or other incident and we'll miss. There's no margin for error."

Ted pulled his knees up, resting his arms against them in a lazy sprawl. "As ya can tell, Char is the optimist between us."

Charlene found a slight smile and offered him a hand. "I'm the realist. I'll take the comm work while you start drying the fields, fix anything else you can and get an inventory of the hand tools. I can see if they have extra hands in Granite or over at the Triple that we can hire for short shifts. Richard, get me a list of everything you need or think you could make work. I'll see what I can drum up."

"Do ya think the Keeles might take a partial payment?" Ted asked, brushing the dust off his hands and the butt of his jeans.

"I'll find out. And while you're making lists I want to know about all of the damages, even the stuff that's fixed. No holding back information, even for the best of intentions. Let's get to work."

20

Richard watched the bolt slip from his fingers and clatter to the floor with a weary horror. It hadn't gone far, but fetching it required moving, and, after nearly a full week of hand harvesting, he wasn't sure if he got down on the floor that he'd be able to get back up again. He yearned for a tub of hot water and one of the bath salt bombs his mother used to buy for him. He didn't care if his father didn't think the salts were manly; they smelled good and did wonders for sore muscles. Then he wanted to sleep for about three days. He knew none of his wistful wishes were going to happen, but they were nice day dreams while he fought to get the combine back together. Charlene had worked some kind of magic and come up with almost all the parts he needed, even if a few of them were from the jury rig list.

As though conjured by his thoughts, Charlene walked into the barn, pulling one of the hover units Richard had salvaged from a junk pile last month. It was loaded with a large crate, several thick loops of machinery belting sticking out of the top. A few sickles and a scythe rode along as well, which meant they needed more repair than the sharpening and grip wraps they did in the field.

"Richard? You in here?"

Despite the protests of his thighs, Richard pushed to his feet. "Back here."

Charlene smiled when she saw him, and he smiled back. Her smiles came quickly these days, and he liked the feeling that he was a reason for the expression. Not that he could tell her so, much to his frustration. Over the last few weeks he'd thought long and hard about his relationship with Anna and concluded that even if she was innocent of her father's schemes, she wasn't what he wanted.

Anna was a woman of parasols and charity balls who would never consider getting her hands dirty to bring a new life into the world, or stand in a darkened field pointing out shooting stars. Life with Anna would be glittering, and beautiful, and boring. He didn't want a life of a standard job, coming home to attend social events and sit in his den drinking whiskey while his wife spent his money. He knew it worked for some people—heavens knew his parents were happy enough—but Richard wanted more. And that's where things got complex. He didn't want Anna, but he had all but offered for her hand. Until he had a chance to talk to her and formally break off his courtship he couldn't pursue anyone else, even if he had definitely had someone else in mind. It just wasn't right.

Charlene scooped up the box, which seemed more awkward than heavy, and brought it over, letting it drop next to his stool. The black and red belts bounced around, but gamely stayed in place, and she leaned against the combine. "I'm pretty sure there is not a damn 1020 belt on the entire planet. But I found six 1030 belts and a 1010. Can we fabricate anything close to a 1020 out of these?"

Richard picked up one of the 1030 belts, running his fingers along the length of rubber and considering the question. "Maybe. The 1030s are technically too long for what we're fixing and the 1010, naturally, is too short. We could try cutting and splicing the 1030s, but that creates a weak point which I don't like."

"Will the 1010 stretch?"

"Not without causing the same problem. We might be able to heat it and stretch it, but we're robbing the material of strength by doing it."

Charlene banged the back of her head against the combine with a little frustrated huff. "Dammit. I was hoping I'd found something helpful. The harvest is too slow. We've only pulled 20 acres in nearly seven days. I out-clevered myself by selecting for thicker stalks and larger kernel pockets on the ogen. It'll hold up under a storm, sure, but it's so much harder to cut it's slowing everything down and forcing us to resharpen too often. I've got a similar problem with the threshing. We can thresh immediately, but it's taking extra time to make sure we've got all the yield. Not that the yield isn't impressive, we're getting over 200 bushel an acre, but…"

She sighed, and he finished for her.

"It's too slow. No one has a working machine we can borrow or buy?"

"I'm working on that angle. The Triple Cross doesn't do grain, just livestock, and they're our closest neighbor. Stacia's got a combine down in Granite, but I have no idea how we'd get it up here. Maybe in pieces and wagons, but we're still running up against time. I need a combine now, not in a week." Charlene held up her hands. "Not that I'm blaming you. You've already pulled off a couple of miracles with the watering programs and re-welding both of the threshing tables. I'm just frustrated. We're so close, and I do not want to make the men harvest in the rains."

Richard nodded and peered into the combine again, following the path of the belts, or at least where the belts should have been. He blinked a few times and then leaned further into the machine, tapping the pulleys and making mental measurements. Charlene bent down next to him and he felt pleasant warmth where her shoulder pressed against his. The scent of lilac hit him, and he inhaled deeply.

"You always smell like lilacs."

She looked at him with a bemused expression. "It's my soap. When I was little my mother used to tell me about the hedges of lilacs which grew up behind her house and how they'd bloom every spring. We can't grow lilacs here, they take too much water, but she would order in lilac soaps and lotions. Madam Aster still brings it in for me."

"I like it." Richard waited for her to tease him, but instead Charlene just gave him one of those shy smiles, the ones he liked the most.

"Thank you."

"You're wel…" Richard stopped midword, "Oh, of course!"

Charlene raised both eyebrows. "Huh?"

Richard stood up and leaned past her pulling on one of the pulleys, tapping the metal behind it. "What about a two part process? It wouldn't be perfect, but it would buy us time until we can get the other belts in."

"I like the sound of it, but I'm not sure what you've got in mind."

Richard pointed at the spot he'd just tapped, "I think I can move one of these pulley sets back far enough that we can use the bigger belt, but it wouldn't feed the upper belt. So the grain would get cut, but the conveyer to lift it to the thresher wouldn't spin. But if we cut the whole field and then gathered and tossed it into the thresher, we'd still be faster than doing the whole thing by hand. It's not an elegant solution, but it's a solution."

He leaned back, rotating sore shoulders and watching her think through the steps. As she had the week before, she caught him by surprise by pulling him into a tight hug. This time he responded faster, closing his eyes to take in her scent and enjoy the brief press before she stepped back. "How long will it take?"

Richard grinned, the weariness easing, "Couple hours I think. Faster if I get a piece of pie."

Charlene laughed, her laughter bouncing around the barn and setting a few birds into flight. "Richard, you get this combine running and I will make you a pie with my very own hands. As Teddy will tell you, that is an event in and of itself. Though for tonight, give me fifteen minutes and I'll see what I can dig up."

Charlene nearly skipped out of the barn, and Richard started sorting the belts, though he couldn't stop smiling. He hoped Anna would return soon because had plans to keep making Charlene Petersmire happy, maybe for the rest of her life.

21

Ogen seed poured in a river of golden grains into the last burlap sack. Ted cinched it up and tied off the top with a second zip tie, tossing it onto the wagon load with a satisfied grunt. "That, ladies and gentlemen, is what a 210 average looks like. An' it's the end of the load we need to ship."

Charlene glanced up from where she was honing the edge on a sickle. She'd lost track of how many times they'd sharpened the devices, some of them right to nubs, finding them useful even once the combine was running. The sun was just setting, kissing the sky with fiery orange and pink, and she looked around at the weary workers. "Then we're going to call it a day. Thank you, everyone. We've still got a day or two worth of clean up to do for the local sales, but you've all earned a break. Gather up the equipment and get the wagons under cover and locked down. Spread the word we're headed in. It looks to be a nice night so we'll pull out the tables and have a celebratory dinner in the yard."

A ragged cheer met the announcement and the men started scrambling to clean up and set things right for the evening. Charlene rose and added the sickle to a growing pile.

"Ted, I should go warn Missus Davidson that hungry hordes are about to descend."

Ted nodded. "Go ahead. If ya think ya can talk her into making slab toast I'd be happy ta eat it."

"I think slab toast has to soak overnight, but I'll ask."

Charlene headed back toward the ranch house, a near twenty minute walk, which was still faster than the hands would be able to clean up. Everything ached, but they had made their deadline, and she wasn't about to complain over some stiffness. Richard's plan with the combine had worked well, and they'd jumped from a less than three acre a day harvest to over five, clearing both fields with time to spare. The threshed stalks still needed to be bound for straw and the last gleaning pass made to sell to the neighbors, but the bulk of the work was completed. Richard had more than earned his promised pie. She wondered if he had a favorite flavor; she'd never asked.

By the time she reached the ranch house, Charlene had decided to open the beer kegs. They usually saved the locally brewed beer for the harvest celebrations after the rains, but given how much had been accomplished in three short weeks and the bonus they'd get at market for such an early delivery, she felt like celebrating now.

She pushed the door open and a variety of smells rushed to meet her, making her stomach rumble. Charlene made her way to the kitchen, laughing when she saw the piles of food on the table and Missus Davidson and Tracy busy at the stove.

"How did you know?"

Missus Davidson peered over her shoulder, giving the stew in front of her a stir. "I made an educated guess based on how close the work was this afternoon. Since I hadn't seen shifts start coming in for dinner it stood to reason we'd all be eating together. I do wish I'd had just a little more notice. I would have done more baking this morning, but what we have will have to do."

"What you have is going to be plenty." Charlene snitched the heel of a loaf of bread, breaking off a piece and popping it in her mouth. Hunger really was an amazing sauce, and the bread had a delightful crunch from sprouted ogen worked into the dough. "I'll go see about getting the tables moved out. I thought we'd eat in the yard and break open the beer. Maybe even get that husband of yours to fiddle for us if you can talk him into it."

"As though he ever misses a chance," Missus Davidson fished in the larger cooler, coming out with several bottles of bright preserves and adding them to the table. "I'll find the hanging lights and bring them out as well."

"Thank you," Charlene turned to go then stopped, "Missus Davidson, I, that is, I would like to learn how to make a pie."

"Oh?" Missus Davidson wasn't facing her, but Charlene heard the smile in the woman's voice. "That's the first time you've shown interest in baking. It t wouldn't have anything to do with Mister Tyler, would it?"

"It might." Charlene's cheeks warmed, and she bit off another piece of bread. She swallowed, "I owe him for getting the combine fixed is all."

"Indeed. Then once we're through this first harvest we can work on it. Plenty of time during the rains to learn to make a proper crust. That's when I usually put the preserves and pie fillings up anyway. I can use another hand."

"I'll plan on it."

Charlene was to the door when Missus Davidson added, "He likes the cherry best."

"That's good to know."

<h1 style="text-align:center">22</h1>

Richard was among the last to come in from the field, the combine chugging its way along until he could maneuver it into the barn. Given the amount of jury rigging the machine had gone through, it was running better than expected, and he didn't see or hear anything rattling in a way it shouldn't. He was looking forward to getting the proper parts and making correct repairs, but that could wait for a while yet.

It only took a few moments to shut the combine down and sweep out the chaff from the teeth. Richard heard the babble of folks coming from outside the shed and hurried out to join the crowd. As he reached the yard he was greeted by the scents of warm bread and the pop of slices of meat being roasted over a large fire barrel. The dining tables were arranged to give everyone room to stretch out with mounds of food piled on a head table.

Richard breathed in the sights and smells, his stomach rumbling, and he hurried to claim a place at the closest table. He was surprised to see not only the familiar faces of the other ranch hands at the tables, but several women and children as well. Richard knew many of the hands had families who lived on small farms of their own, but he had rarely seen any of them save at church.

Someone gave a sharp whistle and the sounds of talking died down. Ted and Charlene stood by the food table, both obviously exhausted but pleased. Charlene caught his gaze for a moment, sharing one of those soft smiles he liked so much before her brother raised his hands, drawing attention.

"Gonna keep this short, cause I know the food is a LOT more exciting than I am. We just wanted ta thank everyone again. We know this doubled up work for almost all of us, but it's going to give us some breathing space and will be worth a good bonus."

Applause rose from the gathering and Ted grinned, in his element as the center of attention. "All right, that said, bow your heads for grace and then eat yourselves silly. No one is expected to start work until midmorning, just be sober by then."

Richard lowered his head, expecting Ted to begin one of the traditional scripted prayers, but instead Ted simply offered a heartfelt thank you to whatever powers might be listening. He praised the workers and asked they might be continually protected in all they did and closed with a simple, Amen.

The *amen* echoed around the tables, and people burst into motion, scooping up plates and joining the line at the head table. Given the abundance, Richard was in no hurry to push into the line. He leaned back against the table, enjoying the snap of the fire and the anticipation of the meal. A shadow passed between him and the fire, Charlene settling on the bench next to him and offering him a mug filled with a foamy brew.

The drink smelled pleasantly of hops and honey, and Richard took the mug, saying, "Thank you. This isn't one of Ted's experiments is it?"

Charlene laughed. "He told you about those, huh?"

"Yes, and about the accompanying hangovers. I fear a Ted-brewed beverage."

"I suspect that's wise, but this is safe. It came up a few months ago from Granite. On the wagon you came in on, truth told."

Richard arched both eyebrows, taking a slow pull of the drink. "It's good. Smooth and a little fruity without taking out the bitter notes."

Charlene raised her own mug. "I'll take your word for it. I know nothing about drinking except for what I like, and what to avoid."

"I did a beer tasting once, but I admit by the last few sips I couldn't tell much of anything different one to the next." He watched her drink, the light of the fire and the hanging lanterns playing gently over her skin. She lowered the drink and he glanced at her lips, forcing himself to look away.

"You should fill a plate before too long, or you'll miss your firsts while other people have started their seconds."

"Maybe, but I'm enjoying the company."

Maybe it was his imagination, but Richard thought she was blushing, and he smiled behind his glass.

"So what happens now? With the harvest, I mean. We've got it in, what's the process of getting it to market?" The question was as much an excuse to keep her sitting with him as it was honest curiosity.

Charlene took another drink before explaining. "We'll take the wagons down to Double Fork. I've already got us a slot on the next transport out to Pristine, so we'll load up and go to the trade market. There's a gentleman we hire out who negotiates pricing and gets us the best possible return in exchange for a percentage. The last gleanings here we'll gather and sell locally at prices we all agreed to at the beginning of the year. Locals get better prices, but that's something that goes around. We'll get a good deal on pork and other necessities we don't grow or breed in exchange."

Richard nodded. "That makes sense to me." He took a swig, realizing he'd reached the bottom of his mug. He wasn't much of a drinker, but the combination of a pleasant night and good company encouraged relaxation. He scooped up her near empty mug and held up a finger. "Stay there."

She arched a brow, but didn't argue the suggestion as he went off to refill the mugs. Richard grabbed a plate as well, slipping in and out of the line and filling it with a couple of hand pies, bread, and cheese before returning to the table.

"It's not exactly a full plate, but Ted is holding up the rest of the line."

Charlene took her mug back with a thankful nod and chuckled. "That sounds typical for Ted. He'll stand there and eat from the platters if he's not reminded to keep moving. Or he'll talk everyone's ears off."

"He certainly has a gift for it," Richard picked up a slice of bread. "Though I am still trying to figure out his accent. I can hear a little accent in almost everyone, but his is very pronounced."

"Yep. He talks like our grandfather. Grandpa came here from Central, but he was working class there, living on some of the islands and growing crops. His accent was always heavy, and Ted adored him and picked it up. After Grandpa died, Ted decided to keep talking that way." She grinned, licking a drop of beer off her lips. "So it's half nostalgia, half habit, and half because he thinks it sounds sexy."

"That's three halves, Miss Charlene."

"When talking about Teddy, you need more than two." She took a drink, pushing her hat back to hang around her neck on its string. "You know, I've never asked about your family. You've mentioned sisters and your parents now and again, but without detail."

Richard chewed through some of the cheese before stretching his legs out in front of him and taking another pull of the beer. "I suppose it's just never come up before. I am disappointingly boring. My parents are alive and well, living on Central. My father is a business man and my mother is the keeper of the household and a strong face in local doings. I've two older sisters who are both married to men who dote on them shamelessly, with seven children between them. I had an older brother as well, but Gregory passed away a few years ago."

"What happened?"

The question was gentle, and Richard met her gaze. He missed Gregory, but time did dull the pain of loss. "Genetics. He was born with a heart defect, and despite the best treatments we could find, and several surgeries over the years, there was only so much the doctors could do. His body rejected two transplants and in the end he just slipped away from us."

Charlene rested a hand on his shoulder. "I'm sorry."

Richard nodded, covering her hand. His head was already a little fuzzy from the beer. It was nice to just sit and talk. "Thank you. I miss him. Gregory was my inspiration to follow my passions. My father would have had me working the family business, but I had no interest in managing accounts and tax law. Gregory told me to do what made my heart happy."

"Charlene?"

Charlene set her drink down as Missus Davidson spotted her. "Yes?"

The cook waved her hand at the house. "Sorry to interrupt, but I need a hand. We need the rest of the bread baskets from the house. Do you mind?"

"No, ma'am. You've worked a miracle pulling this all together. I'm certain fetching baskets is the least I can do."

"Thank you. There's a bundle of them on the back table in the kitchen. Take Mister Tyler with you and you can do it in one load."

Missus Davidson returned to the table, riding herd on the chaos. Charlene chuckled. "You heard her. We're drafted."

Richard tipped his hat, the leather worn and tattered now. It was strange to think of a time when it had been stiff and new. He set his drink aside and rose, offering Charlene a hand up. "I don't mind. A walk will keep the beer from my head."

Her hand was warm in his and he was reluctant to release her, but he did, tucking his hands in his pockets. He kept pace on the walk to the house, noticing how she favored her right side, particularly as she went up the stairs. It was a little thing, but now he was paying attention.

The house was mostly dark, and Charlene moved through it with the ease of familiarity. Richard did his best to keep up, his steps not entirely steady. He managed to dodge most of the furniture until they passed into the kitchen. By some bad luck, one of the prep tables had been moved during the cooking, and he caught the corner with his hip, knocking it over.

Richard scrambled to catch the table and stumbled into Charlene, who also lunged for the falling furniture. They went down in a tangle of limbs and table, Richard twisting to keep from landing on her and ending up on the bottom of the pile. A small sack of ogen flour went flying, hitting the floor and covering everything in a dusting of white.

"Damnation!" He pushed the table off of them with a kick, highly aware of Charlene pressed against his chest. She was shaking, and he looped an arm around her, afraid she was hurt. "Miss Charlene? Talk to me. Are you all right?"

She turned her head, the glow from an over the sink light all he had to see by. Flour dotted her dark hair, and he realized the shaking was contained laughter which spilled over as she nodded. "I'm fine. Oh heavens…what a mess." She kept laughing, covering her lips with one hand and trying to control herself.

"I'm glad you think this is hysterical."

Charlene lowered her hand, her eyes dancing with amusement. "I've never been attacked by a table before, or heard you curse."

"It was a sneak attack. Even a gentleman can be excused when under attack. Vicious, sneaky table waiting in the darkness."

"They do that." She looked down at him, one hand propped on his chest for balance. Richard wasn't sure when the amusement turned to something more serious, but he saw the shift in her expression just before her hand ran down the side of his face.

Her touch was feather soft, despite the calluses on the tips of her fingers, and he shivered though he was far from cold. In fact he was certain the temperature of the kitchen had just spiked several degrees. "Miss Charlene, perhaps we should clean up…" He stilled as she pressed her fingers against his lips.

"Don't," She whispered, her fingers continuing their explorations of his features. Her touch on his lips left him tingling, stealing his breath away before he could think of protest. She brushed his hair back from his forehead, twining her fingers in the golden locks. "I like it longer."

Richard reached up, resting his palm against the curve of her neck. He wasn't sure if it was the drink or the humor of the moment which made him brave, but he pushed his doubts aside. "Then I'll leave it longer." She leaned into his hand, and he pulled her down, watching for any sign of discomfort or resistance and ready to release her.

She folded against him, and, against all good sense, Richard sought her lips. The first kiss was tender and tentative, just a brush of lip to lip which led to another and another after that. She was soft and warm and her lips molded to his, each additional kiss growing in intensity. Charlene didn't just accept his kisses, but met him touch for hungry touch, demanding more. Richard's heart pounded. He slid his free arm around her waist, pulling her against him and kissing her thoroughly despite the fact they were on a dark kitchen floor while a party went on without them.

They broke apart at the same time, and Richard was pleased she was breathing as hard as he was. He wanted to know what she was thinking, but he didn't ask, refusing to break the wonder of the moment. He tucked her against him, pleased at how well they fit together, and guided her head to rest against his chest.

Richard wasn't sure how long they lay there in the silence of beating hearts and he didn't really care. His lips tingled with the taste of her, a sweet femininity touched with the bitter beer and sweat. If he had any lingering doubts about where his heart lay, they were brushed away in the tangled warmth. He pressed a kiss to her forehead. "Miss Charlene."

She snorted, poking him in the ribs hard. "Don't you dare."

Richard blinked, surprised by the sudden little violence. "Pardon?"

"You may not kiss me like that and then call me *Miss* Charlene!"

The irritation in her voice made him laugh and Richard nodded. "That does seem to be pushing it a little far, yes."

"Say it right then."

"Charlene."

"Again."

"Charlene."

"Once more."

"Charlene."

This time, she kissed him, and his reasonable thoughts about getting off the floor and the waiting Missus Davidson were chased out of his head, until he heard footsteps coming up the porch. Fuzzy-headed or not, he knew they shouldn't be caught kissing on the kitchen floor. He would not dare harm her honor or reputation so. Richard pulled back, brushing a bit of flour from Charlene's cheek.

"Someone's coming. We should stop."

She blinked a few times and groaned before getting off of him with a sigh.

"Of course someone's coming, because that's just typical around here. The good stuff always gets interrupted and with our luck it's Teddy." Charlene brushed her hands off and righted the table before looking at Richard again. "We need to talk about this whole kissing thing."

Richard reluctantly got to his feet, searching for a broom. The footsteps had stopped, and he wondered how far their voices might carry. "In my experience talking about kissing is less fun than participating in kissing."

Charlene laughed, shaking her head. "That's true, but my head is a little fuzzy, maybe a lot fuzzy, and I just... I don't want to regret things I did, or didn't do. So I want to know if this was something besides beer-fueled, celebratory kissing."

Richard considered his response, sweeping the spilled flour into a neat pile. "I can't answer that right now. I don't want you to question how I feel because of the beer. But I promise I have no regrets, and I don't want you to have any either."

"That's a rather brilliant non-answer." Charlene picked up the half empty flour bag, setting it aside and gathering the baskets that were the reason they'd come to the kitchen in the first place.

A few quick sweeps and Richard gathered the flour into a dust pan and tossed it away. He set the broom aside, and caught Charlene by the shoulder turning her toward him. "It's not a non-answer." He cupped her cheeks in his hands, holding her gaze. "I kissed you, Charlene, because I wanted to kiss you and because you wanted to kiss me." His lips brushed hers again. "And that's what matters."

She dropped the baskets and wrapped her arms around his neck as the front door opened, Ted's voice booming through the house. "Char? Rick? Where are those baskets? Missus Davidson is fit to be tied. And why the hell is it so dark in here? Ain't ya heard 'f electric lights?"

Frustrated, Richard released her and stepped away as Charlene hurried for the door. "Keep your shirt on, Ted. I knocked over a bag of flour and we had to clean up. I'm coming."

By the time Richard reached the front room Charlene was gone, though Ted still leaned in the doorway. The big man looked Richard over, his stance all too casual.

"I ain't gonna take guesses as to what was going on in here, even if they're pretty good guesses. And cause Charlene's love life, as she continually reminds me, is her own business. I will say though that I've already been to prison once for shooting a man. Ya hurt her and I've got no problem going back." Ted softened the threat with a grin and pushed away from the door. "That said, let's get back before we miss dessert and the music. The night's still young and morning comes early."

23

Thick storm clouds gathered over the ranch house, swirling under the push of unseen winds. Charlene sat curled up on the chair in her room, watching the storm come. Her head pounded in time with her heartbeat, and she wanted to cry, but it hurt too much. The pain had driven her from her bed hours ago, unable to get comfortable no matter how she shifted and too warm under even the light covering of blankets.

She told Richard she had good days and bad days, but this was one of the really bad days, all too frequent when the weather turned. She was glad Ted and Richard were in Double Fork with the grain shipment and not here to see her.

In the distance she saw the double headlights of the combine chugging back from the west forty. Kevin had volunteered to lead the last shifts, and they'd finished the last few acres of the first harvest. Anything which hadn't gone off to be transported to Pristine was already spoken for by other ranchers who were very happy to have an early load.

The sight of the machine turned her thoughts back to Richard. He was on her mind often, no matter how Ted had warned her about pining, the nature of men, and the reach of Anna Reches.

But this was more than pining, even if Charlene didn't dare put words to what she felt, not even in her own head. The kissing was wonderful, not just because it was kissing, but because it was kissing Richard. When she kissed him she felt warm and wanted, all her pains chased away. It frustrated her they hadn't had a chance to talk further in the rush to get the grain to Double Fork. She'd awakened the next morning with the tingle of memory on her lips and wishing he'd been beside her.

She'd hoped they'd be able to take some time for themselves once the harvest was on its way, but after Gravy had taken a fall and broken his ankle, Richard had stepped up to drive the third wagon. He'd held her hand longer than necessary as she'd seen them off with the shipment, and promised they'd talk when he got back. It would be nearly a week…too long to wait.

Charlene pulled her knees tighter to her chest, breathing through another muscle spasm. The agonizing sensation ran from the arches of her feet up her body, and she closed her eyes, pushing back tears and resting her head on the cool glass of the window. That was something else they were going to have to talk about. Richard hadn't seen her at her worst, and she feared it would scare him off. Courting a broken woman was a lot to ask of a man.

She was still at the window two hours later when Missus Davidson knocked on the door before pushing it open. Charlene blinked grogginess away, rubbing a spot of drool off her chin. The older woman tutted.

"Oh my dear, please tell me you didn't sleep like that all night. Again."

Charlene shrugged, shivering in her thin night dress. The heat which had driven her from bed was gone, leaving her cold and stiff. "Not all night, just some of it."

Missus Davidson shook her head, walking to Charlene's side. "There's a comm call from Double Fork holding for you. Do you think you can get as far as your desk?"

"Maybe?" Charlene rolled her shoulders and slid her feet to the edge of the chair. It took several minutes to lower her feet all the way to the floor, and her legs flooded with pins and needles. "Ow."

Missus Davidson helped pull Charlene upright, slipping an arm around the younger woman's waist. "Gently now, we'll just walk it out a bit, and I'll go fetch you some breakfast and your pills."

Charlene nodded, cringing with each shuffling step. They walked a loop around the little room twice before she sank into the chair at her desk. She buried her head in her hands, rubbing her eyes and blotting tears.

"Channel 6, dear," Missus Davidson said before going to get the promised breakfast.

Channel 6 was audio only, and Charlene was glad, slumping against the desk. She brought the screen up, logging in and flicking through the programs to open the long range communications. There was a snap of static and then the line cleared as it connected.

"Charlene Petersmire speaking."

"Heya Char." Ted said. He sounded perky and well rested and Charlene wanted to grump at him, but she held back. It wasn't his fault she was having a rough morning.

"Heya, Ted. You three on your way home?"

"Not exactly."

The unexpected response made Charlene sit up a little straighter. "What does 'not exactly' mean?"

"It means Rick and I are going ta Pristine."

"What?!? Why? What went wrong now?" Charlene tried not to snip, but she sounded sharp even to her ears. Why couldn't a single process this year go without a hitch?

"Don't get riled up. It's nothin' we can't handle. It's just that Mister Jonathan isn't available to do the marketing song and dance fer us. Ol' Donovan Reches hired him off for something else a few days ago."

Charlene rubbed her head. "Not Reches again. I swear he's like a whole stack of bad pennies. I hate him, Teddy. I really do. Every time we turn around he and his are messing things up."

"It gets better. I saw the Keeles in town. Come to find out Reches bought their farmstead at the beginning of the year and insisted they move out before the rains. All in the name of doing what was best for them, of course. Some big song and dance about how he wouldn't want them to have to get through another rainy season when schoolin' on Central starts next month. Otherwise, they wouldn't have gone until after the normal harvest an' we wouldn't be running this tight."

"I reiterate my hatred." Charlene sighed, "So get back to why this means you're going to Pristine. Teddy, you hate the sales and marketing parts of this. You don't even have the mark ups. I sent those right to Mister Jonathan's account. Dammit! If I leave this morning I can get down to Double Fork in two days."

"Because traveling in the rain is ever good for you? Even if you can find someone willing to dodge the starter storms to bring you down since you don't ride horses? Not to mention the last time you rode in a transport you called them an invention of the Devil himself, and it took you three days to recover?"

She could picture Teddy shaking his head as he continued.

"I know I'm not as good at this as you are, but that's why I'm taking Rick. He's been to some of these auction things before. Apparently his folks have business contacts with the trades running accounts. We figure between the two of us we can get everything sold at top prices, with or without Mister Jonathan. Just send me over a copy of the manifests and the mark ups. We'll hire a couple of drivers and send them back with Dale so you can return the wagons."

Charlene chewed on her lower lip. She trusted Ted to try his best, and she believed Richard could succeed in whatever he put his clever mind to, but if Reches had gone as far as buying off Mister Jonathan, could he have influence over Richard? She hated that she doubted him, even in the most abstract fashion. But Richard was, after all, courting Reches' daughter, at least as far as anyone had been told. Richard hadn't told Charlene he wasn't. He'd never said anything about Anna Reches, nor had he formally asked to court Charlene even after the kissing. She wanted to trust him, and firmly pushed her fear aside. Richard wasn't Frank or Jeremiah. He was a man of morals. He wouldn't do anything to hurt the ranch or her. She had to believe that, or she'd go mad.

"All right. I suppose that makes the most sense." The rain pounded on the rooftop, accompanied by a flash of lightning, and Charlene groaned. "You realize leaving now is going to put you on the outside of the travel ban? You won't be able to come home for three months. You can only get a message through during the burst."

"Yeah, and that part ain't good, but I don't see any way around it. We just can't pull this off remotely without a representative, not and get the prices we need. We'll put the time ta good use and work on expanding our sales venues." He paused and laughed, "I can even use fancy words like venue. See if we can get some presales for the late harvest based on the quality of this one. An' it ain't that bad. Half as long as when I was in prison."

Charlene scowled. She didn't want to go three months without seeing either of the men. Finding them each morning had become part of her routine, part of what let her know everything was right with her universe. At least the timing this time was when the ranch was the slowest and she wouldn't have as much to juggle alone, not that there wasn't still plenty to do.

"I guess that's true. Do your best to stay out of trouble, huh?"

"You know me, Char."

Charlene tried to smile. Three months. It wasn't all that long. She could do anything for three months, just one day at a time. "Yeah, that's what I'm worried about."

"I'll be good. Stay dry and get some breakfast in ya."

"I can do that."

"Good. Hey, Rick wants to talk to ya. Be quick about it though cause they're starting to load the transport and I still need the files. See ya in three months. Love ya."

"See ya then. I love you too."

The line went dead and anxiety rolled around Charlene's stomach even as she keyed up the files for Ted. Three months. What could she possibly say to Richard before he left for three months? How could she ask him all the things she wanted to know?

The comm reconnected, and Charlene caught her breath.

"I know, Ted. Just give me a minute. Go get a sandwich or something. We're going to be in the cargo hold, I'm sure they won't load us for a while. We will not miss the damn transport." Richard hrmped, only half speaking into the line, and Charlene laughed when he swore, the humor making it past the pounding of her head.

"Mister Tyler…such language."

He cleared his throat. "Pardon. I didn't realize you could hear me."

She was glad to hear his voice and leaned her head back against her chair. "Most of these comm units have a pretty good microphone."

"Indeed." The background noise behind him died down, and Richard's voice dropped to something more personal and intimate. "I know we didn't get a chance to really talk about us, and I don't want to do it over a comm. I want…" He went silent for a moment, and Charlene glanced at the connection to make sure he hadn't dropped.

"Richard?"

"I'm here. I'm just trying to figure out how to say what I need to say."

Charlene wet her lips. He sounded nervous and that made her less nervous. "I suspect you'd better figure it out quick, or Teddy is going to drag you out of there by your heels."

"That does sound like something he would do." He took a deep breath. "Then I'll try to keep it simple. My contract was for six months. By the time we get back my six months will be over. If it's all the same to you, I'd like to extend my contract. I think you could use my help and a few days ago the strongest, bravest, most beautiful woman I've ever laid eyes on let me kiss her. And if my contract runs out I might not get a chance to do it again."

This time it was Charlene who fell silent. She pushed her hair back from her face. "Well…we can't have that, now can we? Guess we'd better extend your contract another few weeks. I need you to fix the combine with the right belts, and I have it on good authority that woman would like to be kissed again."

"Rick! Get your butt in gear!"

Richard sighed. "I'm being summoned. Please, take care of yourself Charlene." He spoke her name tenderly. "We'll have more time soon."

"I…"

The line disconnected before Charlene could say good bye. The words 'I love you' hovered on her tongue and she wasn't sure if she was relieved or disappointed she hadn't said them.

"2 5 creds per bushel!" Ted crowed, pumping his fist in the air.

Richard laughed and shook his head. "Calm down, Ted. People are staring." He steered the bigger man towards the exit of the conference center, maintaining a steady pace, though he was every bit as gleeful as Ted.

"Let them stare. I bet none of them just closed a 15000 bushel deal at 25 credits per bushel. I wish we could call Char. She's never going to believe it."

"You just want to gloat because we managed this without her or Mister Jonathan."

Richard pushed the door open, stepping out onto the street. Pristine City was in the middle of a delightful spring. The wind that played down the street was filled with the scents of blooming flowers competing with the spicy smoke of a food vendor's truck.

Ted followed, snorting. "Well, of course I want to gloat, but it will also take a huge load off of her. The debt is paid and there's enough left over for bonuses."

"Everyone worked very hard to make this happen. It's about time something broke in our direction," Richard said, checking his watch and angling to the food truck.

"Damn straight," Ted said, a growl to his voice. "I can't believe they lost

Frank and Jeremiah. How hard is it to make sure two men with busted noses get on a transport to prison?"

"Apparently harder than getting you on one. I just hope they find them quickly. Those two were dangerous enough before and now they have additional reason to cause trouble." Richard placed his order for a plate of grilled meats, vegetables, and a thick flat bread he'd become fond of over the last couple of weeks. "I'm headed back to the Pain Center this afternoon. We're going to run the first volunteer tests."

"Ya really think this pain therapy thing is going to work?" Ted asked, placing his own food order before stepping back.

"All of the numbers thus far look right. Doctor Mardsen says he's impressed. If the volunteer tests go well he'll bring in some investors at the end of the month, and we'll see what it would take to produce it on a larger scale. We could help a lot of people."

Ted glanced at Richard side-long, "Not the least of which is Charlene?"

Richard smiled and picked up his plate, tossing down a few bills to cover them both. "Not the least of which."

25

"For the sake of what God gave little green apples!" Charlene mashed the torn pie crust into a ball, starting over again. "I still don't see how you get an even thickness without going completely mad. I always end up with a spot that's either too thick or too thin in the middle." She looked at Missus Davidson who was easing a perfectly smooth crust into a pie tin. "I'd rather keep working on fillings. I don't burn those anymore."

Tracy snickered. Missus Davison gave her a wilting look. "Behave." She turned to Charlene, watching her man-handle the dough. "You've come a long way since we started, but the crust is the most important part."

"Gravy says if I feed the men another doughy or burned crust there's going to be a mutiny. Who knew they'd get upset over extra pie?" Charlene sprinkled flour over the counter again, rubbing the fine milled grain between her fingers. At her request they'd made pies once a week since the rains began, and she saw a very steady progress in her abilities. Not that pie making, or cooking in general, would ever be her favorite thing.

"At first it was a novelty. Now they are expecting quality over quantity." Missus Davidson came over, poking the dough with her fore-finger. "How many times have you rolled this same crust?"

"Erm." Charlene fidgeted, "Three, maybe four?"

"Charlene!"

"I know! I know." She scooped the dough together, putting it in the pile to feed to the livestock. "No more than twice."

"Unless you want it too tough to chew, yes," Missus Davidson handed Charlene the last disk of chilled pie dough. "Again. Don't press so hard and let the pin move in your hands, dear. It is supposed to roll, not push."

Charlene sighed. "Because pushing will tear it. I remember."

"You are simply thinking about it far too hard. I do not believe you can manage the fine manipulation required for gene splicing and not master a simple tapered rolling pin."

Charlene eyed the tapered wooden pin and shrugged. "It's a totally different skill set. I can use my mechanicals to keep the pull constant when I'm splicing. I'm certain the rolling pin is just mocking me."

Missus Davidson rested her hands on her hips. "Then mock it in return if you must, but do not waste any more pie dough. Heaven knows there's only a few more weeks before the weather clears and the time to practice will be lost to chores."

"And the Festivals," Tracy piped up. "Edwin has promised me the most lovely festival dress. He says he wants everyone to see me and be amazed at his good fortune."

"Are you still to wed at the New Year?" Charlene asked, rubbing flour on the rolling pin before she began to work the new wad of dough.

Tracy nodded, dimpling prettily. "Yes. Just as soon as the house is done. Thank you again for letting him work here. He's learned so much from Mister Tyler."

Charlene drove her weight into the crust, trying to hold back jealousy. She wished her future was as certain as Tracy's, or at least that she was certain the man she fancied hadn't changed his mind in the last three months. The message during the burst had been short and to the point: strong ogen sales and futures, some security suggestions and general non-committal well wishes.

She wasn't sure what more she expected, especially as each word was costly, but she was dissatisfied and more anxious than ever for the rainy season to end.

A knock came at the front door, a much louder pattern than the rain on the roof, and Tracy left to see who it was. She returned a moment later, Sheriff Reid a few steps behind her. His overcoat shone with rain, and he held his hat in his hands, doing his best to keep it from dripping on the floor. Once in the kitchen he took a deep breath, his moustache twitching. "It smells very fine in here, ladies. Very fine indeed. My Matilda will be sorry she didn't come along, though I expect she would have insisted on staying to make pies with you and slowed my rounds."

Charlene chuckled. "She would have been welcome. Perhaps if she and Missus Davidson worked together they could improve my crust making skills."

"Maybe so."

But the Sheriff didn't smile, and Charlene raised an eyebrow, trying to keep her tones casual despite the tension building in her gut. "So what brings you by, Sheriff? Not that we aren't happy to see you at any time."

"Unfortunately, a couple of concerns. Would it be possible for you and me to speak alone, Miss Charlene?"

Miss Charlene. It was odd to hear someone who wasn't Richard using a formal address, even if it was totally appropriate from the older man. "Of course." Charlene set the rolling pin aside and rubbed her hands clean on a tea towel before gesturing to the kitchen door. "Why don't we take a seat in the parlor?"

"I'd appreciate it."

He allowed her to show the way to the parlor, which was still full of equipment and seedlings. As Charlene spent much of the rainy season working on her plants, she saw no reason to haul everything back to the seedling lab. The house was much warmer and meant she didn't have to make the trip out in the rain.

She moved a pile of papers from the wingback chairs, setting them on the desk and gesturing to the seats. "Please."

"Go ahead. I'd rather not get rainwater on your furnishings and I won't be here long."

Charlene eyed him and sank into the chair. She might have refused on principle, but truth told her feet didn't mind the break, and she didn't feel like making a point. "You're making me very nervous. What's going on?"

He turned the hat through his fingers, the plastic covering shedding water despite his stated desire not to drip. "We've had a couple incidents I think you should be aware of. First of all, we got a call out for a dead cow over at the Miller's place. They don't do cattle, so it was an oddity. It was one of yours, and it'd been savaged. Not the work of a wild animal, but shot up and dragged while it was still alive and bleeding. It was a mean, painful death. I was gonna have it brought back here, but given the rain and all, the stink was mighty powerful and it was better just to bury it where it lay."

Charlene blinked, swallowing hard. She might have more cattle than she could give names to, but that didn't mean she didn't care about the welfare of each of them. It was a fact of life that they were going to lose animals, but there was a difference between an injured or sick cow who had to be put down and one which had been tortured. It was a personal message for Charlene, destroying what she loved.

"I see." She sucked in a deep breath, rubbing her hands together. "What else?"

"Well, there was a break in down at Madam Aster's place in Granite. A bunch of supplies were stolen, and by the time Old Man Ernest got down to deal with them the thieves were running out, but he swears he saw Jeremiah driving a wagon away. The law folk from Double Fork have been looking for Jeremiah and Frank since they escaped the transport, but with these recent issues, we're pretty sure they're up in this area. I don't think they're alone."

The stony feeling in Charlene's stomach got worse. "They didn't hurt anyone, did they?"

"Not thus far, no. But it doesn't take much to guess why they're back, and I'm worried about you and your folk. The jump between savaging a cow and a person isn't much of a stretch. We need to catch them before it gets that far and get them back on their way to the prison on Pristine."

"I still don't see how they got lost in the first place." Charlene grumbled.

"I don't have an answer for that, Miss Charlene. I wasn't there, though I can guarantee when we left the pair at Double Fork they were contained. We intend to capture them again. However, we don't have them yet. I know you've got a lot of good men here, and that mountain you call a brother, but I'd like to assign a deputy to the ranch. I'd suggest your men start going armed if they don't already."

Charlene frowned, all of her good mood drained away. Guns and other weapons weren't restricted on the ranch and were necessary for dealing with large snakes and the occasional big cat or wild dog down from the canyons, but most of the men didn't carry on a day to day basis. They'd never used weapons against another human being.

"I'll put it before the men and see what they think. I hate giving into the fear of what might happen, but I'd feel a lot worse if anything did happen. I think we'll wait on the Deputy, since that would just make folks nervous. We can manage. I'm glad for the warning."

Sheriff Reid nodded, smoothing his moustache with one hand. "Well, hopefully a warning is all it has to be. We can get someone up here if you change your mind. I won't keep you from your pies. We're taking warnings to all the ranches up in these parts, just in case the attacks aren't limited. I should be on my way."

Charlene inclined her head, rising to see him to the door. "We appreciate your efforts, especially in weather like this."

He smiled in return. "Ah yes, the season of mud and moss, but your fields look none the worse for the extra water. Your folks coming down for the Festival once we dry out a bit?"

"We wouldn't miss it."

They exchanged further pleasantries as he left the house, and Charlene watched him jog to his one horse rig. He slid inside, kicking up mud and heading off into the thickening rain. Charlene leaned against the doorframe, her pies forgotten in the dire warnings playing through her head. She'd set security shifts at dinner tonight and talk to the men about weaponry and other precautions. Then as soon as the rain eased she'd send someone, or a couple someones, up to check on the canyon cattle and the men watching over them.

The thoughts of seeing Frank and Jeremiah again sent a chill through her. She had no doubt they'd be looking for revenge not only against her, but even more against Ted and Richard. She'd rest easier once her men were home and their enemies back in jail.

26

Richard's second trip from Double Fork to Ridgeback was much more pleasant than his first, though with far greater anticipation—and more comfortable clothing. Jeremiah's transport services had been replaced by a young woman named Gracie who drove a smaller wagon but was a much more animated conversationalist. She also drove much faster, leaving Richard wondering a time or two if they were going to stay on the roadway at all.

She and Ted hit it off immediately. It turned out they were both sports fans, though rooted for diametrically opposite teams in just about every sport they could name. As Richard only casually followed any sport, their conversation left him to entertain himself on the long ride back. He didn't mind.

While the heat had returned to Galileo in full force, the effects of three months of rain were everywhere to be seen. Looping green vines crept along the edges of the roadway and wild flowers of every shape and size filled the air with sweet scents and the buzz of busy insects. The farming fields were marked with tall green grasses, and at several points they crossed little streamlets which ran across the rubberized road.

Ted assured Richard that none of it would last for more than a few weeks. After the rains the desert bloomed, and then it slept again beneath the slightly less oppressive winter heat.

As they approached the gate to the Double P, Richard noticed new white poles on either side of the new gate and a much heavier lock, one that didn't budge when Ted gave it a shove. Instead a line of red lights illuminated the top of the gate. Gravy's voice rose through a hidden speaker.

"Double P Ranch. How can we help you?"

Richard grinned, running his fingers over the lights. "Slick system. Looks like there's a voice input right here."

Ted nodded, shaking his head. "When I told Char to bump up the security this wasn't exactly what I imagined." He eyed the spot Richard had indicated and moved closer. "Hey, Gravy. Since when did you become a doorman?"

"Well, hey yourself, Ted. It's been a couple of weeks now. I don't mind so much, and Charlene wanted someone responsible to monitor things. Give me a minute and I'll get the gate. It's open when the lights go green. Then you got three minutes to get through and close it back up."

"Or what?"

"Come ta think on it, I don't rightly know. Likely an alarm of some sort goes off."

Richard eyed the gate and shook his head. "Bet it's more than that. This is set up to run a current. I bet you get a good jolt too."

A few seconds later the lights winked off before turning back on in a cheery green.

Ted snorted and shoved the gate. "Let's not test that theory, huh?"

Gravy's voice echoed again. "That should do it."

"Yeah, Gravy, that did. Thanks. See ya up at the house."

Richard moved through, gesturing for the wagon to pass before closing the gate and making sure it shut tight. He jogged a few steps to catch up to the cart, and pulled himself into the moving vehicle, something he never would have dreamt of doing not so long ago. The technologist in him was impressed with the new system, even if he wanted more information on exactly how it worked, but he couldn't help but wonder what had happened to make it necessary. The sooner he saw all was well with his own eyes, the happier he'd be.

The rest of the journey to the house passed quickly and Richard grinned as the white ranch house rose in front of them. The hands were gathered in the yard, yelling greetings and welcoming them home.

Richard was surprised to see folks weren't only calling to Ted, but to him as well. He hadn't expected to miss or be missed, but he had been. He called back greetings, noticing only when the wagon came to a quick stop that each of the men was armed.

Richard looked around seeing Missus Davidson and Tracy on the porch, but Charlene was nowhere to be seen. He squashed a wave of disappointment. She was likely in with some sick cow or her seedlings. He hopped off of the wagon, crossing to greet the women as Ted made a round of handshakes with the men. Unable to keep from asking, Richard addressed Missus Davidson.

"We seem to be missing someone," he paused, glancing at the space to the left of the steps to make sure Charlene wasn't teasing him, but no one was there. "Where is Miss Charlene?"

"She's on a supply run down to Ridgeback with Kevin. A friend of hers is visiting town so she thought she'd get in a visit and help with the run." The older woman shot Ted a glare, "Someone was supposed to tell us when you got planetside. She'll be disappointed she missed your arrival."

Ted pouted under Missus Davidson's ire, taking off his hat and putting on his best contrite expression. "I didn't mean ta cause a fuss. I just thought it'd be fun ta surprise everyone. Forgive me?"

He made big eyes at her, and the cook snorted. "Heaven forbid you ever turn that wide eyed look to evil purposes, Theodore Petersmire. Why don't both of you get cleaned up?" She then addressed the larger gathering. "Dinner's in thirty minutes. Finish up whatever you're working on. And, Ted, don't forget to pay your wagon."

Ted climbed the stairs and kissed Missus Davidson on the cheek. "Yes, Ma'am. Then maybe you can start catching us up on everything that's happened while we were gone."

"We'll see. Some of it Miss Charlene will want to address herself. You will have to be patient, but she's due back before dark."

Richard nodded, lifting his bag from the wagon and talking over Ted's protests. "We'll manage. Thank you for the welcome." The words were sincere but he still wanted to see Charlene. It was obvious tensions were high, and he wouldn't relax until he'd seen her, no matter how glad he was to be home.

27

The sun had well and truly set, stars winking into brilliant life as Kevin and Charlene rolled up on the house. In the back of the wagon, sprawled amidst the supplies, Daria slept, snoring gently. When Charlene had received the message Daria was in town, she hadn't expected to find the woman drunk and dancing on the bar at the Bottomless Barrel. She still wasn't entirely sure what had happened except for some rambling line about catching Emilio playing hide the salami with a starlet backstage. Daria and Emilio had only married a little more than a year ago, and Daria had been sure he was her ticket to a life of adventure and luxury. Apparently sharing him wasn't part of the adventure she'd expected.

Charlene climbed slowly out of the wagon, moving around to lower the tailgate. "Daria, you've got to wake up, because there is no way I'm carrying you into the house, and Kevin has to get the supplies under cover."

The woman ignored her, continuing in her drunken snooze.

"Need a hand?"

Weary from the trip Charlene nodded, catching Daria by both ankles and pulling her to the end of the wagon. "Yeah, Ted. Can you take her into the guest…" Charlene's thought processes came to a screeching halt and she spun around, throwing herself at her brother in a hug. He hugged back, lifting her off her feet before gently returning her to earth.

"When did you get back? You were supposed to let us know when you were leaving Double Fork!"

"Yes, a fact I've been scolded for twice now."

Charlene's heart did a little flip-flop. She tried to keep her tones casual as she continued. "Did Richard come back with you?"

"Of course." Ted waved vaguely at the rest of the ranch. "Not like I'd let him run off or something. He's off working on the combine. He had an epiphany while we were off planet about a way to fix it and decided to get started."

Charlene glanced towards the equipment barn, wishing she could go find him right now, but she had to deal with a drunk guest and a load of supplies first. "Good. Glad to know he's earning his keep."

Ted snorted, knocking her hat off and mussing her hair. "Uh huh." He glanced at Daria. "She staying fer a while?"

"Morning probably. At least until she's sober and I can figure out what happened. I expect she'll want to go over to her parent's place after a day or two, but I couldn't take her to them like this. Can you put her in the guest room while I help Kevin get things stored for the night?"

"I guess. Sure. But then I think a few explanations are in store, right?"

Charlene nodded even though she didn't want to. Once Ted got his teeth around something there was no way to make him let go. It'd be best just to answer his questions even if the answers would worry him. "Yeah, probably. Go ahead and get Richard up here too, please. I may as well explain things to both of you at the same time."

Ted scooped Daria up, the lanky red-head nothing to his strength. "Good enough." He grinned, never looking at his burden, only at Charlene, "I missed ya, Char. Ain't had anyone to order me around for weeks. I almost started thinking for myself and we all know how devastating that would be."

"Oh shut up, you big lug." Charlene buttoned up the tail gate before adding. "I missed you too."

It didn't take long to get the supplies under cover as they only bothered to unload the few things which might suffer from spending the night outside and not in the cold lockers. Everything else was left under a tight tarp as a job for the next morning, and Charlene sent Kevin to go get some rest.

Charlene walked across the yard, limping after too long on the wagon. She was aware there were two figures sitting on the house steps, backlit by the porch light. Richard rose as she approached, his features crinkling with concern. He took her hands, kissing her knuckles before guiding her to sit on the steps.

"I'm glad to see you, and so sorry you didn't know we were coming. I thought Ted had sent ahead, and I certainly would have if I'd known he hadn't. Let's get you off your feet."

Ted gave them a lazy grin, and Charlene stuck her tongue out at him, stretching her legs out in front of her. "Shut up."

"I didn't say nothing."

"Then shut up saying what you're not saying," Charlene sat between the two of them, leaning lightly into Richard's shoulder and trusting the semi-dark to cover the warming contact. Maybe she was imagining it, but she thought he leaned back, shifting his arm so it was behind her back.

"Yes'm." Ted paused, then reached over and tapped the small caliber gun which rode on Charlene's thigh. "So I know it's late and stuff, but this is a new accessory. It seems like everyone's got one but me. I'm feeling left out and a might bit jumpy." His tones were purposefully light, but Charlene heard the tension. "As I recall ya ain't much of a fan of guns all together save as a necessary evil for putting down an injured cow or chasing off a critter. I never thought I'd see you wearing one."

Charlene chewed her lower lip, wishing they were talking about grain yields or pies, or that she was kissing Richard, especially the last. Anything but the shadow of trouble that was Frank and Jeremiah. "Yeah, well… It isn't loaded. I'm too worried I'd accidentally hurt someone to carry a loaded gun."

"It don't do ya any good ta have it if it ain't loaded, Char."

"It's psychologically comforting," Charlene retorted. "If you're jealous, I know you've got one of your own up in your room. Start wearing it."

Richard cleared his throat. "I think, Miss Charlene, the concern is more why you are wearing it, and the rest of the men too. Until today I can only remember seeing a gun a few times when we were worried about wild animals. What changed?"

"Frank Hanns and Jeremiah Walker changed." Charlene couldn't help the bitterness. She'd never been close to Jeremiah, relying on him to help ferry folks around, but not much else. Frank, however, was a different story, and his continued betrayal hurt. "In the last three weeks we've had three dead cows, four if you count the one the Sheriff buried, a busted up fence line, and one of the field generators used for target practice until it stopped working. We're responding as fast as possible, but we've never caught them at it. The Sheriff says they've been spotted down in town off and on, and he's certain someone is funding their troublemaking and helping them hide, but no idea who. He offered us a deputy up here, but if twenty of us can't spot trouble coming then I'm not sure what another man is going to do any differently."

She sucked in a deep breath, muscles tightening up with each word. The whole situation was upsetting. "You've seen the updated gate, and we're in process of replacing all of the perimeter fencing. It's a damn good thing you got a good price on that harvest, because I've already spent most of what's left over after paying off the Keeles and the bonuses."

Ted squeezed her knee. "Sounds like it's a good thing we got back when we did. We'll have a war council tomorrow and go through everything, the list of what's been done, ideas for new things to do, and how we're going to catch these bastards."

"All while giving people a chance to attend Festival down in Ridgeback and preparing for second harvest and the return of the cattle from the range," Charlene added wryly. "Because the needs of the ranch aren't going to slow down while we try to keep everyone and everything safe."

"We'll manage." Ted promised, covering a yawn. "We always do, though I will manage better after a couple hours of shut eye."

Charlene nodded. The situation hadn't really changed, but somehow it was more conquerable with Ted's solid support. "Trent and Gravy are on watch tonight. We'll work you two into the schedule tomorrow, but you can sleep for now."

Ted rolled to his feet. "Then I'm going to get to it." He looked between Charlene and Richard, neither of which had moved. "Don't you two stay up too late staring at each other." He started across the yard towards the bunk house, calling over his shoulder. "And don't do nuthin' I wouldn't."

Charlene snorted, "Well…that leaves it wide open then."

28

Richard waited until Ted had completely disappeared from sight before he slipped his arm around Charlene's back, pulling her up against him the way he'd wanted to since he'd seen her across the yard. She rested her head on his shoulder and sighed. "This wasn't the way I pictured your homecoming."

"It doesn't matter. I'm just glad to be back and glad for a few moments where we're not racing around to take care of someone or something else."

Charlene sighed. "Likely too few moments. I should check on Daria at some point and make sure Ted put her on the bed and didn't put a pillow over her face."

Richard blinked in surprise. He couldn't picture Ted behaving like that towards anyone, much less a woman. "I take it they have history?"

"She was his fiancée years ago." Charlene said, "She grew up just one ranch over on the Triple Cross, closest thing to a neighbor you get out here, and we were fast friends. When we were little Ted teased us both equally, but then puberty set in. Ted fell hard and fast. I really believed Daria loved him as much as he loved her. They were going to get part of the Double P and part of the Triple Cross as a wedding present and start a ranch between the two. Just after my parents died Daria called the whole thing off. She kept working here for a while, then married Emilio which is how a position opened up for you. I honestly never expected to see her again."

"Huh. I never would have pictured Ted as the loved and lost. He seems to like women too much to settle on one." Richard thought on what he'd just said and shook his head. "Though maybe that's one of those things where one begets the next."

"Something like that. He's not had anything resembling a serious relationship in the near five years since."

"He doesn't seem overly unhappy about it," Richard chuckled, looking down at her. "Though I'm not entirely sure why we're discussing Ted."

"Because it's tragic…and means we're not talking about us."

The pale porch light played over her face, and Richard stroked his fingertips over her cheek feather light. "I suppose that's true. I guess it's just hard to know where to start." He chuckled, "Kissing is more fun than talking about kissing."

"Well, we're not doing either now." Charlene muttered, making a face at him. "And I guess the starting point is that there is an 'us', at least in my mind there is. Those kisses weren't just drunk comfort."

Richard smiled at the question in her tone, turning so he was looking at her squarely. He didn't want her to doubt his sincerity. "Those kisses were not just drunk comfort. I'm pretty sure we weren't even that drunk. Even if we hadn't kissed there would still be an 'us'. I'm not sure exactly when it happened, but you've taken up a constant residence in my thoughts. I look forward to seeing you each day and wondering what you'll do or say that impresses me next. I've never known anyone like you."

"Even if you wanted to strangle me that first day?" she teased, and Richard kissed her forehead.

"Even then. You were lovely in your anger, and surprisingly reasonable in your end approach. I may not have wanted to see you as much those first weeks, but that's nothing against how much I wanted to see you the last few months. I missed you, and I hoped you missed me."

"More than I missed Teddy."

Richard threw back his head, laughing. "I should certainly hope so!"

Charlene smiled. "I kept looking for you through the days when you were away. I'd think of something I wanted your opinion on or just some good company. I didn't realize how many little moments we had until I wasn't having them anymore."

"Indeed. I kept turning around expecting to find you, and was disappointed when you weren't there." He smoothed her hair, letting his fingers dig into the knot at her neck, loosening the pins until the braid dropped.

"So, there's an 'us'." Charlene reached up, tugging the tie from the tip of her braid. "What does that mean?"

Richard ran his fingers through her hair, letting it twine around his fist. This was the part of the conversation he was dreading. He'd tried to work out exactly what he would say, but all his rehearsed lines and explanations sounded lame as he sat with her. "Unfortunately it means I'm going to have to beg you for patience."

Charlene arched both eyebrows. "Not exactly what I expected. Why do you need my patience?"

"Because," he took in a deep breath, "because despite the feelings we both have, I can't court you yet and you deserve nothing less than that. I don't just want to pass the hours together or keep each other warm at night, to borrow a phrase from Ted."

"I agree with that part. I'm not a casual fling kind of woman. So what is keeping you from court…" She stopped, staring at him and pulling away, though it left a few long hairs wrapped around his fingers. "Oh merciful heaven, you're still mooning after Anna Reches!"

Richard shook his head, grabbing her shoulders before Charlene could stomp away. "Not mooning, Charlene. Not in the slightest, not anymore. But there was a time when she and I were very close. I came to Galileo intending to offer for her."

"You're not making me feel better."

He kept his grip light; if she really wanted to she could get away. "I'm trying to explain. This isn't a matter of want; it's a matter of doing the right thing and polite society. Out here maybe it doesn't matter so much, but in the circles she moves in and the ones I once did our situation was much speculated on and anticipated. If I just start courting someone else without officially breaking my association with her, it would reflect badly on both myself and her. I don't think it's fair to sully her reputation, and I'd rather not damage my own." He tried a little smile, "We don't want my sisters showing up to try to determine if I've lost my mind entirely, and I'd rather not be disowned. So it's just a matter of doing things right."

Charlene sighed. "And you couldn't have done this *before* kissing me?"

"Not for lack of desire. Anna has been off planet."

"Miss Reches."

Richard paused, "Pardon?"

"I know it's petty, but will you call her Miss Reches? Hearing her given name on your lips..." Charlene met his gaze, her expression fierce, "It kinda makes me want to find her and rip her perfect hair out."

Richard wasn't certain how to take the admission. It was rather gratifying to see Charlene jealous over him, not that he wanted the women fighting, but it spoke to the depth of her emotions. He smiled, touching his forehead to hers. "Possessive?"

"It's a personal failing. I'm trying to find patience, but once I decide I want something I have a hard time being told I have to wait. I don't want to share you with her, not even your thoughts or your words. I loathe the woman. She and her father have been nothing but trouble to the Double P since the moment they came to Galileo."

Richard nodded, though he still wondered how much Anna was her father's pawn. "I am not overly fond of her father. He offered me a very nice set up if I would try to get you to sell to him or could bring him information about your processes. For all that I do not agree with his methods or desires, he can be very persuasive." Richard trailed off, puzzle pieces clicking together in his head. It had never made sense that Frank had betrayed the ranch, but what if Donovan had made him an offer too? He kissed Charlene's forehead and released her. "Stay right there. I'll be right back."

He sprang to his feet, running across the yard. It was a long shot, but Frank had given him papers intended for Anna's father. He'd forgotten about them until now, but was certain they were still in his vest. He'd been too upset to remember them when he'd last dined with Donovan, and hadn't worn the vest since. But if there was anything there that could firmly tie Frank Hanns to Donovan, it might be enough to connect them now too.

———

CHARLENE STARED AFTER RICHARD, not sure if she was angry or bemused. She'd expected a discussion about balancing work and personal lives, and a repeat of the kisses she'd been dreaming about for three months. She hadn't expected him bring up Anna Reches and certainly not to run off in the middle of the discussion.

She leaned back on the stairs, not the most comfortable of places, watching the stars wink at her from above. A bright star raced across the heavens and Charlene heard her mother's voice in her head. *Wish upon a falling star, my darling girl. Then catch the wish and hold it to your heart.*

"I wish…" Charlene shook her head, her hair tickling her cheeks, "I wish you were here now."

She watched the sky until her elbows began to ache and she had to change her position. What was taking Richard so long? Had he made it as far as his bunk and dozed off? It didn't seem likely but he was taking his own sweet time.

She pushed to her feet, both knees popping in discouraging harmony. Charlene paced the length of the porch twice before the sound of approaching feet turned her attention. Richard was returning, a fold of papers in one hand. He had a pocket light out and was skimming the pages quickly. Charlene wasn't sure she would have tried reading by pocket light and walking at the same time, particularly in the dark, but he managed admirably.

He stopped at the steps, only then looking up and offering her the papers. His eyes danced with satisfaction. "Take a look. I wasn't the only one Mister Reches offered work to, though I'm not sure I'd call those terms working ones."

Charlene took the stack, leaning back against the porch rail to get better light on the printed information. She started from the top and had to stop three paragraphs in and begin again more slowly. It was a letter of contract between Frank Hanns and Donovan Reches. Frank was to have been paid 10,000 credits for each cow or flat of seedlings he could smuggle away from the Double P. There was even a bonus for damages done to slow the harvest with a special note that Donovan didn't want the ranch destroyed, just inconvenienced and demoralized.

Her stomach clenched, her eyes filling with angry tears. "What is wrong with this man? There are hundreds of ranches on planet, thousands in the Cluster. If he really wants a place he can buy into a lot of them, or just plain purchase the land and start his own place. What benefit is it to keep harassing mine?"

"I'm not sure." Richard admitted, "Though I suspect it may be because you keep telling him no. Donovan Reches isn't the kind of man who likes being denied whatever he's set his sights on."

"Well he's going to have to get over it. He can't have the Double P, our methods, or animals!"

Richard's hands came to rest on Charlene's shoulders. He nodded, meeting her gaze. "Damn straight. While these papers don't prove that Donovan is supporting Frank and his band of ruffians, I think it's likely and this should be enough for the Sheriff to investigate."

"Festival gatherings start down in Ridgeback day after tomorrow. We can take it to him then. It'll be easier than trying to track him down while he's helping get everything set up. He always shows up at the first night dance. His wife insists."

Richard nodded again, brushing the tears off her cheeks with strong fingers. "Good. Then we have a plan." He cupped her face in his hands. "I'll find Miss Reches and talk to her too."

Charlene rubbed her cheek against his fingers. His hands were warm and his touch made her body hum with desire. "Does that mean I can't kiss you now?"

"Technically?"

She dropped the papers, catching him by the front of his shirt and pulling him down to her. She didn't want him to finish the sentence, claiming his lips with hers. He didn't hesitate before kissing her back, his kisses wanton and demanding as though he could fill the lost time with his lips alone. Three months of suppressed need raced through her, and Charlene pushed him back until they were out of the light and his back pressed up against the wall of the house.

If she couldn't kiss him again, or even acknowledge there was a relationship between them for a few days, she was going to get her fill now. And it wasn't as though he was protesting. She caught his lower lip between her teeth, nipping lightly before drawing her lips down across his jaw. Stubble tugged her mouth with a tickling whisper and Charlene smiled as she ran light kisses along his throat.

Richard groaned, one hand clenching in her hair and the other running down her back and hooking around her waist, pulling her bodily against him. His breath came fast and his eyes closed, his head tilted to give her better access.

She kissed and licked her way around to the tender spot just beneath his ear and bit down.

He gasped, arching against her and gathering a fist full of her shirt, pulling it free from the back of her pants. His fingers sought her skin, but he hesitated. "Charlene…" He swallowed hard, his voice a breathy whisper. "If you keep doing that I am going to forget all about social responsibilities and respectful behavior."

"Is that supposed to be encouraging or discouraging?" She murmured against his throat. He tasted of dust and sweat, a perfectly lovely combination as far as she was concerned.

"Yes? Both? I don't know."

Charlene laughed, licking the shell of his ear. Carl never liked it when she was aggressive and had pushed her away, but Richard was entirely different and she loved the little sounds he made and the way his body shifted against hers.

He sighed, muttering. "Evil woman."

"That sounds very complimentary."

"It is." He used the hand in her hair to make her stop, meeting her gaze, his expression flushed, blue eyes wide. "But I am going to insist we stop, because I want to do right by you." He smiled, tugging her hair. "Not that I don't want to make love to you under the stars, but I want more out of our first time than a hasty stolen moment wondering when someone is going to disturb us. It also seems to me a few blankets seem in order for such a thing."

"Mmm, that's sensible." She made a face at him before kissing his neck one more time. "If you can be sensible, so can I." Reluctantly she loosed her grip on him and took a step back, smoothing down the front of his shirt. She felt his muscles tense under her hands and wished his shirt was gone. "Have your talk or whatever, but don't make me wait too long. There's only a certain amount of socially responsible and respectable a girl can take."

Richard stole another light kiss before taking her hands and pressing a kiss to each palm. "I promise. Just a few days to work through a couple things, then we'll announce our courtship to everyone and withstand the groans and the 'I told you so's." He squeezed her fingers. "And because we could both use something to look forward to, will you come to the Festival dance with me?"

"I'll come, of course, but I don't dance. I used to, but my joints just don't work that way anymore."

Richard grinned. "We'll see about that."

29

Despite their agreement, Richard was certain it would be difficult to ignore their blossoming relationship, but Charlene proved remarkably adept at avoiding eye contact and keeping her expression so smooth he couldn't guess what she was thinking. The morning started out with slab toast to celebrate the start of the Festival week before settling into the familiar, and much missed, rhythm of a normal day on the ranch. Richard checked in on his favorite calves, both of whom had put on weight in the last three months, but were happy to lick grain off of his hand and butt him in greeting.

Ted's war council mostly consisted of Charlene reviewing everything they were already doing, and Richard sharing the letter between Frank and Donovan. It was agreed Ted, as the ranch manager, would talk to the Sheriff about the letter, and they'd keep pushing forward on the new fencing and security shifts. Richard wished he had more suggestions of how they could keep the outlaws off of the ranch, but most of his suggestions for dealing with outlaws came from audio programs or the old holos he'd watched with Gregory, neither of which seemed practical in the actual situation.

He was helping Ted sort the latest load of supplies when Charlene and Daria came down to hook up the small wagon to the cart horse who kept lipping Charlene's hair. In the light, Richard could see Daria was a stunning woman. Long red hair hung down to the small of her back in haphazard curls, framing a sweet, heart-shaped face and storm grey eyes. Her dress was cut to emphasize her abundant figure, and Richard looked away before Charlene noticed him looking.

Ted glanced up once and frowned before he opened another box labeled 'parts' and started sorting.

"Ted, I'm gonna run Daria over to the Triple Cross. Do we have anything else that needs to be dropped off over there?" Charlene's question was rushed, and Richard saw she was hooking up the rig as fast as possible. He thought it likely she hadn't realized Ted was in the barn and was trying to hurry Daria away as fast as possible.

However, the red-head didn't want to cooperate. She grinned, licking full lips and looking over the men. "Don't know why we're in such a hurry. I haven't seen Ted in over a year and I've not even met my replacement."

She strode over to the table, standing too close to Ted and thrusting a hand at Richard. "Hey, sugar. I'm Daria Frebon."

Richard took her hand, though he noticed she was paying more attention Ted than him. "It's nice to meet you, Miss Frebon." He released her, gesturing absently to the table. "You might want to step back a little. We don't want to spill anything over. I'm sure you understand what a pain it can be to track down spilled nuts and bolts."

"Oh, indeed." Daria stepped back, but towards Ted, not away. She looked down at him, then pulled his hat off. "Heya, Ted, you seriously gonna ignore me and not even say hello? I thought we were still friends."

Ted snatched his hat, putting it back on his head. "You thought so. I don't, and I've made that clear. Ya wanna visit with Charlene, that's fine, but leave me be. I got work to do."

"Daria, we're set. Let's get going, okay?" Charlene interjected, but Daria frowned, resting her hands on her hips.

"Ted, stop being an infant. All of that was years ago, and it's not fair of you to hold it against me."

"Fair? Damnit, woman, do we really have ta have this conversation every time ya poke your nose around?"

"A good churchgoing boy would have forgiven me."

"A good churchgoing woman wouldn't be whoring around the Cluster."

"THEODORE!" Charlene snapped, but it was too late. Richard watched the color drain from Daria's face and had just enough time to get out of the way as she caught the edge of the table. She flipped it up and kicked the table leg, sending everything, Ted included, toppling.

She spun on her heel and stalked to the wagon, pulling herself up next to Charlene. "Go to hell, Teddy."

Ted rolled over in the dust, glaring at the woman. "Meet you there! Charlene, get her out of here before I say something that I regret. I don't wanna see her back on the Double P again."

"Don't worry. You won't."

Charlene shot Ted an apologetic look before snapping the reins and getting the cart horse on the move. No one spoke or moved in the barn until the sound of the wagon had faded. Richard offered Ted a hand up.

"Well, that was unique."

Ted snorted, righting the table. "I guess that's one word for it." He tossed Richard a small bucket before getting one for himself, and started gathering the small parts which were scattered all over the floor. "I try hard not ta fight with her, and Charlene usually does a really good job of running interference so we don't talk to each other. It's better that way."

Richard nodded, shaking dirt off of a handful of screws. "My father told me once that while hell hath no fury like a woman scorned, worse was the fury of the woman who got what she only thought she wanted."

"Well, it's too bad if she changed her mind. I did my best to do right by her. Seems like it ain't so much to ask fer her ta just leave me alone." Ted set several large caps on the table and scowled. "And she didn't have ta kick the table. It's gonna take hours ta make sure we got everything and no one steps on a nail."

"I'm sorry for inadvertently giving her the idea."

"Eh, she would have come up with it herself anyway." Ted tipped his hat back, so he could see more easily. "No more talking about the she-devil. Sounds like ya know enough of the story anyway. Did ya get that present all set up for Charlene?"

Richard nodded, not resisting the change of topic. He felt sorry for Ted and for a pain which had gone on for so long. It seemed to him that the pair weren't suited for each other, but neither of them could leave the past alone, picking at it like a scab when it'd be better to truly forgive and move on.

"Yeah. I'm all ready with it. I'm hoping I can catch her tonight after dinner. Do you have the second part of it?"

"Yeah. I had Missus Davidson check it yesterday. She says the sizing is correct and wishes you the best of luck. I'm pretty sure you and Charlene are the only ones pretending that we don't all know yer sweet on each other."

Richard paused, looking over the table at Ted and raising both brows. He started to protest, then stopped. "Yeah, maybe. I just need to do this right, and that means waiting a little longer before making any kind of public thing of it."

"I don't rightly see how it's any big deal. Ya like her, she likes ya in return, sweep her off her feet and carry her off inta the sunset. Fortune favors the ballsy."

Richard snorted, adding more pieces to his bucket. Trust Ted to make a common turn of phrase tawdry. "It's a pretty picture, but I don't want to just sweep her off her feet for a night or two. I want a future together, and I want to start everything off on the right foot."

Ted snorted. "Well...I can't say I mind really. You make her happy. I've seen enough to know that. You understand her limitations without resenting them. You've even got her to back off on some of the stuff she shouldn't be doing anyway." He grinned. "Though I hold with what I said before. Screw it up an' we won't be friends anymore."

"If I screw it up I'm not sure who I'll be more afraid of, you or her." Richard's tones were light, but he promised himself he wasn't going to screw this up. Not this time.

30

The cart horse lipped at the grass, ignoring Charlene while she swore at the wagon, which sat at an odd angle at the edge of the road. Charlene wanted to kick the old wagon, but she knew that wouldn't fix the issue and would hurt her foot. The back axle had shorn in two when the damn horse had startled over a snake soaking up the afternoon sun on the rubber road. Like many other things, the little wagon was on the list of items which needed updates and repairs, but far enough down the list that neither had happened yet.

Charlene sighed, pulling the bag of hand dyed yarn Daria's mother had given her for Missus Davidson out of the wagon. There wasn't much else she couldn't do without. Not for the first time she wished the hand-held comms which were so popular on other planets would work on Galileo, but wishing wouldn't get her any closer to home.

Using her belt and a length of rope from the wagon, she fastened the bag onto the horse and led him down the road. Without a saddle, the horse was too tall for her to mount easily, and even if she found something to climb up onto, the idea of riding bareback made her cringe. She'd have to walk, a thought which made her more and more nervous as the sun tipped the horizon. She shouldn't have visited for so long, but Missus Frebon was a chatterbox and there never seemed to be a polite way to end the conversation before she launched into her next point. Charlene was very fond of the woman, who was much like a second mother, so she endured far longer than she should have.

Charlene kept herself on the edge of the road, setting as fast of a pace as she could handle. She'd missed lunch—the tea and cookies at the Triple Cross hardly counted—as well as her second pain pill, the combination making her dizzy, and her steps less certain than she wanted. As the dark settled in around her she cursed herself roundly for not packing the standard emergency kit in the wagon. She knew she should have taken the few minutes to fetch the extra supplies; she'd often scolded the men for skipping the step because they weren't going very far. Now she was an example of why it mattered. It was only about a half hour to the Triple Cross by wagon, but a lot longer on foot.

The noises of the evening rose, and Charlene was desperately aware of the empty gun she carried and how easy it would be to carry her off with no one knowing any better for hours. Adrenaline and fear pushed her along, stumbling over stones and spring foliage until she forced herself to lead the horse to the middle of the road. They were much more visible, but there was less to trip over.

Charlene cried out in relief when she reached the fence line which represented the border of the Double P. She ran for a few steps, tumbling to the ground when her knees protested the action. Frustrated, she forced herself back up and returned to a walk she could maintain. All too slowly she reached the main gate, running her hands over it and entering her access code so she didn't have to disturb Gravy.

She was halfway down the lane when she saw someone approaching, a broad shadow against the faint light coming from the house and the barns. He raised an electric lantern, and Charlene put a hand up to shield her eyes. "Hey, you're blinding me."

"Charlene?" Kevin's voice was puzzled, and he lowered the light. "I'm sorry. I didn't expect to see you out here. Everyone thought you stayed over at the Triple Cross with Miss Daria."

Charlene raised both brows, too weary to be tactful. "Did anyone actually call over there to find out?"

"I…erm…I don't know?"

She held out the reins of the horse. "Take him back to the barn and give him a rub down please. I'd do it, but I'm just too tired. The wagon is busted around half ridge. We'll need to send folks after the wagon in the morning."

"Yes, ma'am." He took the reins, looking at her with concern. "Would it be easier if I helped you ride him in?"

"No. I can manage okay, but if you want to ride him, he deserves to have to work a little for his supper."

Kevin shook his head. "I think it'll be better if I walk you back to the house. Ted will clobber me if he hears I rode off and left you walking in the dark on your own."

"Mm…" Charlene nodded, continuing to put one foot in front of the other. If she stopped she was afraid she'd fall down and not be able to get going again. "He just might at that."

They walked the rest of the way in silence, and Charlene didn't stop until she'd climbed the steps of the porch. Missus Davidson met her at the door. The older woman looked her over and didn't ask any questions, simply helped her up the stairs and into the bathroom.

Charlene managed a thank you before stripping out of her sweaty, dirty clothing and turning on the water. She stayed until she was clean and the water ran cold, letting her thoughts drift as the heat chased away many of her fears. Wrapped in a thin robe, Charlene limped into her room and picked up the thigh holster, removing the small caliber gun. Deliberately she pulled the box of ammunition from her closet and loaded the weapon. Ted was right, if she was going to carry the weapon she needed to trust herself enough to load it and use it.

She set the gun on her desk with the holster and sat on the end of the bed, forcing a comb through her hair. She was tired, but if she didn't work her hair out it would be a tangle of snarls in the morning. Besides, the action was soothing.

A soft knock sounded at the door. Charlene blinked a couple times, realizing she'd been drifting. "I'm awake."

Tracy opened the door just enough to peek in. "Sorry, Miss Charlene. But Mister Tyler is downstairs and wants to talk to you."

"Did he mention what about?"

"No, ma'am."

Charlene pursed her lips. She didn't want to see anyone right now, but if it was important enough that he'd send Tracy up at this hour, he deserved her attention. "Bring him up."

Tracy blinked, startled. "But…to your room? And you're in a robe!"

"For hell's sake, Tracy. I know, but I can't take the stairs right now. So either he has to come up, or he'll have to wait until tomorrow. We'll leave the door open if folks are so concerned about who I may or may not have in my room. Just tell him and let him make the choice. I'm going to change."

Tracy stammered and Charlene waved her off, getting to her feet and finding her night gown and a robe. If the bedroom or the informal dress insulted his sensibilities then Richard would have to wait.

31

Richard stood at the top of the stairway, wondering why they didn't just turn one of the downstairs rooms into Charlene's room given she had so much trouble with the stairs. A lot of the lower floor was taken up with the kitchen, but with some creativity an addition could be put on back to give the kitchen space and a bedroom suite added. A small voice argued that it could be a master bedroom, big enough for two, but he didn't entertain the thought very long. They weren't quite to that point of courtship, and it was maddening to consider possibilities which he couldn't act on.

He looked at the stacked boxes in his hands. They weren't really enough reason to disturb her after what had, by all rumors, been a long day, but by those same rumors he wanted to see her. He walked down the hallway to the open door and knocked before looking inside. Charlene was curled up in a chair next to a simple desk. She was dressed in a robe which showed a trail of lace at the hem and neckline, hinting at the nightgown below. Her skin was tinged pink from the heat of the shower and her hair hung wet and loose around her shoulders. Richard's mouth went dry.

Charlene looked up, tilting her head to one side with a soft snicker. "You're staring."

"I…" Richard forced himself to step into the room, ignoring the feeling he was doing something illicit. "I suppose I am, but there's a lot to stare at." His gaze dropped to her feet and he smiled. "For instance, you have very nice toes."

"Toes. I'm certain they were the first thing you noticed." She laughed, but her eyes were tired. She waved at a wooden fold out chair nearby. "So, not to be overly blunt, but what can I do for you? Not that I'm not happy to see you, but my very nice toes are one of many body parts that would like to be in bed."

Richard settled into the chair, eyeing it as it squeaked. He set one of the boxes on the foot of her bed, holding the other across his lap. "I know, and I do apologize for keeping you up. Kevin came in telling stories about you walking most of the way back from the Triple Cross, and I needed to know you were all right."

"Tired and stiff mostly, but all right, just angry for not remembering the emergency supplies. I was in such a hurry to get Daria away from Ted that I broke my own rules. I wish we'd looked at that wagon during the rains." She offered him a lopsided smile. "If we were officially courting I'd let you kiss me better."

Richard blushed before breaking into good natured laughter. It wasn't her fault they were waiting, and he deserved a little teasing. "If we were officially courting I would be certain to oblige you. But as it is I do have something to offer besides kisses. This was something I had hoped to do after dinner, but I think it will help you now."

She arched both brows, curious. "You have my undivided attention."

Richard's hands tightened around the box, and he was hit by a wave of nerves. What if the therapy rig didn't work for her, or if she thought he was being impertinent? She hadn't asked him to solve her problems. He pushed the doubts down and offered her the package. "Ted told me it was traditional to give gifts during Festival."

Charlene took the package, and he saw the slight shake of her hands as she gathered it onto her lap, pulling the thin ribbon bow loose. "Technically," she said with a grin which reminded him of the interlude the night before, "we give gifts at the end of the Festival, but I'm certainly not going to complain."

She removed the brown wrapping and unfolded the box inside, looking at the contents with puzzlement. She drew out several sets of small flexible pads with soft fabric on one side and wire leads on the other, following the wires to where they connected into a larger box with a belt hook on it. "Um…" Charlene's brow furrowed as she sorted through the pieces, finally holding two up and looking at him. "You win. I have no idea what you've gifted me with except there are a lot of wires involved."

Richard smiled and knelt by her chair. He picked up the two smallest discs and removed a thin sheet of plastic from them before pressing them on the back of her hands, one for each. "Close your eyes."

Charlene eyed him, but did as she was told. Richard picked up the lead box, pressing a button. Immediately the disks warmed, sending an electrical pulse into her hands. Charlene blinked, opening her eyes and looking down at the pads where they lay still against her wrists.

"Oh, that feels really good." She sounded surprised and Richard's smile widened.

"It should. I've been working with the Pain Center on Pristine for the last three months to get everything right. It's a mobile version of their Cempack treatment machine. The box with the battery and settings can be hooked to a belt, and the pads go on your joints in pairs, as few as two at a time: hip, knee, ankle, shoulder, elbow and wrist. The combination of heat and electrical massage is good for easing pain and loosening up stiff joints. It should be flexible enough to be worn under clothing, though I'm not entirely sure how it will interact with other machinery so maybe stay out of the equipment barn. It's still imperfect, but it should make you feel better, and if you wear it for a few hours, then take it off, the effect should carry on for a while. It's not a cure, I know that, and I know you don't need to be fixed, but it's something I can do to make things easier for you." He knew he was babbling and forced himself to stop.

She was silent for a long moment. When Richard looked up he saw tears on her cheeks. He covered her hands, kissing each one. "Charlene? What's wrong? I can turn it off if it's hurting you. I might have to adjust the settings. If you don't like it you don't have to use it. Please don't cry."

She shook her head, blotting the tears. "No, it's not that. It's…" Charlene searched for words, explaining. "When you are always in pain you get to the point you don't realize how much you hurt, how much you're just ignoring until it's gone. The relief is…I don't have words for it. These aren't sad tears."

Richard smiled, watching her face. Every bit of work and every late hour was worth the delighted expression. She flexed her fingers against his hands, making a little startled noise as the program changed to a deeper massage. A light blush ran over her cheeks. "Well, that one is a little startling, but not in a bad way."

"There are three different levels of massage. I preprogrammed a few cycles, but you can play with it. The Doctor on Pristine suggested not using it for more than 15 minutes per hour, especially at first and not always in the same places. I suspect you'll have to experiment a bit."

He reached behind him, picking up the second larger box and setting it on her lap. It might have been more comfortable to return to the chair, but he liked the view where he was.

Charlene arched an eyebrow. "You've already given me more than plenty, Richard."

"Maybe, but I don't want you to have any excuses."

"Excuses?" Even as she asked the question Charlene pulled the second ribbon free, pushing the paper off the box. Her fingers moved quickly, more confidently than they had on the first package and Richard was filled with pleasure that his machine had given that to her, allowed her to be more herself.

"Mmhm." He waved at the box. "You'll see."

She made a face and pulled the top off the box, catching her breath. Her eyes widened as she slowly drew back the tissue paper and lifted the fabric from within. The light raced along the rich red silk gown, making it shimmer. It was a lightweight design with delicate flutter sleeves and a scoop neckline which remained modest, but far more daring than anything he'd ever seen her wear. Cream and gold ribbons crisscrossed the bodice leading to a cream lace over skirt which hung over more red silk embroidered with tiny flowers. Dainty cream colored dancing slippers with gold laces completed the package.

Charlene's mouth moved, but it took a few moments before sound came out. "I can't wear this."

"Why not?"

"I…I wouldn't know how." She ran her fingers over the silk, "I'd be afraid of getting it dirty or ripping it."

Richard laughed, resting his hand against the side of her face. "Then it gets dirty or ripped. It's just clothing, beautiful clothing, yes, but still just clothing. I want you to feel as beautiful as I think you are and thought this might be nice. But mostly I didn't want you to have any excuses not to come and dance with me. The seamstress guaranteed me the skirt is full enough for dancing and lightweight enough you'll be comfortable. And if that won't work then wear your most battered trousers and shirt and we'll surprise them all."

Charlene rubbed her cheek against his fingers. "Well, when you put it that way. I'll wear the dress because if only because that will be much more of a surprise. Thank you, for everything."

He brushed his thumb across her lips, adding the moment to ones he would always remember. "You're welcome."

32

Charlene turned slowly in a circle, watching the lacy overdress follow the sway of the silk skirt. The woman who looked back at her from the mirror didn't look familiar, dressed in the red silk gown with her hair piled up high and pinned with tiny pearl clips. She'd pulled out the cosmetics she hadn't used since leaving Central, adding a touch of color at lips, cheeks, and eyelid and Charlene was pleased with the effect. Her spin brought the pain therapy box into view, and she smiled, running a finger along the plastic.

Richard was right that the massage unit wasn't a cure, but, even with only a day's use, it was better therapy than she'd had in years. She felt loose and warm. Maybe dancing wasn't so far out of the realm of possibilities either.

"Miss Charlene." Missus Davidson's voice came from the bottom of the stairs. "Gravy is here with the wagon. Are you ready, then?"

Charlene scooped up her evening bag, a small pouch which matched the dress and carried a lipstick and her gun. It seemed odd to take the weapon to a dance, but after her night alone on the road Charlene wasn't leaving it behind despite her reluctance to carry it in the first place. "I'm coming!"

She twitched her dress a final time before shutting off the light and walking down the stairs. Gravy and Missus Davidson stood arm in arm near the bottom step, both dressed in their church best. Missus Davidson looked up first and her mouth formed an 'o' before she smiled.

"Oh my dear, you look marvelous."

Gravy turned as well, arching shaggy eyebrows. "Indeed she does." His features softened. "You look like your mother, Miss Charlene, and that's no little thing. I suspect you will be the belle of the ball."

Charlene blushed. "I don't have any real interest in being the center of attention."

"Just one particular man's attentions, I'm sure." Missus Davidson said with a knowing smile. "You've our blessing, not that you need it. He's a good man."

"I think so." Charlene laughed, pulling a shawl around her shoulders. "Even if you're not supposed to know yet."

Gravy snorted. "We have eyes, girl. You two are about a subtle as a rutting bull. I suspect the whole ranch figured it out before you did. And as my Missus here said, we approve. Now, let's get you lovely ladies to the dance."

The whole ranch figured it out. The thought struck Charlene as amusing. Even if they didn't need it, she was glad to get approval from the hands. She wasn't sure what changes courting Richard would mean, but she wasn't afraid to try.

Gravy led the way out of the house, holding the door for the two women. Edwin had picked up Tracy earlier, and the rest of the men, those who weren't working the security shifts, went down early in the morning to help with set up on Matilda's request. Gravy had exchanged the wide wagon for a small carriage borrowed from the Triple Cross. The carriage had high sides and even a roof to keep off wind and rain, not that it looked like there was any threat of poor weather.

He lifted each of the women into the carriage, placing Missus Davidson to ride next to him and Charlene nearest the outside. As they rolled away she waved to Kevin who had drawn one of the evening shifts. He waved back with a smile, and Charlene made a mental note to talk to Ted about giving Kevin a raise. He was the youngest of their hands, but he'd certain proved himself capable.

The journey to Ridgeback passed both too slowly and too quickly, and Charlene found herself leaning forward with anticipation as the lights of the city came into sight. Additional strings of bright lights had been strung from building to building and along the stone cliffs which surrounded the town, like bright stones on a necklace. They came around the back side of the city and parked at the church, joining many other rigs and wagons. Gravy helped them down then waved them on while he saw to the needs of the horse.

As they approached the town square, music rose up to greet them, and Charlene swayed as she walked. More lights decorated building fronts, mostly white and blue to represent the rain which had fallen and passed. Desert flowers bloomed on every side, brought to life for a few short weeks and adding a spicy aroma which heightened the scents of food as they drew closer.

Gravy caught up just as the women reached the edge of the square. One set of dancing had just ended and the next was starting. Gravy caught Missus Davidson around the waist, giving Charlene a rakish grin before he spun his wife into the dance. Charlene laughed, clapping along with the other on-lookers while the dancers spun and leaped around the square.

She spotted Ted amongst the dancers, a girl on each arm. They didn't seem to mind dancing as a threesome, nor did any of them know the steps, which they also didn't mind, frequently bumping into others and apologizing. Charlene absently wondered if Ted had been sampling the various spirits which were making the rounds, or if he was just happy to be out in society. Either, or both, was entirely possible.

"You look amazing." The whisper came at her shoulder, startling Charlene. She spun, smiling when she saw Richard standing just behind her.

He was dressed for the evening in a pair of dark trousers and a newly pressed white shirt. Over the shirt was a buttoned vest in the same red as her dress, a black bow tie at his throat. She suspected he'd brought his coat and hat, but even in the dark of early evening it was simply too hot to wear them. His hair brushed across his forehead with a boyish charm, and she was pleased he hadn't let Missus Davidson cut it too short. The look suited him.

"If I look amazing it's all because of the dress."

Richard shook his head. "No. I barely noticed the dress even though it's very nice. You look amazing." He smiled, taking her hands and pressing them to his lips. "I'm glad you came." His smile took on a more playful air, "And not only because Ted made a bet with me that you'd, in his words, weasel out at the last minute."

"The two of you bet on me staying home?" Charlene raised both brows, resting her hands on her hips. "And what, exactly did you bet?"

"Cattle mucking," Richard laughed at her expression and shrugged. "I thought you knew. There's a lot of betting that goes on between the men, almost all of it payable in chores. Everyone has things they hate doing. Comes up in card games too."

Charlene shook her head, but smiled. "I can't believe a well bred man like yourself partakes in this behavior."

"Oh, I hesitated at first, but the part of me which hates mucking cattle was stronger than the part of me which doesn't hold with gambling."

"Ahh…so we've corrupted you. I consider it a job well done." She teased.

Richard took her hands again. "I truly don't mind."

The music shifted, and he grinned, pulling her into the square. Charlene started to protest. It had been so long since she'd danced in public. She felt like everyone was staring at her, even though she rationally knew it wasn't the case. He dropped his hand to her waist, pulling her in close, and she placed her hand on his shoulder. "Richard. I'm not sure I remember the steps."

"Don't think about the steps. Just trust me and I'll remember for both of us."

He didn't give her any more time to fret, leading her right into the middle of the dancers and keeping her so busy she couldn't think of anything but following where he lead. He was an excellent dancer and following wasn't nearly as hard as she thought it might be. They bumped into another couple once, but the bump was met with good-natured laughter.

Charlene lost track of how often the music changed, sure there was some rule about dancing over and over again with the same man, but she didn't care. Richard's blue eyes held her captive as much as his warm grip, and she rarely looked away.

Finally, he spun her off of the dance floor and towards one of the long tables which surrounded the dancing so they could both catch their breath.

"For a woman who doesn't remember the steps, you are remarkably agile, Miss Charlene."

Charlene wished she had a hand fan, not wanting to blot the cosmetics from her skin but aware she was sweating. "It's easy to look agile when you have the right partner. I'm certain your toes must be bleeding from all the times I stepped on them."

"To be honest, I hardly noticed. I was too busy deciding if I should defend your honor from all the admiring glances you were getting." Richard's eyes crinkled at the corners when he laughed, and she didn't bother looking away.

"I never noticed. I only saw you. I was trying to save your feet."

"Just as well, I'm not good at duels. I'm not even sure how defending honor would work out here." He flicked the hair off his forehead and squeezed her fingers. "I'm finding myself a bit parched after all that. Would you care for some punch? I may even be able to find some of the meats which have been, I admit, tempting me all afternoon."

"Both sound really good. I think I'll take a moment to freshen up while you do that."

Richard nodded, kissing the back of her hand, lips lingering on her skin, before releasing her and heading for the food tables. Charlene watched him go and pushed up off of the bench. Rising was easier than she expected, and she couldn't help the warm smile that brought. She was still a bit stiff, but it was so much better that she nearly danced her way into the General Store where facilities had been made open to the general public.

She made use of the lav and washed up, taking a moment to freshen her lipstick and repin one section of her hair. On her way back to the table she exchanged pleasantries with the store owners and some of the other women of the town. She was so often at the ranch that she couldn't say she knew most of them well, but enough for casual greetings.

When Charlene reached the table there were two plates and cups where they'd been sitting, but Richard was nowhere to be seen. Charlene picked up her glass, sniffing the contents. It was fruity with an alcoholic undertone, so she sipped versus gulping, still looking for Richard. She sat down and as she did so the crowd parted enough for her to see him, bending over the hand of Anna Reches.

Charlene jumped to her feet, the punch spilling from suddenly nerveless hands to splash on the ground. Richard had said he needed to talk to Miss Reches, but Charlene hadn't thought he'd do it tonight. She frowned, wondering if Richard had known Miss Reches was going to come and hadn't said anything. He wouldn't do that.

Would he?

She chewed her bottom lip and forced herself to sit down. Miss Reches looked like an angel in a white and silver gown which was much more appropriate for a ballroom on Central than a Festival dance in the middle of a dusty square. There was no way the white chiffon would last the night without damage, but then again Miss Reches probably only intended to wear it once.

The pace of the music changed to something slow and swaying, a song Charlene usually liked, but when she was watching Richard lead Miss Reches onto the floor all the notes sounded sour. She fumbled around behind her until she found Richard's full glass and emptied it in a couple of long swallows. The alcohol burned, not unpleasantly so, particularly in contrast to watching the dance. Charlene admitted Richard and Miss Reches made a striking couple, his red and black to her silver and white, both crowned with golden locks and though his skin was darker than hers it only served to highlight her fashionable paleness.

Charlene looked away, wishing she had more punch. He had promised her he wasn't mooning over Anna Reches, that he just needed to break up with her so they could officially court, but a slow waltz in public didn't seem very much like a break up.

She picked at the plate of meats. What had been a treat was now just something to do with her hands while she tried not to fret. The direction of the dance brought Richard and Miss Reches past Charlene's position, and she couldn't look away. Richard didn't meet her eyes, but Miss Reches' did, her icy gaze filled with triumph as she laid her head on Richard's shoulder. Her lips moved as she watched Charlene, ~Mine...~

Charlene muttered a string of curses and got to her feet, very nearly slipping in the spilled drink. Maybe all of this was part of Richard's master plan and would lead to what she wanted in the long run, but Anna certainly didn't know, and Charlene didn't have to watch it. She made it to the edge of the square before she heard footfalls behind her. Charlene turned, expecting Richard and blinked when the follower proved to be Daria.

"Hey, Char. You seem to be going in the wrong direction. The party is back there." Daria was dressed the way Charlene now wished she were, in a black divided riding skirt and a silky green blouse which made the most of her red hair. Daria paused, raising both eyebrows. "Uh huh. I've seen that look. Whose hair do we need to tear out? Please tell me it's that Anna Reches woman who's dancing with the tall drink of water you're so fond of. I've always wanted to get a fist full of those ringlets. They're just unnatural, ya know."

Charlene managed a smile at the thought of Daria dragging Anna Reches around by the hair. "It's her, but…" she took a deep breath. "Richard has it under control. He's breaking up with her."

"Uh huh. Maybe it's none of my business, but that didn't look very break uppy. It kinda looked all snuggled up and heading for a really good roll in the hay." Charlene paled and Daria made a face. "I'm sorry. I just made it worse didn't I? Hi, my name is Daria, and I live with both feet in my mouth."

"It's all right, I just. Can we not talk about them?"

"Sure. Sure. We'll talk about something else."

"Miss Charlene?" A young man, no more than 14 approached, his head held at a quizzical angle.

Charlene turned away from Daria. "Yes?"

"Oh, good. I'm supposed to give you a message. Someone by the name of Kevin sent a comm in to the General Store. He says he needs you back at the ranch in a hurry."

Of course. Charlene puffed out a breath. "Did he say why?"

"Not as I know, Ma'am. I'm just delivering the message. Madam Daisy might know more."

"If Madam Daisy isn't too busy to remember her own name," Daria murmured.

Charlene closed her eyes and counted to ten before opening them again. "Thank you. You can tell Madam Daisy you gave me the message." The teen slipped off, and Charlene gave herself a shake. "It really never fails. I need to find Ted or Gravy and get a lift back. Kevin is a solid hand, if he says he needs me back there it's for a good reason." She wasn't happy to be leaving the celebration, but she didn't mind not watching Richard conduct his break up anymore.

"I've got a carriage. I borrowed Daddy's rig when he and Mama decided to stay home. We can zip out and see what's up and then come back nice as you please. Bet we'll even be back before they set out the desserts."

Charlene smiled and hugged her friend. "I'm glad you're back. Remind me why it was I let you leave?"

"Because I was in love, of course. People do strange things when they're in love. It makes us all fools and crazy people."

Thinking of Richard, Charlene nodded. "It does at that. Let's get going."

33

Anna Reches smelled like she'd been dipped in a rosebush. Richard did his best not to sneeze while he led her through the steps of the waltz. They didn't speak while they danced, the layers of her dress floating around them until Richard decided he was dancing with a powder puff. He was relieved when the dance came to an end and took a step back, bowing and kissing her gloved hand before tucking it in the crook of his arm and guiding her away from the square. He hadn't expected to see her tonight and approaching her had seemed like a good idea until he'd seen the stricken look on Charlene's face. Now, he cursed himself for a fool.

He simply wished to get this conversation completed as fast as possible so he could return to the woman he thought of as his and apologize.

"Richard!" Anna's voice was sharp, breaking across his thoughts. Richard blinked, realizing by her tone she'd been talking to him for several moments. She looked into his face and smiled a wispy smile. "My goodness, you are distracted tonight."

"I apologize. I am simply lost in my thoughts and the enjoyment of dancing. Though I thought we could go for a short walk, I'd like to speak to you more privately. It is a little difficult to get a word through in the ruckus."

Anna laughed, and Richard was annoyed by the titter. "Of course, though I must admit I've missed the noise. So many of the places I've been are so quiet. One of the benefits of travel is coming to appreciate every-thing," She paused, looking at him significantly, "And everyone, you leave behind."

Richard cleared his throat, inclining his head before leading her away from the square. They walked in silence as he drew her down to where one of the local artists had turned a space between two shops into a foun-tain display for the Festival. He'd watched the water jumping from pipe to pipe with fascination earlier in the afternoon, and it seemed like a good place to find a moment's rest.

"Where are..." Anna jumped as water arced from a metal wrought flower at her side, passing over their heads and landing in the mouth of a frog made of copper. She shook her head, her curls brushing around her neck and clasped her hands together, "Oh, how marvelous!"

"Yes. It's rather impressive. I'm told it took the whole of the rains to create, and this is the only time when they have enough excess water to run it."

They walked through the display, the splash of the water creating a faint mist the deeper they went.

"You've taken me somewhere like this before," Anna observed. "Back in college. Do you remember? When you first kissed me."

"I remember." Richard led her to a bench in the heart of the display, helping her to settle though he remained standing, watching the jumping water.

"Richard, my dear boy, whatever is the matter? You act like something terrible is about to happen. This is a night for celebrations, you know. A Festival."

"I do, yes." He paced a few steps, tucking his hands in his pockets. "But it's also a night about change, celebrating the way the desert blooms after the rain. A lot of marriages and even babies will be started this week. A lot of changes and growth, and I think it's time I did some of my own."

Anna looked up at him, her eyes shining with excitement. "I do hope that means what I think it does."

Richard bit his lip. This was more difficult than he wanted it to be. He didn't wish to hurt her, but his heart was no longer his own to give.

Somewhere along the line Charlene had claimed it, and he'd been happy to let her. "It doesn't, and for that I'm very sorry."

"What? What do you mean?" She whispered, her face falling.

"I mean, Anna…" He knelt next to her, taking her hand between his. "That I am calling off our association. I am very fond of you and I have no regrets about the time we spent together, but I think we have grown apart and I do not see a future for us. It would be very unfair for me to lead you on. I meant to have this conversation some time ago, but you left planet and I felt it would be improper to discuss such things over the comm or in letters."

"But it's not improper to discuss them at a dance?" She looked at their joined hands, tears welling up in her pretty eyes. "I do not understand. I thought everything was wonderful. What went wrong? What changed?"

"I did. I'm not the same man I was when I came to Galileo. That man was young, a little foolish, and even a little selfish. I didn't know what I really wanted, caught between everyone else's desires. I thought I'd come to prove something to you and to my family, but I ended up proving something to myself. I have a life here, a life I love and people who are a part of that. I'm happy with that life, but it's not a life that would ever give you the things you want, and if we were to pursue our relationship, in the end we would make each other very unhappy."

Anna frowned, dashing the tears away. "It's that woman, isn't it? The one you work for. I saw you dancing with her." She shook her head, brushing drops of water out of her hair. "Good heavens, Richard, what future do you have there? What does she have to offer you? A dust farm in the back of nowhere? You're not thinking straight. I know I was gone for a long time, and I know how a man has physical needs. I don't blame you for, what is the vulgar term, sowing your wild oats? That doesn't mean you need to devote yourself to what is obviously a mistake."

Richard frowned. "Charlene is not a mistake. Nor am I sowing any wild oats. She and I have never done anything improper."

"Then why are you throwing me away for her? I can give you everything, the manor on Central, a proper place in society. I can be all those things you need to be who you were born to be." She lifted his hand to her cheek. "My father will hire you and we'll run away. You'll never again have to do work which leaves you with dark skin and harsh calluses.

You're just confused. Come home with me and we'll work everything out."

Richard gently pulled his hand away from her. "Anna. I'm not confused. Maybe for the first time in my life I know what I want. Not what my parents want or society wants, but what I want. Charlene understands that. She makes me a better man. She needs me and I love her."

Anna struck snake-quick, slapping him across the face. The blow was softened by her silk gloves, but he was shocked she'd slapped him. "You are an idiot, Richard Tyler. You could have everything. Maybe we wouldn't be happy, but we would be successful and there's a lot of unhappy which can be soothed by success."

She rose to her feet, pacing away from him. Her voice was cool, the playful nature he'd become accustomed to banished along with the tears. "My Father warned me that you were too honest for our world, but I assured him I had you well in hand. You should be congratulated for surprising me. I generally read men well enough to know just what cards to play to get what I want. I believed I had your number."

"So you were playing with me and willing to let it go as far as marriage?" Richard rubbed his cheek. "Why?"

"Means to an ends. It is a favorable match as far as society is concerned and would merge your family wealth and good name with mine. Your skills are not without merit and would bring in a good living and increase my Father's company and holdings." She looked over at him, her features softening, "I am truly fond of you. Think about it Richard. We could make things work for both of us, tonight doesn't have to end in sorrow. I don't even mind if you want to have the woman as a mistress. We'd both be traveling for our work and causes. It wouldn't be such a big thing for you to stop by and see her, especially if it would smooth the path for buying that ranch Father is so obsessed over. There couldn't be children with her, naturally, but we could have our own little brood, and you'd enjoy the process of getting them. I guarantee that."

Richard slowly pushed to his feet, shaking his head. He met her gaze, stunned it had taken him so long to see through her ruse. He'd been more naïve than he'd known. "I don't know you at all, Miss Reches, and it seems very clear to me that you don't know me either. I'm just glad all of this came out before I was fool enough to offer for you. I'd hoped we'd remain friends, but I see even that is quite impossible. If you'll allow me, I'll see you back to the gathering and then I do not wish to see nor speak to you again."

"If that is what you wish." She looked out into the darkness, raising one hand in a beckoning gesture. "But I can't have you running about loose tonight either. Your timing is poor. I'd hoped to keep you here out of harm's way, but given our discussion I will have to turn that responsibility over to another. I'm sure you remember Mister Walker. He has a few things he would like to discuss with you, in detail."

Four men emerged from the shadows, two of them carrying thick metal rods as long as Richard's forearm. Jeremiah led the group of thugs, his gaze burning with hatred. His nose hadn't healed straight, and by the way he listed to one side, Richard was certain the man wasn't sober.

Anna drifted past the men, a white-clothed demon among devils. "Don't kill him. I want him alive to see the results of his refusal." She paused, purposefully meeting Richard's gaze. "One thing to think about before I go—if you're here, then who, pray tell, is with your woman?"

Richard had only a moment for the horror of the question to set in before the men closed ranks around him and the first stroke fell.

34

Charlene dropped from the carriage and approached the gate to the Double P. The alarm lights winked brightly in the darkness, pulsing red. She ran her fingers over the gate, inputting her code, but nothing happened. Frowning she hit the intercom. "Kevin? Can you hear me? Something's not working with the gate. It won't take my code."

There was no vocal response, but the lights flickered, turning from red to green. She heard the click of the gate latch unlocking. Something felt wrong and Charlene frowned. "Thanks, it's open, but I can't hear you. Trouble with the comm might be why it didn't take the code. Give me a test?"

Nothing.

Charlene frowned, her hand resting on the gate. Three minutes until it would relock. She looked at Daria. "Something's not right." She stopped, seeing the look on Daria's face. "What?"

Daria pointed towards the north, her face pale in the wan lantern light from the carriage. "Fire." She swallowed and shuddered. "Can't tell if it's your property or the tree line up on your north edge."

Charlene's stomach dropped, and she spun around, staring at the horizon. She saw the winking orange light, and made guesses at the distance. "Far northern line, but those trees are just scrub to mark the edge of the property and keep folks out of a gully. It's nothing for the fire to jump

176

into the field." She shoved the gate open. "I'm going to raise the alarm here and check the suppressors, but I'm worried about the comms. I'm not sure if I can get a message out as far as Ridgeback if I can't even reach Kevin. I'll try from the house, but I need you to go to your folks' place and call for Ted."

"Char, I think you should wait for help."

"There isn't time. I've got men here who stayed behind. I have to help them if I can. Get going!"

Charlene pushed the gate closed behind her and broke into a run, hiking her skirt up so it didn't trip her. She couldn't keep up the pace all the way to the house, but she was going to try.

35

R ichard staggered under the heavy blows of fist and rod, grateful for the dark and the confined space which blunted the swings. He had no delusions he could win this fight without help, but the gathering was too far away and too loud for anyone to hear the fighting or a call for help.

Anger and fear combined with adrenaline into a desperate strength—anger that he'd been deceived and fear for what might be happening to Charlene. The only choice left to him was to hurt someone badly enough the others hesitated and gave him a chance to run and even the numbers up. His gaze flashed over the four in no more than a second, and he focused on Jeremiah. The others didn't have a personal stake in this, but Jeremiah was bat-shit crazy and if he dropped the rest might leave.

Thus decided, Richard hesitated just long enough for Jeremiah to close in and rammed into the man, shoulder first. Jeremiah's breath rushed out on a long curse. Richard used his momentum to drive the man into and on top of the stone bench. Richard got his legs on either side of the bench, holding Jeremiah's knees down and driving a fist into Jeremiah's chin. The first blow snapped Jeremiah's teeth together with a click. The second spun his head, splitting his lip.

Satisfaction rose in Richard's gut, pushing aside the pain of bruises and scrapes. He took little joy in hurting someone, but his tolerance had limits, and anyone who threatened Charlene or the Double P deserved whatever punishment he could dish out.

He landed a third punch, setting Jeremiah's nose to bleeding before he was hauled away and thrown backwards into another display. He hit the pipes and something stabbed into his back, ripping through vest, shirt, and flesh followed by a terrible gurgle as water splashed ineffectively against him.

Two of Jeremiah's cronies held Richard down by the shoulders, the third pulling Jeremiah off of the bench. Far from being grateful, Jeremiah shoved the man away, staggering to where Richard was held.

Jeremiah brought his weight down on top of Richard, pushing him harder onto the metal which was skewering him. Spittle fell into Richard's face as Jeremiah snarled.

"Forget what that Reches woman said. Yer gonna die." His hand flashed to his waistband, coming up with a knife. "Jus' carve ya inta pieces an' watch ya bleed."

Richard pushed against Jeremiah, but he had no leverage and each squirm brought more pain and bleeding. Jeremiah ran the tip of his knife down Richard's cheek, drawing a thin line down his skin. "I'll take an ear first." He brought his knee up towards Richard's groin, though the position of the fountain kept the strike from being effective. "Or maybe we'll see if yer bitch likes ya neutered."

The ratcheting sound of a shotgun being cocked broke through the hiss of Jeremiah's foul breath, followed by Ted's voice. "Do *not* call my sister that."

Richard didn't pause to try to figure out how Ted had known there was trouble. The moment Jeremiah looked away, Richard shifted his weight up onto his shoulders, even though it drove the offending metal deeper, and kicked out as hard as he could. The kick wasn't precise, but it didn't have to be, hitting Jeremiah in the chest and throwing him backwards and away from Richard's face.

Beyond Jeremiah, Richard saw a gathering of six men, all of them armed. Sheriff Reid casually leveled the shotgun at Jeremiah's head. "It'd be best if you all put your weapons down and got on your knees. You're under arrest. I'd hate to end the night with bodies."

As though he hadn't heard the warning, Jeremiah leapt at Richard, the knife outstretched. The gun roared, and Richard watched as Jeremiah sagged to the ground, his chest a shattered ruin. The man looked surprised, balancing briefly on his knees before falling face first into the dirt. Casually, the Sheriff ejected the cartridge.

"Got a second shot if anyone would like it."

The remaining men knelt, dropping weapons and placing their hands on their heads. Ted ran forward, pulling Richard free of the fountain before he could protest.

"Hell and damnation, Rick. Doncha know four on one ain't good odds? Ya at least should have invited me ta the party. I could've handled two 'f them easy."

Richard shook his head, but decided it was unwise as his world spun. "Something I'll keep in mind if I'm ever accosted again." He blotted the side of his face with his sleeve. The cut there was shallow, but oozing nonetheless. "How'd you happen to come by with an army?"

"Doin' what Char told me to, 'f course. I brought the papers to the Sheriff, and we went down to visit Reches, but ain't no one home. Yer just lucky this is the easiest way back ta the party, and we heard the scufflin'." Ted frowned, leaning over to get a look at Richard's back. He tugged the shreds of the shirt aside and whistled low. "You're leaking." He looked over his shoulder, "Doc Kirtlin! I got a patient for ya."

Richard's head reeled, spots filling his vision. He didn't think that was good. "I thought Doctor Kirtlin was a woman."

"There are two. The old man and his daughter. They share a clinic."

"Oh. Is it bad?"

"How am I supposed ta know? Yer bleedin' pretty fiercely and there's a hole in your hide where there ain't supposed ta be. Don't move. For all I know ya skewered yer spleen. We'll get ya settled where the doc can look at ya an' then I'll go find Charlene. She can kiss it better and we'll compare notes."

Charlene.

Richard shook his head, pushing his hand against his back to staunch the blood and forcing himself straight. "Find her first! I'll manage. We have to go. Miss Reches said something about Charlene being in bad company, and I didn't see Frank here but he was running with Jeremiah before."

"Shit!" Ted swore, grabbing the Doctor by the arm and pushing him towards Richard. "Patch him up. I'll be back." He didn't ask anything else, taking off with a speed Richard had never seen from the big man.

The Doc, an older man with a thin moustache which matched his thinning hair, glanced after Ted and then got a better look at Richard, raising both brows. He checked the wound, and moved to Richard's less injured side and got a bony shoulder under him. "We'll just take you to my clinic I think. I need better lights and Ted can find us there easily enough." His voice was soothing, though his grip was solid, and Richard found himself steered to the clinic whether he wanted to go or not.

Once inside, Richard sagged onto a stool, not protesting when the Doc cut his shirt and vest off or started prodding at the punctured skin. All of Richard's thoughts were for Charlene and the mistake he'd made by leaving her alone. He prayed she was still at the dance and Anna's words were just bluster, but he feared he'd lost her for good.

36

Charlene's breath came in gasps as she broke past the fields, stumbling for the calving shed and the nearest all in alarm. She hadn't seen any of the men who'd remained behind yet, a fact that bothered her even more deeply than the fire. The closest field to the fire line had already been harvested, but there was still plenty of stubble to burn and carry the flames to the rest of the ranch. They had to get it out.

She pushed open the door and slapped the alarm, sucking wind. Her feet throbbed from running in shoes completely unsuited for the activity, and she knew she couldn't stand there and wait for the men before she acted. The shoes had to go though, they were shredded through the toes, and she'd fall and kill herself crossing the fields like this.

With the alarm blaring in her ears, Charlene ran for the house, tripping when she hit the top step. The skirt of her dress snagged and ripped as she pulled herself up, and she winced, but didn't stop. The house was dark. Charlene didn't bother with a light, flinging herself up the stairs. Her knees were screaming; the therapy treatment had been very effective for a night of dancing, but adding a run down the lane and up the stairs was more than she had bargained for.

She flipped on the screen and the long comm at her desk, squirming out of her dress and laying it across the bed. The screen blinked a few times before settling into the normal loading routine while Charlene pulled on the first clothing which came to hand.

The machine beeped and flashed. 'No connections available.' It was the same no matter which channel she tried. The Double P was cut off. She cursed and pulled on her boots, followed by the thigh holster and gun, a defense that seemed insignificant against fire and hurried back down the stairs and into the yard.

No one else was there.

"Dammit," Charlene snarled, frustrated. There should have been five men on duty, including Kevin who had called her. Where were they?

She walked further down the open yard, looking where the fire was growing stronger beyond the fields. The flames were still only yellow and orange dots on the horizon, but larger than they had been. The only thing she could think of that would keep the men from responding to the alarm was that they were already fighting the fire. She could see the suppressors in the fields weren't working. They should have been lit up and the only light was the distant flame. She forced herself to ignore the additional paranoid thought that something, or someone, might be keeping them from responding.

When another two minutes yielded no response, save for the cows in their southern pasture, Charlene hurried down to the equipment shed. Most travel around the ranch was done on foot or on horse, saving precious fuel for the large equipment, but there were two small four-wheeled cycles they used for emergencies and moving mud. She couldn't take a horse towards the fire and walking was too slow.

The check for fuel and keys took seconds, as did loading a water extinguisher and a foam one onto the back of the cycle. Maybe the small extinguishers couldn't make any difference to the blaze in general, but they could contain small flames to clear her way.

Charlene climbed onto the machine, setting it in action, slowly at first and then with confidence as the motion became familiar and remembered. She took the longer route around to the top of the field, reasoning that bouncing over the furrows and the crop stubble would take more time and could easily throw her from the bike. A smoother path was worth the few added seconds, and gave her enough time to wonder if Daria had made it home, and how long before the others would arrive.

A smaller portion of her mind wondered if Richard was still dancing with Anna Reches. The vision of them stuck in her head, taunting her even as she tried to focus on the issues at hand. Charlene came around a slight bend and saw the tree line burning, sending great gusts of black and grey smoke into the air. It hadn't made the leap to the field and her heart rose. A human-sized shape darted in front of her, and she shrieked, hitting the brakes and steering hard to the right. The bike's front tires hit the first furrow and flipped, throwing Charlene into the field.

She landed hard, rolling across the furrows and stubble, inhaling a mouthful of dust and dirt. When the world stopped spinning she spat dirt and blood, pushing up on her hands.

A shadow crossed between her and the fire, and Charlene looked up with tears in her eyes. Frank peered down at her from under the wide brim of his hat, his eyes shadows. His lips twitched in a cold smile as he crouched to her level. "Hallo, Charlene. It's time we had a little talk."

37

The pain spray was cold against Richard's back, and he did his best not to shudder. He'd already endured a brisk scrub and the removal of pieces of metal and skin from the wound, which was the worst of his injuries. The Doc had offered a sedative which would have helped treat the pain and relax Richard's aching muscles, but Richard refused, worried he'd fall asleep. He couldn't do that until he knew what had happened to Charlene. He prayed she was safe, and Miss Reches had just been sprouting empty threats.

"Mister Tyler!" A young voice Richard didn't recognize called from the door, the boy peering around the room until he found Richard. "Sir, Mister Petersmire says you need to come and right now. Miss Charlene can't be found and there's a fire at the Double P!"

Richard tried to get up, but Doc Kirtlin pushed him back down with firm hands. "Hold still, boy. Another few stitches and you'll be good to go, but I'm not having you running about while you still have a hole in your back. Pretty sure the emergency will still be there in a few minutes, and you can't help anyone if you pass out from blood loss."

"Yes, Sir." Richard muttered. He wanted to protest, but knew better than to argue with the man putting stitches in his skin. He waved the boy back toward the door. "Get going. Tell Ted I'll be there in just a moment and not to leave without me."

Doctor Kirtlin placed another stitch, adding, "You can tell him I'll come along as well, since I'm sure they're wondering. It's too rare to have a fire without injury and my girl is on labor watch over in Granite."

The boy took off, and Richard closed his eyes, trying to be patient. Fire. There were few things the ranchers feared more than fire. It was why he'd spent so much time working on the suppressors, which he prayed were working. If there was nothing to slow the fire the ranch might be gone by the time they got there.

One more stitch and Doctor Kirtlin snipped the thread free, covering the wound with a plaster and smoothing it over Richard's back. "Don't get that wet for at least a week." He added a layer of gauze wrapped all the way around Richard's torso and secured with metal clips. "Have either myself or my daughter take a look in four weeks, sooner if it's weeping past the plaster or smells off." He handed Richard a blue plaid shirt. "This was left behind a while ago. It'll be a bit big, but the Missus washed it, and I don't see the previous owner claiming it."

"Thank you."

While Richard buttoned the shirt the Doctor added emergency supplies to a tall handled box, snapping it closed. He led the way out of the clinic, closing the door behind them and locking it before beginning down the street in the opposite direction of the party still going on in the square.

Richard took a step in the other direction then stopped and followed Doctor Kirtlin, trying not to yell at him to hurry faster. "Excuse me, sir? Aren't they going to be back with the wagons at the church?"

"Maybe a few folk, but the rest will be at the fire station. We've got a motored truck for these kinds of emergencies. It's a lot faster than wagons. We'll take the big truck ahead and let others follow with wagons." He glanced over at Richard. "That attack on you, you think the fire is related, given you're working for the Petersmires and provided the paper trail between Reches and the outlaws?"

Richard frowned, his stomach churning with fear and worry. "I think it's likely. Just before I was attacked Miss Reches said something about someone being after Charlene. I think they separated us on purpose."

"I met Mister Reches once. He struck me as the kind of man who gets a bit in his mouth over something and can't let it go, no matter how it hurts him or anyone else."

"That's what I'm afraid of." Richard swallowed back worry. Charlene was worth more to Reches alive, but that didn't mean they couldn't or wouldn't hurt her. He wished he'd never left her side that he'd just sent broken up with Anna via a comm message, polite society be damned. He couldn't change any of that, but provided they all survived the night he'd never let Charlene go again.

"Here we are." Doctor Kirtlin broke in on Richard's thoughts and Richard looked up to see men running about, loading hoses and scrambling up onto a large tanker truck.

The engine started up with a rumble, belching dark smoke into the air as the truck began to roll. Ted hung off of one side, stretching out a hand towards Richard. His broad features were compressed in rage. "Grab on!"

Richard caught the offered hand, jumping as Ted pulled him onto the tanker and making space for the Doctor to be hauled up next. As they found places to sit, though it was more simply just holding onto whatever they could, Ted met Richard's gaze.

"Miss Reches is cooling her heels at the Sheriff's office. She says they've been planning all this for weeks. She's very smug 'bout the whole thing. Char…" He snarled, a wild angry noise. "Char got a call back ta the ranch right 'bout the time you an' I were distracted. She ain't in town. We've been tryin' but the long comm ta the Double P is out. She's on her own til we get there."

"How long will it take?"

"With this thing? Faster than wagon. Twenty minutes maybe."

Richard scowled, facing forward and watching the scenery whip by. Twenty minutes too long.

38

Charlene swallowed back terror, pushing herself off the ground. She was bruised and scratched, and grateful she hadn't broken her neck in the fall. Her right leg was twisted in a way that looked wrong and felt worse, but she couldn't tell if it was broken or just dislocated.

Frank leaned back into his heels, running a finger along her cheek before slapping her hard enough to make her ears ring. "Nothing to say to me, huh? After everything we've been through together?" He pushed the brim of his hat up so she could see his face, and Charlene gasped. Frank's right eye drooped and there was something wrong with the angle of his cheekbone. A thick scar ran from his chin to the corner of his left eye, puffy and badly healed.

"Pretty ain't I? Your brother did a number on me, you know? We just don't have the kind of clinic that does reconstruction. I thought about letting them take me to Pristine, just long enough to patch this up, but then I decided you should see what you did to me. My outside as broken up as my insides."

Charlene didn't meet his gaze, looking away from the madness in his eyes. "I didn't do anything to you, Frank. I was honest. I told you I wasn't interested. I'm sorry you were hurt, I am, but you brought it on yourself. You didn't have to betray the ranch. You could have worked here for a long time, and we would have been glad to have you."

He gave a short bark of harsh laughter, catching the front of her shirt and pulling her to her knees, leaning forward until his face nearly touched hers. "Yes. I could have stayed and watched you and the city boy court and wed and have nice fat babies all while knowing if not for him it could have been me." He touched his lips against her cheek. "Should have been me, you know? Why wasn't it me?" His breath was too hot and smelled of bile and alcohol. Charlene dropped her right hand, fumbling with the thigh holster until the safety strap flipped back.

"Frank, let me go. You were a good friend once. Don't let this be something you can't come back from. We can call the Sheriff and make sure you get the help you need."

Frank twisted the fabric under his hand, tightening her collar until she couldn't breathe. She grabbed his hand, digging her nails into his wrist. "I can get what I need on my own. I can take what I need."

He covered her lips with his, further straining her breath, and Charlene's eyes widened in panic. She shoved the little hand gun against his ribs and pulled the trigger until it clicked empty.

The roar of gun fire deafened her, and Frank's body fell to the side, dragging Charlene with him until she managed to wrench her shirt out of his grasp. He sucked air to speak, but it gurgled uselessly in his perforated lungs and after a moment he stopped breathing. His empty eyes stared at her, accusing and raw.

The gun dropped from Charlene's numb fingers. She crawled away from Frank's body, heaving until she'd emptied her stomach. She dragged the back of her hand across her mouth, tears dripping down her cheeks. She hadn't wanted to kill Frank, and even though she'd been acting in self defense she felt soiled, as though she would never get the smell of him off her hands and out of her mind.

Moments passed until the sharp crack of flame on green wood pulled Charlene out of her numbness. The fire had jumped to the field and was surging along the rows. No matter what had just happened she had to get away, or she was going to be just as dead.

She dragged her way to the overturned bike, pulling herself up against it. Her right leg only held weight for a second before buckling, and Charlene screamed a wordless cry of pain and fear into the night sky. She grabbed the lighter of the two extinguishers, pulling it free from the bike.

In the distance she could see the control shed Richard had claimed as his own. Why weren't the fire suppressors going?

Charlene measured the distance and the feasting fire. It was too far from her to the shed, and there was no way she could get there dragging her leg, even with the extinguisher to clear some kind of path. Getting back to the house was likewise impossible. Her gaze moved along the fire line and the burning trees. The gully. There was nothing to burn there. She'd be safe, but it meant she'd have to get through the fire line.

She pushed the bike, trying to get it upright, but without the leverage of two working legs it only wobbled. Charlene watched the way the fire was burning, bending with the slight breeze. If she could make it to the furthest end of the trees and blast the area with the extinguisher she might be able to get through. It wasn't a good option, but she didn't have any of those and she didn't want to die.

Charlene murmured a desperate prayer and pushed away from the bike. She hobbled as long as she could, keeping as much weight off her leg as possible, but eventually she collapsed. Determined, she crawled forward, her eyes locked on the break where she thought she could get through.

The closer she drew, the hotter the flame, and she tried using the extinguisher, but found it created more smoke than put out fire and didn't open enough of a hole. She pressed forward, but she smelled and felt her skin and hair burning and had to turn back. She dragged herself as far away from the fire as she could, curling up against the security fencing she couldn't get through or over.

Each time the flames licked closer, she gave a burst with the extinguisher. It helped, but it was only a matter of time before she ran out of fuel. The tears returned and she didn't fight them, tears for what might have been.

"Teddy…" She whispered between shallow breaths. "I'm sorry. I never meant to leave you alone." She knew her brother would blame himself, and she ached for the hurt it would cause him. In her mind's eye she saw his face as it had been at their parents' funeral, anguished and lost. She closed her eyes and the vision was replaced, showing her instead Richard. A hundred little moments flashed through her mind and she regretted too many days lost to pride, too many things unsaid in fear. "Richard…" She heard the fire snapping closer and curled even tighter. "I'm sorry. I love you."

39

"I t's the north forty!" Ted yelled as the truck pulled into the lane. "But I don't see the generator lights. The fire system isn't working!"

Richard banged his fist down on the cab of the truck. "But they should be! The last test went perfectly. Even if all of the generators didn't go on, some of them should have. They're not daisy chained anymore! I need to get to the control shed."

"We got ta take the truck up that way anyway; it's the closest route from here."

The truck stopped at the gate, and Ted swung down to the ground, entering his code. Richard heard swearing when it didn't work and instructions to run the gate down. He climbed back as far as he could, sheltering behind the water tank. The firetruck surged forward and after two strikes the gate broke, swinging open and setting off a piercing alarm.

Sherriff Reid and Doctor Kirtlin joined Ted. Richard started to climb down before Ted stopped him.

"We're going ta the house first. If someone has Charlene that's the most likely place ta hold her."

"Then I'm coming with you."

Ted shook his head. "You can't. No matter what's wrong with those fire suppressors, you're the only one who has a chance in hell of fixin' them. There's another truck coming, but if we don't beat this back now we're gonna lose the ranch. We have to hold this line. You know if Char were here she'd tell you to save the damn ranch before her, so go already!"

Richard hesitated, torn between what he wanted to do and what he should do. Finally, he nodded, ducking next to the tank again and holding tight as the truck started across the field. The trip was agonizing as they raced across the furrows, each lurching moment ripping at the stitches in his back and the bruises on his body.

As they drew nearer the flame, the other men, much more experienced than he, began hooking up hoses to the back of the truck and spraying water on both sides. Richard saw the shed, which was surrounded by flames, but not burning itself. He worked his way around to point out the location. "I've got to get there!" Richard yelled, and the hose worker nodded, yelling to the others and redirecting the spray.

Richard waited until they were a few yards away before jumping off the slowly moving truck. He rolled when he hit the ground, more from momentum than planning, and staggered to his feet, running for the shed. The plaster on his back ripped partially off, taking skin with it, but it was the least of his concerns. If there was a later, he knew he would consider his actions insane, but in the moment they seemed not only reasonable, but the only possible course.

He kept his head down, pulling the neck of his shirt up across his nose and mouth, and kept running until he reached the door. It flew open at the lightest touch, the latch smashed in. Inside, his precious screens and data units were spread about, many broken beyond repairs and all damaged. He stared at the mess, barely able to comprehend what had been done, his mind refusing to wrap around such wanton destruction.

Solve the problem now, fix the rest later, he thought, digging through the debris to his storage locker. He grabbed the belt with his hands-on tools and the key to the generators and slipped it around his waist. It fit high enough to rub his back painfully, which he did his best to ignore.

Richard ran out of the shed, getting caught with a spray from the truck. It wasn't enough to knock him off his feet, but it was enough to soak him instantly in the combination of water and retardant foam. He added wetness to his list of things he was ignoring and ran for the first generator, his dance shoes slipping on the sandy soil. If he could build up a line of suppression here then he could press closer to the fire one machine at a time.

It took only a couple minutes to reach the first field generator and Richard twisted the key in the lock, pulling the cover open. There was no damage here. He keyed in the manual commands, his fingers flying over the screen and keyboard. The generator groaned as power flooded the unit. It telescoped to its full height, bright white lights surrounding the top of the generator blinking to life before it began blowing water and fire foam in a ten foot radius.

A ragged cheer rose from the fire truck, but Richard barely heard it already sprinting for the next unit. There were ten generator units across the top of the field and Richard fell into a rhythm, never looking back and only as far forward as the next twenty foot sprint through the water and foam. He slipped a few times, shoes meant for dancing giving him no traction, but kept his mind focused on the goal. Ten units. Save the Double P. Beg Charlene to forgive him. See if the hair clip he'd bought for Anna could be exchanged for an engagement ring.

Richard didn't know how long it took to get to the end of the line. Time didn't mean anything; he was lost in his need to get to the next station as fast as his feet would carry him. He closed the last panel, sagging against it and watching the water fly and the fire recede. It wasn't perfect. They were going to have to bring the truck in for the tree line, and he needed to activate the rest of the fields just in case the fire jumped, but it was a significant win.

He rubbed the ash and foam off his face, it was still hard to breathe, and headed for the edge of the field where he could get out of some of the spray and start down to the next row. He only got a few yards before the sight of an overturned wheeler caught his attention. The vehicle had no business being out here.

Richard's heart was in his throat. He ran to the bike, getting a shoulder under it and pushing it upright. It was damaged and some of the paint burnt, but both were minor issues. A fire extinguisher still strapped to the back caught his eye. Whoever had brought the bike here had come to face the fire, or at least to keep it at bay.

He turned the bike headlight on to provide more light and caught his breath when it illuminated a body. Richard rushed to the prone form, deciding after a few steps that it was a man. He didn't stop, bending down and catching the man by the shoulder to roll him over. Frank's ruined face stared back at him, his chest a bloody mess that reminded Richard of

Jeremiah's fall. Richard yelped and released the man, jumping back. His foot hit something metal and he looked down. A gun. He picked the weapon up, running his fingers over the grip. Charlene's gun.

Richard looked back down at Frank's body and kicked the man viciously. It wasn't as though he could do any more harm to the bastard, but it brought some measure of satisfaction. Richard took the gun to the bike, tying it in with the extinguisher.

Mist from the fire suppressors continued to block the sky, building up on Richard's skin. He shook the moisture away and slowly began riding toward the fire line. He'd start at the top of the field and work his way down. She had to be somewhere. She had to be alive. She just had to be. "CHARLENE! Charlene where are you? It's Richard. Help me find you!"

If it killed him, he was going to find her.

———

SHE WAS WET. The thought broke through Charlene's haze. And cold. She shivered, shifting against the fence and trying to put the significance of the events together.

It wasn't so hot.

She was alive.

Someone was calling her name.

Charlene opened her eyes, but everything was too bright and it hurt too much. She tried to call out but all that came was a croak. Frustration rose and she threw herself forward, only to land on her face on top of the solid mass of the extinguisher. "I'm here." She whispered through cracked lips. "Don't leave me out here."

———

IF HE HADN'T BEEN WATCHING CLOSELY Richard never would have seen the movement, buried so close to the fence. He left the bike running, jumping off of it and dashing towards the motion. For an instant he thought it might be a calf, but then the form fell forward and he knew it wasn't a cow. He slid to his knees, horrified at the blackened cloth and blistered skin that met him. As gently as he could, he rolled Charlene to her back. She made a muffled sound, and he touched his fingertip to her lips. "Don't try to talk, Charlene, please. I'm going to take you back to the house. It's going to hurt and I'm so so sorry for that, but you're hurt really bad and there's a doctor at the house."

Her fingers clutched his arm and her eyes flickered open. "Richard."

"Yes. It's me."

"Not a hallucination?"

"No. I promise." He shifted to pick her up. It broke his heart when she screamed in agony. He got her onto the bike in front of him, letting her lean against his chest where the wet shirt pressed against her burnt face. He drove as fast and as smoothly as he could, racing for the ranch house and the help he hoped waited there.

Turning into the yard, Richard was greeted by organized chaos. Half a dozen men, including Donovan Reches, were seated in the middle of the yard with Sheriff Reid and some of the ranch hands watching over them. The ranch hands didn't look happy and occasionally took the opportunity to kick one of the captured outlaws. Sheriff Reid pretended not to notice.

"Where's the Doc?" Richard called, trying not to shout in Charlene's ear.

Sheriff Reid looked up, his brow immediately furrowing with concern. "In the house. One of the hands got shot. He and Ted are trying to save the boy. Is that..." He stepped closer and swore, "Get her inside. The other Doctor Kirtlin should be here any minute."

Richard nodded, turning off the bike and leaving the keys. Someone else could move it, he didn't care. He raised Charlene into his arms. She barely whimpered, which seemed a bad sign. As smoothly as possible he carried her into the house, calling for Ted. The big man came out of the kitchen, his eyes widening.

"She's not?"

"Dead? No, but she's hurt bad."

Ted gestured towards the parlor. and Richard saw blood on his plastic gloved hands. "In there. Kev..." He shook his head. "Kevin was shot. Doc is trying to save him. Char's gonna have to wait if she can."

"We'll manage," Richard turned toward the parlor. Kevin was just a kid. He was too young to be shot and fighting for his life. Richard lowered Charlene to the sofa remembering the last time he'd carried her into this room. He knelt at her side, holding her hand between his, promising himself she was going to live.

The door pushed open and the younger Doctor Kirtlin entered. She turned on more lights and got a good look at her patient, her brow furrowing. She began taking vital signs, all of her attention for Charlene, though she spoke to Richard.

"There are wagons coming into the yard to pick up the prisoners. Go tell them I need one for the wounded, right now." She met his gaze, her hand resting on his shoulder for a moment. "We need to get her to the hospital at Double Fork and maybe the burn unit on Pristine. I'll do more harm than good trying to do much here."

"But she's going to make it?"

"I don't know."

40

Two months later...

*Tw*o *months later...* Charlene's hand itched horribly. She groaned, trying to reach for it but she felt so heavy. Soft hands touched her shoulders and face before retreating.

"She's coming around."

"Do you want me to get the brother?"

"Not yet. Let her get her wits before he smothers her with his exuberance. Bring up a food tray though. Something very gentle and some ice chips."

"Yes ma'am."

Charlene heard footsteps receding, and she slowly opened her eyes. The room was dim, and she could hear the little beeps and whooshes of machinery and smelled antiseptic. "What?" She managed one word before her throat closed, so sore.

"It's quite all right. Your throat is going to be sore for a few days. You've had a breathing tube in place." The white clad doctor moved to where Charlene could see her, glancing at the machines to see the read outs. The name Wong was printed on her uniform. "You gave us a scare, young lady, but I think you're through the worst of it."

Charlene nodded, continuing to take in the details of the hospital room. She'd visited the rooms in the pain center often, but this was her first time in a formal hospital. "Where?"

Doctor Wong smiled, her pretty eyes crinkling at the corners. "You're at Mercy Hospital on Pristine. You've been our guest for the last two months. You were burnt up pretty good and your lungs full of a lot of things they shouldn't have been full of. We had to put you to sleep in order to let your body heal. You're going to be okay, but it will take you a little while longer to get your strength back."

"Oh."

"Oh indeed."

The nurse returned with a food tray, and Doctor Wong helped Charlene to suck a handful of ice chips before she tried a few bites of a wobbly red gelatin which tasted of sugar and some fruit Charlene didn't recognize. Once she was finished, she leaned back against the pillows, exhausted by just the few motions.

"If you think you're up to it, you have a visitor."

Charlene mmed, remembering someone had mentioned a brother. For all that she was raw she wanted to see him. "Ted. I'd like...see him."

Doctor Wong nodded and sent the nurse out again. She return a moment later with Ted on her heels. He stood in the doorway for a long moment until Charlene raised her hand. "Hi."

The word was like permission, and Ted bowled through the medical personnel dropping to his knees next to the bed and grabbing both of her hands, squeezing tight. "You're awake!"

"You're...too hard, Ted. Ouch."

He looked sheepish and loosened his grip though he didn't let go. "You scared us so bad, Char. I thought ya were gonna die. You looked so awful."

She shook her head. "Too stubborn."

"Damn straight." Ted blinked. Charlene saw tears in his eyes. "Don't ever do that again, okay? It was bad enough seein' ya with stitches, much less all burnt up."

"Didn't mean to." She squeezed his hand back. "Try harder to behave."

"Yeah, well ya can't run away for a bit so at least we can keep an eye on you. But yer tired, I can let ya rest now that I know you'll wake up again."

Charlene nodded weakly, then whispered, "Richard? Okay?"

"Who, him? He's fine. He's at the Double P. We've been rotating who was here and who was there, cause we knew you'd be mad if we neglected the ranch, even wi' good reason. The second harvest is in full swing, and we had to get the cows back down from the canyon so we could start marking up the breeding pairs. Richard is almost as good at organizing all this stuff as you are, though he's gonna be pissed that I was here when ya woke up."

"I think…He found me?"

"Yeah. And don't worry about the rest of what happened. Judge Frebon already determined Frank's death as self-defense and fully justified. More than fully if you ask me. Ya did the right thing. Rat bastard."

Charlene shuddered, seeing Frank's crazed eyes all over again, feeling his touch too hot on her skin. She whimpered, and Doctor Wong touched Ted's arm. "No more of that. Let her get some more sleep. It'll all get better from here on out."

"Dammit, I'm sorry, Charlene. No more about that ever again, I promise." He stood up and leaned in to kiss her cheek. "I'll come back soon. You just focus on getting well."

She nodded and closed her eyes, asleep in minutes.

41

For the second time in a few months, Charlene felt like she was looking at a stranger. The woman who looked back at her from the mirror was too pale with hair far too short and eyes far too haunted. She ran her fingers through her hair, the dark locks only a few inches long. The cut made her features look sharp, but the burning had ruined her hair, her eyebrows and eyelashes only just now looking normal.

Doctor Wong, a familiar friend these days, swept into the room looking Charlene over with approval. "Well, while you're still skinnier than I'd like, you're at least moving in the right direction. I'll sign you out with a note you're to keep eating at least four to five small meals a day and spend at least three hours on the pain massager. Be careful of too much sun. Over time you'll brown up again, but most of your skin is new and going to be very susceptible to burning. Use the sun block."

"Yes, Ma'am."

The two exchanged a hug, and Charlene rose, feeling the odd lightness of the silk skirt swaying around her calves. She'd given Ted instructions to get her pants and shirts which he'd happily ignored, allowing himself to be guided by the store associate who favored light weight silks and bright colors. It wasn't a terrible look, but Charlene had no idea when she'd wear the clothing once they were back home.

As though summoned by her thoughts Ted knocked on the door before sticking his head in the room. "The car is here. Are ya ready?"

Charlene nodded, picking up the small bag with her few possessions gained while she was in the hospital. "I am. I want to go home."

42

Richard stood on the newly painted porch of the ranch house, his nerves increasing as the minutes ticked by. Missus Davidson and Gravy were nearby, young Miss Tracy away with her fiancée for the afternoon, and the rest of the hands waited in the yard. Kevin wasn't among them, having left planet three days ago. Richard had heard Kevin's side of the story and believed the man thought Frank was just coming to get a few personal items. He never should have let the outlaw in, it was a poor decision, but Kevin had lost his left leg from the knee down after being shot and that was plenty of penance for anyone. Not that Kevin believed it, and despite forgiving the man, Richard hadn't tried to stop him from leaving.

The narrow wagon came rattling down the road, Charlene sitting on the driver's seat next to Ted. She looked like a butterfly dressed in cheerful silks which fluttered in the wind. They were very different from what she usually wore, but Richard liked it. As the wagon stopped, Ted bowed to the assembly. "Hey folks, look at what I found. I think we'll keep her."

Charlene laughed and slipped down from the wagon, passed from ranch hand to hand, exchanging hugs and cheek kisses. The dizzy dance of greeting carried her across the yard, ending up at the porch where

Gravy and Missus Davidson came down for greetings of their own. Charlene never looked at him and Richard wasn't sure if that was good or bad.

She turned back to the men and waved her hands at them. "All right, I'm greeted. There will be plenty of time for more talk later. Go earn your keeps and get my fields harvested." She smiled, the orders fully teasing, even if the work did need to be done, "Beer all the way around tonight and slab toast in the morning, providing you haven't eaten me out of house and home while I was away."

Another cheer greeted the announcement and the men dispersed, taking Ted with them and leaving Charlene and Richard alone. Richard descended the stairs, taking her hands in his. Her skin was smoother than he remembered and paler, but just as welcoming. He bowed and kissed her knuckles. "Welcome home."

Her fingers closed tight around his, and she met his gaze with a soft smile. "Thank you. I see you've been busy while I was gone. New paint everywhere, and I believe those are real curtains and shutters on the windows."

Richard laughed, glancing over his shoulder at the cheery blue window shutters and the accompanying flower boxes filled with cactus plants. "Indeed they are. We're pushing the kitchen back as well and putting a master bedroom on the main floor, but the last of that has to wait until the harvest is shipped. I found a wish list in the parlor and I thought I'd see how many items I could cross off." He led her up the stairs, guiding the way to a porch swing. "Including this. It wasn't that broken, just needed some new springs and a pad."

Charlene blinked and reached out a hand, running it along the ornately carved frame of the swing. "I remember watching my parents sit here at night. They made plans for our future on this porch swing. I didn't know Ted kept all the parts when he broke it. Apparently, it couldn't handle vigorous teenaged making out." She settled into the swing making space for Richard beside her. "I can't believe you managed so much in just a couple of months."

"It wasn't so hard once I got it all organized. Several things just needed a bit of work with a hammer and a screwdriver and that is something a good technician excels at."

"Dare I ask how we afforded it all? I saw the rest of the fencing was in place, and that cost should have absorbed all of the excess from the last harvest and part of this one."

Richard wondered how she was going to handle this part, but he didn't shy away from answering the question. "I paid for a lot of it. That machine I made for you is a hit at the Pain Center, and the production is expanding not only for them but for other planets in the Cluster. They figure there's some 1.5 billion people who could benefit from the massagers on Central alone, much less the outer planets. I get a percentage of every unit sold, which is adding up faster than I thought it would. It felt right to put some of that into the Double P since I never would have started working on the project without you."

Charlene pursed her lips, thoughtful, before nodding and giving the swing a little push. "I hope you kept track of what you spent. I'd like to see the totals."

"You're not paying me back."

She arched both eyebrows. "I might."

"I won't take it." He returned with a grin, glad to see her arguing with him. He'd worried about how she'd come back, if after everything she'd been through she'd be his Charlene. And while she was a little more wan, and her eyes weren't as innocent, she was still herself.

"Stubborn man."

"Yes."

They sat in silence for a long moment, the rocking of the swing and soft squeak of the springs the only sound. Charlene rested her head on his shoulder. "So...you know you're well beyond the terms of your contract, Mister Tyler. Even with that extension we talked about."

She was teasing. Richard slipped his arm around her shoulders. "I suppose I am at that. Would you care to renegotiate, Miss Charlene?"

She turned to face him. "Well, I suppose that depends on what you have to offer."

Richard cradled her cheek, running his thumbs gently along her skin. "Everything. All of my heart and my skills and my love, for you and for the ranch. I love you, and I love it here, though I never thought I would." He made a face. "But I still don't want to muck the cattle."

Charlene leaned up, her breath whispering against his lips, and he smelled lilacs. "We all do the work that needs to be done, but I'll keep it in mind."

"Does that mean I can stay a while longer?"

"I was thinking forever."

Their lips met, and Richard pulled her into his arms. Forever sounded pretty damn good to him.

MISSUS DAVIDSON'S NO-FAIL PIE CRUST

Yield: 2 single-crust pie shells or 1 double-crust pie

Ingredients:
   2 cups all purpose flour
   ½ teaspoon salt
   ½ teaspoon sugar
   ½ cup shortening or lard
   ½ cup butter, into small squares
   Ice water to make a soft dough

Combine flour, salt and sugar in a medium bowl. Cut in shortening and butter until lumps are the size of peas. Gradually add ice water to form a soft, but not sticky, dough. Divide into two disks, wrap in plastic wrap and refrigerate for 10 minutes. Shape as desired (but don't over roll!). Bake single crust pie shells as directed at 400 degrees. Bake double crust pies according to filling instructions.

ABOUT THE AUTHOR

Hi, We're Jadelynn

Referring to ourselves in the plural isn't an affectation. Or not just an affectation. Jadelynn Asher is a pseudonym for two friends who turned to each other one day and said "could we really?" One of us (Jana) has the writing chops, having worked as a writer for (ahem) uncounted years. The other (Jacob) loves romance stories and reads and writes about them and complains when people get their stories wrong. It was during one of his rants that the assembled friends (many of them writers) challenged him to write his own. Cringing at all that work, he deferred. This scene played out with minor variations for a while when Jana said "you know, if you have the story, I could make the writing happen." And we decided that our friendship could probably stand the nonsense working together would entail and we gave it a shot. You can judge for yourself if the results are a success!

We'd love for you to join our newsletter at www.jadelynnasher.com. Choose highlights to know when a new book is coming out, or chatty to get frequent emails waxing philosophical about writing, writing romance, cooperative writing, and publishing in general.

About *Desert Rains…*

Desert Rains was a book which came out of nowhere during a difficult summer. I've been writing and submitting books for a long time and was in the midst of working on an Urban Fantasy when one afternoon the entire outline of *Desert Rains* spilled onto a notebook. The story wrote fast and furious and I fell in love with the folks of the Double P Ranch. It's my hope you'll love them as much as I do.

If you enjoyed this story, please take the time to share with others by gifting a book or posting a review on your favorite online retailer or on Goodreads.